LEFT AT THE ALTAR

BOOKS BY AJ CAMPBELL

My Perfect Marriage
Did I Kill My Husband?
First-Time Mother

Leave Well Alone
Don't Come Looking
Search No Further
The Phone Call
The Wrong Key
Her Missing Husband
The Mistake

AJ CAMPBELL

LEFT AT THE ALTAR

bookouture

Published by Bookouture in 2025

An imprint of Storyfire Ltd.
Carmelite House
50 Victoria Embankment
London EC4Y 0DZ

www.bookouture.com

The authorised representative in the EEA is Hachette Ireland
8 Castlecourt Centre
Dublin 15 D15 XTP3
Ireland
(email: info@hbgi.ie)

Copyright © AJ Campbell, 2025

AJ Campbell has asserted her right to be identified
as the author of this work.

All rights reserved. No part of this publication may be reproduced, stored in any retrieval system, or transmitted, in any form or by any means, electronic, mechanical, photocopying, recording or otherwise, without the prior written permission of the publishers.

ISBN: 978-1-83618-690-8
eBook ISBN: 978-1-83618-691-5

This book is a work of fiction. Names, characters, businesses, organizations, places and events other than those clearly in the public domain, are either the product of the author's imagination or are used fictitiously. Any resemblance to actual persons, living or dead, events or locales is entirely coincidental.

To Andy

*Thank you for choosing me to be your bride!
Every day with you is a blessing.*

*Love always,
Amanda x*

ONE

'Are you sure?' Alan asks with a wide grin. He winks at me.

I cock my head to the side and look at the man sitting beside me who, in less than an hour, I'll be calling my father-in-law.

'I've never been so sure of anything in my whole life.' I take a deep breath, inhaling the sweet smell of the red roses from my bouquet and the peppery scent of Alan's aftershave. 'Thanks for doing this... you know... for giving me away.'

I'm lucky. Alan's a good man. He's going to make the best father-in-law. Charismatic, kind and fun, I warmed to him from the first day I met him.

'The honour is all mine, Hannah. I mean it. I can't wait to officially welcome you into the family.' He has trimmed his grey beard for this special day and looks super smart, dressed in his tuxedo and crimson bow tie to match the colour of my sister's bridesmaid dress. I was surprised when Johnny decided on tuxedos for his wedding outfit and groomsmen. I thought he'd have gone for something more casual. I smile. But that's Johnny – always surprising me.

I never understood the saying that you'll just *know* when

you meet Mr Right until I met Johnny. We've only been together for a little over a year, but from our first date, there was no doubt he'd become the love of my life.

He's good-looking, too, but not overly so. It's his prominent dimples that appear when he smiles, so they're almost permanently there, that I love so much. He's what my mum would've described as a wholesome boy-next-door, friendly and approachable. I felt like the luckiest woman alive when he got down on one knee and told me he wanted to spend the rest of his life with me.

I was apprehensive about a winter wedding, concerned about the weather, but I had little choice given the circumstances.

I touch my belly. A moment of sadness overcomes me. I immediately retract my hand.

No.

Not today.

I promised myself I wouldn't think of our angel baby today. But it's challenging. Despite the months that have passed since that traumatic night, it hasn't got any easier. The loss lives in every breath I take.

My fingers lightly brush the lacey sleeve of my dress. I stare out the window, thankful to see the sun shining, radiating a golden warmth into the car.

I'm tingling with nerves and excitement.

This is going to be a perfect day.

Alan adjusts his bow tie. 'Nervous?'

'Just a bit.' I giggle like a loved-up, giddy teenager. Butterflies are out in force, making me feel slightly nauseous, as I have all week, but it's the excitement of what's to come rather than nerves.

'You've got a lot to look forward to. Here we go.'

The driver turns into the treelined avenue leading to the

church. In the distance, guests are arriving, many wrapped in winter coats to stave off the cold.

A phone buzzes. At first, I think it's mine, but Alan reaches into his jacket pocket and pulls out his. 'What? Slow down. Slow down,' he says to the caller. A deep frown appears on his forehead. 'Hang on.' He leans forward and taps the driver on the shoulder. 'Do another lap, could you, please?'

The driver, a short stocky guy I've only met once when he brought his Rolls-Royce over to show to Johnny and me, nods. 'Sure can.'

'What's happening?' I ask curiously when Alan ends the call.

'There's been a hold-up. Nothing to worry about.' He puts the phone to his ear, uncrossing his legs and recrossing them in the other direction.

I'm unsure if it's my imagination, but his face appears to have paled.

'Are you OK?' I ask.

'All good!' He abandons the call and grunts.

'What's going on, Alan? You're making me nervous.'

He fiddles with his bow tie. 'Nothing. Nothing.' He smiles. But it's not his usual affable smile. It doesn't reach his grey-blue eyes. He takes my hand and squeezes it, a gesture of reassurance. 'Just relax.'

I take a deep breath and slowly blow it out, trying to shake off the distraction and return to the excitement blossoming inside me. The anticipation of what's to come is almost too much to bear. I smile. In less than an hour, Johnny and I will be married. It's what dreams are made of – a perfect fairytale with me a princess for the day.

I face the window again. The driver turns the corner, and the joyful smile lighting up my face is wiped in one awful moment.

I do a double-take.

My blood runs as cold as my thoughts.

India is climbing out of a black sports car. Though it isn't the sight of my younger sister that has frozen my blood, but the man who has slipped his arm through hers.

What the hell is India doing with Dean Ferguson?

TWO

It can't be. I must be wrong. It makes no sense.

I haven't seen Dean Ferguson for a long time. And I never expected to see him ever again. I gulp. But he's found me.

My stomach turns. But not from excitement this time.

I blink hard. Among the nerves and anticipated joy of meeting Johnny at the altar, I must have got it wrong. I twist around, straining to get another glimpse out the back window. All I can see is the back of two people fading into the distance, walking to the church, one unmistakably my sister and a man who could be anyone.

Then he turns around.

And I know I'm definitely not mistaken.

He appears to be looking directly at me, snarling. He's grown his hair long. It's past shoulder length now. But I would recognise that mean, contorted face anywhere.

I clutch the door handle.

India is coming to my wedding on the arm of Dean Ferguson.

This isn't a coincidence. Dean is doing this on purpose. He's here to haunt me. There's no other reason for him to be at my wedding.

The driver swings another left. We're three-quarters around a circuit back to the church.

This should be the best day of my life, but I can't concentrate.

I need to warn India.

Alan is busy on his phone, calling someone who doesn't appear to be answering.

I open my bag, a beaded clutch, and grab my phone. Crushing waves of nausea pulse through me as I search my contacts.

Alan sighs. There's no mistaking the look of anxiety on his face. 'Are you calling Johnny?'

'No. I need to speak to my sister.' My throat tightens as if someone is strangling me. 'Is everything OK?' The vibe in the air has changed from one of extreme excitement to an icky sense of foreboding.

'I was about to ask you the same thing.' He frowns. 'You've gone very white.'

I laugh his observation away. 'Just nerves.'

He makes another call.

We turn the final corner to the church again. The squishy leather seat squeaks as Alan fidgets beside me. It's unbearably stuffy in here. I remove the white, faux fur shrug from my shoulders and open the window. A cold stream of air filters through the car, but it doesn't cool me down.

My call to India rings straight to her voicemail, where her soulful voice tells me to leave a message. I will myself to control my nerves that are now racing out of control. I must calm down. I'm a bride about to arrive at the church. Turning up in this state isn't an option. It's a day to look my very best. But I can't wipe the image of Dean Ferguson's arm looped through my sister's from my mind.

Alan runs his hand through his hair. He leans forward to speak to the driver. 'Carry on, can you, please?'

Panic grows within me. Something isn't right. 'What's going on?' I grasp Alan's forearm. 'Tell me.'

He glances up to the roof of the car and turns to me, slowly puffing out a long breath. If I'm not mistaken, tears swim in his eyes. 'I don't know how to tell you this, Hannah. But...'

'Tell me.' I shake his arm. 'What is it?'

His voice falters. 'Johnny... he's not coming.'

THREE

I laugh incredulously.

It's one of Alan's jokes. He's always mucking around, playing games with us all, fooling around like the family clown. 'Stop it.' I gently punch his arm.

'I mean it, Hannah.' He vigorously shakes his head, his face stern. 'Johnny's not coming.'

The past months of planning this big day flash through my mind. Apart from our outfits, Johnny and I have done it together, from organising the church to finding a hotel to hold the reception and choosing the menu.

Don't get me wrong, I knew straight away that I wanted to spend the rest of my life with Johnny. But he was the one who pushed for this wedding. I would've waited until after our baby was born. But he didn't want a child out of wedlock. 'Let's do this properly,' he said.

The driver turns up the music that I didn't even notice playing. It was just a background whisper to my muddled thoughts, but now an unknown artist's music pumps as fast as the adrenaline racing through me. 'Can you turn that down, please? I need to make a call.'

I stab Johnny's number on my phone and turn to Alan. 'I need to speak to him.'

Alan holds his phone in the air. 'I've been trying him. He's not answering.'

The bitter waft of betrayal catches in my throat. Alan was right. The call goes straight to Johnny's voicemail. I try again. He has to pick up. Johnny never fails to answer my calls. 'He must be somewhere where there's no signal.' I try again, still in denial. I'm not thinking straight. If he doesn't have any signal, the call would go straight to his voicemail. 'How do you know?' My voice cracks with fear – and panic for what my future could now hold. 'How do you know he's not coming? Who told you?'

'He didn't turn up at the pub where he was meant to meet the lads for a drink before they went to the church.'

'And...?'

'He called Tom and said he'd changed his mind.' Tom is Johnny's half-brother. Alan's voice wavers. 'He couldn't go through with it.'

The man who I was looking forward to calling my father-in-law blurs before me. I must be dreaming. I pinch my arm to wake myself up.

But it's no dream.

It's as real as the bouquet of red and white roses splayed across my lap.

'That can't be right.' Johnny wouldn't do this to me. The pitch of my voice rises higher and higher to dizzy heights. 'This must be some kind of joke.'

I open the window further. 'I need to see him.' I call out at the driver, 'Please, take me to Johnny's apartment now!'

The poor guy stops the car. He turns to face us, blushing, and his confused eyes dart from me to Alan.

'No. Take us back to the hotel, can you, please?' Alan says in a sombre tone. He rests his strong hand gently on mine. 'He's not coming, darling.'

I bite my lip with a deep sense of dread.
Is Dean Ferguson part of this?

FOUR

My blood runs as cold as ice. I'm beside myself with panic. I turn to Alan. 'When did you last see him?'

'Yesterday when he dropped Lucas off.' Alan and Angela, Johnny's stepmum and Tom's birth mum, had agreed to look after my boy for the weekend.

'What time was that?'

His eyes widen, and he lets out a long breath. 'Just before five.'

I think back to yesterday. I last saw Johnny around four, when he picked up Lucas from my house. But it doesn't take an hour to get to Angela and Alan's house from mine. It's only a ten-minute drive. So what had he been doing with Lucas for the other fifty minutes?

'How did he seem?' I ask.

Deep creases line his forehead. He pauses as if he needs to consider his answer. 'A little tense as any groom would be.'

'Did he say something to you then?'

'What do you mean?'

'Did he give any indication he was going to do this?'

Alan shakes his head. 'I'm as shocked as you, Hannah.' He

adjusts his rectangular-framed glasses. 'I don't understand. As far as I knew, he couldn't wait to—' He stops as if he senses what he's about to add will upset me even more. 'He was tired, he said. He hadn't had a good day.'

'He'd been to see that client up north,' I say. 'And got stuck in traffic on the way back.' My breath quickens. 'What else did he say?'

Alan shakes his head. 'He couldn't wait for today, he said.'

I wind up the window, shivering. The furnace from earlier now feels like a fridge.

So what changed? Could Dean have got to him, told him everything?

I find India's number again. Although my older sister, Carrie, is on my favourites list, India isn't. That doesn't mean I love her any less, far from it. It's because Carrie is more needy than India's free spirit, and I speak to Carrie daily. India, on the other hand, lives abroad. The only way I know her current location, unless I've had a recent text with an attached photo of another breathtaking view, is to look at her Instagram account. She runs a travel page and corresponding blog of her adventures around what she terms the unexplored world that is now funding her alternative lifestyle.

Again, the call goes straight to voicemail. This isn't anything out of the ordinary. Despite being glued to social media, India rarely answers her phone. After I leave a message, a call comes in. It's Carrie. She is marrying Tom – Johnny's half-brother – next weekend. Having two family weddings so close together wasn't ideal, but Johnny and I had little choice.

The family dynamic is a little too close and complicated for my liking. But Carrie and Tom were engaged before Johnny and I even met, so who am I to complain? You can't help who you fall in love with.

'Are you OK?' Carrie asks.

'What the hell's going on?' I don't recognise the strong

woman I am in the pathetic whiny sound coming out of my mouth.

'I don't know. Tom arrived at the church and said Johnny wasn't coming.' She sounds breathless, as if she has been running around looking for my fiancé herself.

'Put Tom on,' I say.

'He's talking to the priest.'

I imagine Tom telling the confused congregation the wedding is off, and the rest of the day's events are cancelled.

'I don't believe it.' I swear. I rarely use the F-bomb. But sometimes it's the only suitable word.

'I know, none of us can,' Carrie says.

'Have you seen India?' I ask.

'Briefly. She left with her new guy.'

'Did you recognise him?' It's a silly question. Carrie only saw Dean once, briefly, but I'd told her what a rogue he was – like his brother back then. They were both involved with rather unsavoury characters. It's possible he could've changed, I suppose. Who am I trying to kid? People like Dean Ferguson don't change. They are the dregs of the earth, rotten through and through.

'Recognise him? What do you mean?' Carrie asks.

'Nothing. Where's Lucas?'

'He's with me. He's all confused, wondering what's going on.'

I think of my sweet little boy, all dressed up in his tuxedo and red bow tie. A mini version of Johnny for the day, who I was expecting to walk down the aisle in front of Alan and me. He'll be distraught. I lower my head, wondering how I'm going to explain this nightmare to him.

'Get back to the hotel as quickly as you can, please,' I say to my sister. The desperation in my voice is palpable.

This can't be happening.

FIVE

There must have been some kind of mistake.

I'll get to the hotel, and Johnny will be waiting for me. I'm so sure, I'd swear my life on it. But as we drive along in silence, doubt creeps through me.

The driver hooks a right into the impressive gates of Maple Manor, a Georgian estate set in immense grounds that has been converted into a luxury hotel and spa.

Johnny brought me here in the early days of our relationship. As the car ambles along the long gravel driveway flanked by bare cherry blossom trees, the memory of that night toys with me. The game of tennis we played upon arrival. The afternoon in the spa relaxing by the indoor pool. The five-course meal as we chatted and laughed, discovering more about each other and our pasts we cared to share. It was perfect, as has been every day we've shared together since... until today.

When he emphatically told me that night I now knew everything about him, I assured him there was nothing more for him to learn about me either. At least nothing I could admit to. He didn't need to know about the way Charlie had treated me. And I was too ashamed to tell him.

Alan gets out of the car and comes to open my door.

I climb out of the car to join him. 'I want to go home.'

'Understood. We'll get you packed up, and I'll take you. Unless you want to go with your sisters?'

'I don't care. Whoever can get me there the fastest.'

Hotel guests, blissfully unaware of my distress, turn to admire the bride as we walk into the grand entrance. The wedding gown I couldn't wait to wear now feels like a trap I have to get out of. The receptionist, a gregarious lady, who greeted Carrie and me when we'd arrived late yesterday afternoon, stares at me, scratching her head. I can't look her in the eye. And I certainly can't talk to her. She leaves the desk and walks towards us, but Alan quickly waves her away.

We take the lift by the imposing staircase to the bridal suite on the third floor. I rush inside. Alan follows me to the living area, a large room with a vaulted ceiling, exposed beams and a cream décor. It leads to an expansive terrace with unobstructed, breathtaking views across the large lake and surrounding gardens that taper down to a dense forest.

I stood on that terrace early this morning in my bathrobe, sipping tea while marvelling at the extensive grounds covered with a dusting of snow. It was cold, but I didn't care. My cheeks ached from smiling, and the day hadn't even begun.

Carrie had joined me. Her voice rings in my thoughts. 'Just look at you! You're glowing. Totally radiant. And you haven't even got your dress on yet. I hope I look this good when I marry Tom. Only a week to go. I'm so excited. Who would've thought we'd be getting married so close together?'

Alan sits on one of the thronelike chairs by the fireplace and picks up the remote control. He sighs deeply. 'I'll wait here while you pack your stuff.' He presses a button on the remote control. A football match appears on the flatscreen on the wall. 'If you need me to do anything, just shout.'

I haul the train of my dress up the hallway and enter the

bathroom. My mind is in turmoil. I stand in front of the ornate mirror. My winged eyeliner has smudged. I rip the bobby pins from my hair holding the French braid in place. I smack my hands on the marble vanity unit and silently seethe in the mirror as if I'm talking to Johnny, 'Why have you done this?' I drop my head, trying to control my breathing. I need to hold it together. Lucas will be here any minute. He can't see me in a mess. He'll be confused enough as it is.

I perch on the edge of the claw-footed bath, taking deep breaths as I stare at my wedding shoes, a dainty pair of court shoes with kitten heels.

I need to see Johnny.

Now.

I kick off my shoes and slip out of my dress. The lace-sleeved gown falls in a pile onto the floor. I stand for a moment, staring at it, overcome with emotion. I was so excited to walk down the aisle to meet Johnny in this dress. I rip off the lace garters I'd borrowed from my sister and the silk stockings and kick them at the bin with a loud grunt. Grabbing one of the luxury bathrobes hanging on the back of the door, I slip it on.

But as I open the door leading to the bedroom, I abruptly stop.

I gasp out loud, unable to believe the sight before me.

SIX

I blink, wondering if I'm dreaming. My muscles stiffen.

Red rose petals shaped in a big heart cover the king-sized bed. Large bunches of red and white roses matching my wedding bouquet fill crystal vases on each bedside table. The fresh, floral smell is overpowering. A white envelope stands against one of the vases.

A gut-churning sensation claws at my throat. I grab the envelope.

My name is written on the front.

And there's no mistaking it's Johnny's neat handwriting.

With a trembling hand, I rip it open. My heart hammers, every beat a reminder of the fate the day has delivered. Inside is a white card with a handwritten note. I mutter the message, "'Welcome to your happy ever after, my darling. Here's to the beginning. Forever yours, Johnny X.'"

Some sicko is playing games with me.

I return to the bathroom where I drop to my knees in front of the pristine white toilet and promptly throw up, continuing until there's nothing left inside of me.

Coughing, I wipe my mouth and stand, turning to the

vanity unit where I stare in the mirror. Mascara runs from my beautifully made-up eyes, smudging my cheeks. I swipe my toothbrush from the holder and clean my teeth. But however much I brush, the rancid taste of deceit refuses to leave my mouth.

I call Alan into the bedroom. 'You need to come and see this.'

He enters the room, as dazed as me to see the overindulgence of passion, love and devotion glistening from the bed. He goes to speak but no sound leaves his mouth. There are no words.

I grab the handwritten card and give it to him. 'This isn't the mark of someone who was about to bail. Is it?'

His eyes widen as he reads the loving words Johnny has written for me.

'I don't understand,' I say. 'What's got into him? You don't go to all these lengths only to leave your wife-to-be at the altar. You don't, do you?'

'When did he do all this? It must've been after we all left for the church,' he says.

'So he went to all the effort to decorate the room and then not turn up. What the hell is going on, Alan?'

He looks as perplexed as I am.

He follows me to the living area and leans against one of the chairs, his arms ramrod straight.

I call the reception desk. The line rings and rings. 'They're not answering. I'm going downstairs to speak to the manager.'

I slam down the phone and rush past him into the bedroom, where I change into the jeans and jumper I arrived in yesterday. I stare at the bed. The amorous sentiment is in Johnny's nature. He's a romantic. He often turns up at my house with flowers and a bar of Lucas's favourite chocolate. But most importantly, from the moment I'd introduced him to Lucas – and he's the only man I've ever granted that privilege to – Johnny has treated him like his own son.

I return to the living area, slip into my trainers and open the door. 'I'll be right back,' I mouth to Alan, who is now conversing with someone on his mobile. 'I'm going to find out what's going on here.'

Not bothering to wait for the lift, I take the stairs two at a time to the ground floor, hurrying along the thick carpeted hallway. I can't get that note from my head. *Forever yours*. Johnny wrote those words but didn't turn up to marry me?

In the grand reception area, a line of couples four deep is waiting to check in. The duty manager, a tall and lanky guy with a thin face, greets me. 'Miss Young!' His neck twitches. A sombre façade has replaced the overwhelming enthusiasm from when I spoke to him at breakfast this morning. He guides me to one side, away from the throng of guests. 'Our sincere apologies for the circumstances.' He runs his fingers around the inside of his shirt collar. 'I've instructed my staff to take care of all matters for you. I'm sorry we didn't get to your room in time. I—'

'When did Johnny come here to decorate the room?' I try to remain calm. This poor guy is not at fault.

He hesitates as if he isn't sure how to answer me. 'Mr Caxton came here late yesterday afternoon, just before you arrived.' His neck jerks. 'He left written instructions on how he wanted the room decorated for... for your arrival this afternoon.' He slowly turns his head as if he can no longer bear to look at me.

I bite my lip, unable to understand why someone would go to all that trouble if they had even the tiniest doubts.

'Mum, Mum!'

I turn to see my beautiful little boy running towards me. The constant in my life. The person I'd do anything for... absolutely anything. His cheeks are as red as his bow tie which sits crooked at his neck. He's smiling, pleased to see me, but I can detect the confusion in his innocent face.

Carrie walks behind him. Seeing her in her red bridesmaid's dress is heart-wrenching. My jaw locks. I can't cry in front of my boy. Carrie's eyes dart from Lucas to mine. She shakes her head, her face displaying the shock and disbelief that is smeared all over mine.

Lucas stumbles but corrects his step. 'Mum! Is it true?'

I open my arms to catch him.

His face is a picture of raw childhood pain I never want to witness again. 'Is Johnny not going to be my dad anymore?'

SEVEN

I hug my son tightly as if I never want to let him go.

It takes all my effort to hold back the tears pleading to burst. But I have to. I've only just become accustomed to the news myself, so I haven't given thought about how I'll break it to him.

'Where's India?' I ask my sister.

'She said she'd meet us here,' Carrie replies.

'Is it? Is it true?' Lucas's muffled voice asks into my shoulder. He lifts his head. Tears roll down his face. It's an excruciatingly painful sight. 'What's happened, Mum?'

Be honest with kids. That's the motto I've brought my son up by, except, of course, where his real father is concerned. I never want him to know what a monster he was. It will disturb him for life.

'I don't know, darling.' This is the truth: I simply don't know. I'm as confused as everyone else. I run my hands through his mop of blond curls. I love his hair, even if it does remind me of his father's. 'I need to speak to Johnny.' I wipe away his tears with my fingers as Carrie and I exchange looks of despair.

'But I love Johnny,' Lucas cries. 'I want him to be my dad.'

'I need to speak to him,' I repeat, controlling my rapid breaths.

He grows hysterical. 'Call him, then, Mum. Just call him.'

'I've tried, but he's not answering his phone at the moment.' I take his hand. 'Let's go upstairs to the room.'

In his usual manner, Lucas talks all the way up the stairs. From the day he found his voice and learnt to say 'Muma', he hasn't stopped.

Johnny excels at chatting with him. A little after we met, he bought a PlayStation under the pretence he'd wanted one for as long as he could remember. But secretly, I think he believed it was a way to bond with Lucas, as he only ever bought *Hot Wheels*, *Lego* and *Astro Bot*, never any adult games.

My stomach coils with sadness as I think about how Johnny transforms the spare room in his apartment, which he uses as a study, into a bedroom when Lucas stays. He bought a solar system duvet set, as Lucas is captivated with the planets, and a string of fairy lights with astronauts, spaceships and rockets that he threaded around the bookcase. And he studies the planets, learning all kinds of weird and wonderful facts, so he always has something new to tell Lucas about Mars being as cold as the South Pole or that there are mountains on Pluto.

Alan opens his arms when we arrive back to the suite. 'Come here, buddy.' He bends to swoop up my son.

'Why didn't Johnny come?' Lucas clutches his hands around Alan's neck.

'Why don't we leave your mum and aunty here and go and find some ice cream.' Alan manages a smile for him. 'Or chips. Which would you prefer?'

'Both.' A film of snot bubbles out of Lucas's button nose. He wipes it away with the back of his hand.

Carrie snatches a tissue from a box on the coffee table and cleans him up.

'Both, it is,' Alan says to Lucas. 'Let's go.'

'Did he not mention anything at all about this to you?' Carrie asks Alan.

'No,' Alan snaps. It's so unlike him, my sister and I are both taken aback. He is usually so chilled-out.

Alan nods at me. 'We'll be back in a bit.' He lifts Lucas into the air, turning him like the propellers of a helicopter as he walks out the door.

An odd sensation creeps through me. Johnny was close to his dad. Much closer than most father-son relationships. So I find it hard to believe he never told Alan his plans to dump me at the altar.

EIGHT

My mind is in overdrive. Alan is the most trustworthy person I've ever met. He'd tell me if he knew more. I shake my head. My emotions are getting the better of me.

'What the frickin' hell?' Carrie says. 'When I next see Johnny Caxton, he's going to get a big, fat piece of my mind. Tom's livid with him, too.' She sweeps past me. 'I need to get out of this dress.' She opens her overnight bag and pulls out the leggings and shirt she wore when she picked me up from home yesterday.

I grimace. Pressure is building behind my eyes. 'I've got a damn headache coming on.' I rush to my bag and find a couple of tablets.

I fight tears as I swallow two paracetamol with a glug of water. We'd be having our photographs taken right now under the archway entwined with winter roses that I spotted in the churchyard during the wedding rehearsal. I thought it was the perfect spot. The family went to a local pub afterwards, where Tom ordered champagne. I can just hear his cheery voice now: 'It's never too early to celebrate.' He popped the cork of the first bottle, filling champagne flutes and handing them around. 'To Johnny and Hannah. May you live happily ever after.'

I flop down on one of the posh chairs. Its appearance is better than its comfort. I try Johnny's number another time, only to get his voicemail. I scream in frustration. 'I don't understand it.'

'Me neither.' Carrie takes the chair beside me. 'Tom is distraught. We all are. Not as much as you, obviously.'

I bite my lip and look up at the ceiling, unable to stop the tears now flowing freely.

Carrie snatches a tissue. 'I'm so sorry, Han. This is just awful. I'm truly shocked.'

The pain is cutting, slicing through my heart like a butcher's knife. I can't imagine ever feeling OK again. I wipe the tears away, allowing more to fall until I'm sobbing. My shoulders shudder relentlessly as raw emotion escapes from me in loud wails. But at least they'll be out of my system before Alan returns with Lucas.

I sniff and wipe my nose again, tossing the tissue in the bin. 'I'm trying to make sense of it all. Something happened on the way to the church. Get this. I saw India get out of a car with a guy I could've sworn was Dean.'

'Who, Dean Ferguson? Her new boyfriend?' She stares at me, confused. 'Are you sure?'

'Dean! Yes,' I say. 'Did you see him at the church?'

She nods. 'Only from afar.'

'Did he look familiar?'

'No.' She squints. 'Are you sure you're not mistaken?'

'No,' I cry. To be fair, she only saw him briefly once, after the inquest. And the circumstances were hardly favourable. And he's changed. He's still a hefty guy, but he's lost a lot of weight.

'How the hell did India get hooked up with Dean Ferguson?' she asks.

'That's what I want to know.'

'Was this before or after you found out Johnny wasn't turning up?'

'Before.'

'India can explain when she gets here.' She shakes her head in dismay, peering around the room. 'I guess we need to get this lot cleared up. Where do you want to stay tonight? You could come to ours.'

'I don't want to see anyone. I just want to go home.' I hold up my phone and clutch it in my hand with hope. Hope that the man who has just jilted me at the altar will call me. 'Unless, of course, Johnny calls.'

I momentarily imagine the phone ringing, his name flashing across the screen, and me answering it to hear him begging for forgiveness. In a moment of madness, he got cold feet and deeply regrets his actions.

I snap out of my fantasy world and stand. 'Come and look at this.'

I take her hand and lead her to the bedroom. The door is open, but the duvet is clear. 'Damn. Alan must've cleared it all away.' I frown. That's strange. I can't understand why he would've done that. It wasn't his place to. He must've thought he was doing me a favour.

'Cleared what away?' my sister asks.

I gesture to the bed, explaining the overindulgent display of rose petals waiting for me when I arrived back from the church. I grab the note beside the vase of flowers and show it to her. 'This was left here.'

'It doesn't make sense,' she says. 'Why would he do this?'

My phone rings. I run to answer it, the smidgen of hope that it's Johnny fading fast.

India's name flashes across the screen. 'I've been trying to call you,' she says. 'I'm so sorry, Han. I can't believe what's happened.'

'Where are you?' I ask.

'I'm on my way to the hotel,' India says.

'Don't come here. Can you meet us at my house?'

'Sure. I'll go straight there.'

'The guy you brought to the church,' I say. 'What did you say his name was?'

'Dean.'

'Dean what? What's his surname?' My stomach turns. I don't know why I'm bothering asking her. I know what she's going to say.

She lowers her voice. 'Dean Ferguson. Why?'

'I'll talk to you when I see you.' I end the call.

If there's any colour left in my cheeks, it melts away faster than an ice cream left in the sun.

'What happened at the church?'

Carrie frowns. 'Do you really want me to go over this?'

'Yes!'

'Really, Han?' She looks wholly uncomfortable.

I glare at her.

She sighs. 'Everyone was arriving and getting seated. Tom and Johnny weren't there, of course. I put it down to them sneaking another quick pint at the pub. Then I thought perhaps they'd got caught in traffic. I then realised Tom had been trying to call me. He turned up, as white as a sheet. Said Johnny had called him to say he...' She pauses as if trying to break the truth to me in the kindest way possible. 'He'd changed his mind. He... he suddenly felt... trapped.'

'Trapped!'

NINE

Carrie and I turn to a knock at the door.

The dying delusion reappears that I'll answer it to Johnny's face full of regret. 'Who's that?' Carrie says. We stare at each other, a sliver of hope swimming in our eyes.

I rush to the door, only to find Angela, the family matriarch, who should now officially be my mother-in-law. I clench my jaw. I can't think of her in those terms anymore. The only relationship Angela and I will maintain going forward is boss-employee.

I haven't thought about work, but I'll have to at some point. The time will come when I'll have to face them all again in the offices where Johnny, Tom and I – and Carrie until recently – work at Caxton Events, an exclusive events management company that Angela and Alan own.

As I said, the situation is domestically close.

But none of us could've predicted that when Carrie coaxed me into moving to the area last year, after persuading Angela to give me a job, I'd end up falling in love with the boss's son. The game of love forges its own rules.

Angela brushes past me in a pale blue smock dress and a

matching fascinator in her shoulder-length hair, which she has styled into a French pleat for the occasion. She closes the door and turns to face me. 'I'm so sorry, Hannah. This must be dreadfully humiliating for you.'

I go to add that the sadness and confusion far outweigh the humiliation, but I don't get the chance to.

'I'm afraid that the guests who were planning on staying here tonight are on their way back from the church. I've suggested that the hotel determine how many people are still intending to stay and use the wedding food to feed them accordingly. They might as well have the meal I've paid for. Otherwise, what's the hotel going to do with all those four-course meals?'

It could go to the homeless, but I don't have the bandwidth to argue with her. Angela is a complicated character. Generous to a fault, straight thinking and demanding but most definitely a person with whom I avoid confrontation at all costs.

I knew we should never have let her get involved. I told Johnny it was a bad decision. We initially booked one of the much smaller suites on the lower floors of the hotel because this bridal suite was almost triple the cost. I'm generally a no-frills girl, and I didn't see the point in spending all that money when we would've been content anywhere as long as we were together. But Angela insisted on paying for the bridal suite, as well as forking out for the wedding meal. 'You only get married once.' I recall her raised eyebrows as if I was a naughty schoolgirl who'd done something wrong when she added, 'Hopefully.'

I didn't want to be beholden to her. But Johnny put pressure on me. He doesn't like upsetting Angela. Mainly because he doesn't like upsetting his dad. Alan's first wife died in childbirth, and he met Angela soon afterwards, so she has practically brought Johnny up. They have a complex relationship. He respects her, but I think that secretly he's often perplexed at his father's choice of lifetime partner.

'Come on, Han,' he'd said. 'It'll really help. They can afford it.'

With the cost of the wedding heading north with colossal speed, I buckled. We've had so much to fork out for. And there's the deposit for the house we've also been saving up for. I groan. The house of our dreams we are due to move into in the new year that will no longer happen.

'It appears many guests have decided to stay,' Angela says.

Carrie and I exchange looks of disbelief disguised in silent, small shakes of our heads.

'A little insensitive, I thought,' Angela continues. 'But be that as it may, I assume you'll want to get away from here as soon as possible. I'll call a taxi.'

'It's fine,' Carrie says. 'I have my car here. I'll drive her.'

'Take me to his apartment,' I say. 'I want to see him.'

Angela juts out her chin. 'That's probably not a good idea.'

'Why?'

Strangely, she stumbles on her words as if she doesn't know how to best answer me. It's odd. Angela is eloquently spoken. 'Let's allow things to calm down.'

'What are you keeping from me, Angela?'

'Nothing at all.' She vigorously shakes her head. 'I knew nothing about this.'

I eye her suspiciously.

She resumes her usual brusqueness. 'I'll go and manage the guests who are staying. I don't expect to see you at work this week, Hannah. Take the week off.'

I don't believe it. Even at a time like this, work is on her mind. I've never known anyone so obsessed with their job.

'And rest assured,' she says as she leaves the room, 'I'll be having words when I see that Johnny Caxton.'

My phone buzzes. I'm constantly on edge, waiting for word from Johnny. He owes me that much, surely? But it's only Jenna from the office, who works closely alongside Johnny, expressing her concern for me.

'It's going to be hell facing all these people. Bloody hell, Johnny.' I slam my hand to my forehead. 'How could he have done this to me, Carrie? Why?'

My sister takes my hand. 'Come on, let's get you home.'

'What about Lucas? I don't want to go down there to find him. I can't face anyone at the moment.'

'I'll go and get him.' She digs her keys out of her bag and hands them to me. 'You go and get in my car.'

I rush around the suite, gathering my stuff. Everywhere I look, reminders of Johnny cut me to the quick. A stray petal between the pillows. My wedding gown on the bathroom floor. The card scribbled with *Welcome to your happy ever after, my darling. Here's to the beginning*. It's crippling.

With my bags packed, I try to phone him again. The least he could do is call, or even send me a message. But the disappointment continues coming at me like a boxer who is hell bent on defeating their opponent.

I peer around the room for the last time before closing the door on what should've been the happiest chapter of my life that has turned into the saddest.

Angela isn't the only one who will be having words with Johnny Caxton when they next see him.

And I don't care what she says.

I'm going to his apartment now.

TEN

I head to the hotel's back entrance to avoid bumping into anyone. But a couple holding hands and pulling cabin bags are waiting as I exit the lift. They smile and thank me, the flush of excitement of a weekend away together evident on their glowing faces. Another wave of sadness rips through me. That should be Johnny and me.

A gust of cold air hits me. The wind has whipped up, sending a flurry of snow circling my head. I shiver. Once I'm inside Carrie's car, I turn on the ignition and ramp the heating up to maximum. I don't want it to be cold when Lucas joins us. I stare out of the windscreen, tapping my foot on the floor. Come on, Carrie.

Dean Ferguson resurfaces in my thoughts.

It's too much of a coincidence. He has something to do with why Johnny backed out today. I'm sure of it.

The sudden urge to be in the safety of my own home is overwhelming. I peer towards the hotel, willing my sister to get a move on. I'm distraught. Of course I am. The pain is raw and pounding, but there's also an overriding fear driving through me.

The car door opens, startling me. Carrie gets in.

'Where's Lucas?' I ask.

'He's still eating his chips, and he hasn't had his ice cream yet. Alan said he'll drive him back later. We thought it'd give you a chance to catch your breath.' She fastens her seatbelt. 'We can wait for him if you want.'

'Leave him if he's happy.' I clear my throat. 'Drive me to Johnny's apartment. I need to have this all out with him.'

'But India's waiting for us at yours. Anyway, Han. I think Angela was probably right. Let the dust settle for a few hours. We can go later. You don't even know if he's there.'

'You're probably right.'

Carrie drives us back to mine. I constantly check my phone, but the only messages clogging my inbox are from guests who should now be toasting the bride and groom.

'How the hell did India get mixed up with Dean Ferguson?' Carrie says.

'Heaven only knows.'

India is waiting outside my house when Carrie pulls up. She's tanned from life on the Gold Coast of Australia where she's been living for the past three months, working in a bar part-time while running her digital travel business and enjoying beach life. She's halfway through her month's stay back here, but I haven't seen much of her. I've been busy with the wedding, and she's been catching up with friends.

She hugs me. 'I'm so sorry, Han. What a bastard.'

It's wrong to hear that word used about Johnny, especially coming from India. She's a gentle, peaceful soul. She rarely has a bad word to say about anyone. But I can't blame her. If a guy did to either of my sisters what Johnny has done to me, I'd probably express myself the same.

'Get me inside,' she says. 'It's freezing.'

I open the front door with an increasing sense of dread. I'm due to exchange contracts on the sale of this house on Monday, and Johnny and I will move into our dream home in the new year. The exchange was meant to happen yesterday, but a technical hitch with the purchaser's solicitors meant it didn't proceed. If there are any small mercies in this fiasco, that is one of them.

It's as cold inside as it is outside. But I hadn't expected to be returning for a few days. I lock the door and override the heating to throw out hours of warmth for the evening ahead.

Carrie heads to the kitchen, calling over her shoulder, 'I'll open a bottle of wine.'

'Not for me.' I need to keep a clear head. Wine and my mood won't marry well. If Johnny gets in contact, I want to speak to him sober. And if he doesn't, I don't want the effects of alcohol to drag me any further down the well of sadness I'm already heading to the bottom of. Besides, the threat of a migraine still lingers.

There's also the conversation I need to have with India.

'Aren't you driving?' I call out. If Carrie opens a bottle of wine, she won't stop until the last drop has gone.

'Tom's getting a lift here, and he said he'll drive home.'

'I'll have tea.' I rush back to the front door to double-check I've locked it. I don't normally use the bolts at the top and bottom, but I feel the need to today.

I join my sisters in the galley kitchen that widens to accommodate a square table, two chairs and a large dresser that dominates the far wall. Small but cosy, Johnny calls it.

We don't go out much because of Lucas, but Johnny loves coming here. We've spent many evenings at this table with a takeaway curry and a bottle of red wine, discussing the future we planned to spend together. I wanted another child. I press my hand on my belly and look up to the ceiling. He wanted five, more if possible. I bite my lip. It's heartbreaking our dreams are now in the past tense.

'I'll have tea, as well,' India says.

Carrie fills the kettle and flicks the switch.

I can't believe I'm here. It's surreal. I should be sipping champagne with my husband right now, or having our first dance. I pull a chair from beneath the small table for India. 'Sit down.'

India frowns, collecting her mane of long dark hair and pushing it over her shoulder. It tumbles down her back. She's a petite woman, but strong from all the yoga she practises. Her eyes are big and blue just like Carrie's. They're both attractive, but India's easygoing lifestyle affords her features a more relaxed appearance than Carrie's uptight, rigid expression. 'I don't like the sound of this – being summoned by big sister,' India says in jest, attempting to lighten the mood, but it's beyond salvageable.

I fetch the stool from the living room we use when Johnny comes over. It's another small room with an original cast-iron fireplace and a blue sofa I bought from a charity shop when I moved in. Johnny attached the flatscreen TV on the wall to the side of the fireplace to afford more space. A jumper of his is thrown over the arm of the sofa. The moccasin slippers I bought for when he stays are sticking out from under the coffee table.

Reminders of him are everywhere.

I return to the kitchen, where Carrie is serving three cups of tea. She has used Johnny's Star Wars mug that Lucas bought for him last Christmas. I can't bear to look at it. I sit on the stool and come right out with it. 'I need you to tell me about Dean Ferguson.'

India's eyes dart from me to Carrie. 'Why?'

'Because he's trouble,' I reply.

India crosses her arms. 'Explain.'

'First, I need confirmation he is who I think he is.' It's fruitless. I know exactly who he is. 'Does he have a brother?'

India leans back in the chair, squinting at me curiously. 'Yes. He had a brother, but he died in a dreadful accident. Well, to be honest, he said it could've been murder.'

ELEVEN

My voice wavers. 'Murder? That's crazy. He's crazy. What did he say happened?'

'Charlie fell off the roof of his house. Or someone pushed him.'

My chest tightens. I stare at Carrie. 'I knew it.'

'You knew what?' India says.

'I think Dean has something to do with why Johnny didn't turn up today.'

'Han, careful,' Carrie says.

India's eyes flit from me to Carrie. 'What on earth do you mean, "careful"?'

Carrie glares at me.

'Come on, Carrie. She's our sister,' I say. 'I have to tell her.'

'Tell me what?' India's face reddens. 'Can one of you tell me what the hell is going on here? You two have always kept secrets from me. Ever since we were kids. It's not fair.' She slaps her fist on the table. Only gently. Aggression isn't in her catalogue of emotions. But still, tea wobbles in the cups. 'And seeing as it's concerning the guy I'm involved with, don't you think I have a right to know?'

I get up and pace up and down the kitchen, my fists clenched into tight balls. 'I used to live with Dean's brother Charlie.'

India sits upright, her lips parted.

'I only met Dean a couple of times.' I think back to those few occasions. 'For some reason, Dean made it clear he didn't like me from the word go. But Charlie said I was being paranoid. Dean worked on an oil rig so Charlie didn't see much of him.'

'Good grief.' India nods. 'That's him. We *are* talking about the same person.'

Carrie rolls her eyes. 'I think we've already established that. Perhaps I should open that bottle of wine.'

My phone beeps. I grab it from the table and tap the screen, still clinging onto the thin threads of hope. But it's only a text from a friend. I ignore it.

Panic consumes me. I rush to the back door and check it's locked.

'So how come you never told me about this Charlie?' India asks.

'You weren't here.'

'How long were you together?'

'About eight months, but it was pretty intense. I moved into his house a month after we got together. He was a builder.'

'That's right. Dean told me. He was doing up the rundown house where he died.'

I nod. 'It had a single-storey extension out the back that had a flat roof.' I tell her how Charlie had transformed that roof into a small balcony. He replaced the bedroom window with double doors to provide access and built railings around the outside for, ironically, safety. 'He used to sit on the railings when he was smoking.'

'And that's what he was doing the night he died?' she asks.

I nod. 'And taking drugs.'

'Drugs? Dean never mentioned drugs.'

I nod again. 'And he'd been drinking. He'd been out with his mates, and there was beer with the drugs on the table of the balcony. There was an inquest.' My stomach twists and turns. The day is taking its toll. 'They concluded it was an accident. That's what's on the death certificate. But Dean blamed me. He reckoned I pushed him. He's a psycho. I'm telling you, India. You need to keep away from him.'

'Charlie was so nasty to her.' Carrie grabs my hand and shows India the ugly red scar at the base of my thumb that oozes anger for how it came about. 'He did that. He held her hand on the grill. And he hit her. Repeatedly.'

India stares at me, aghast. 'Why didn't you leave?'

'Because I was twenty years old.' My voice lowers at the shame that still haunts me about the whole affair. 'And I had nowhere to go. Dad was dead. We'd moved Mum into the home. You were away. Carrie was preparing to join you.' I withdraw my hand. 'And he threatened me. Said if I ever left him, he would come after me. I was saving up to get away.'

'This is freaking me out.' India's eyes dart nervously between Carrie and me.

'Where did you meet him?' I ask.

'Online. He contacted me about my blog. I can't even remember which one now, but he was interested in visiting the country I'd written about.' She scratches her head. 'Croatia, I think it was. Anyway, we developed a friendship, especially when I found out about my mole.' She holds up her hands, making air quotes to emphasise the word friendship.

Earlier in the year, she'd gone to the doctor's, concerned about an odd-looking spot on her leg. It turned out to be cancerous. She wasn't going to come to my wedding, as she was due to have it removed, but she got lucky, and the operation was brought forward. She only decided last minute to come back to see me get married.

'He had a cancerous growth removed from his neck a while ago, so he understood what I was going through.' She sips her tea. 'I thought he was a decent guy. He made me laugh.'

'I reckon he's done it to get to me. I mean, it can't be a coincidence.' I glance anxiously from one sister to the other. 'Can it?'

'But why does he want to get to you?' India asks. 'And why now?'

I shrug. 'How do I know what's going through his warped mind?'

Carrie stands. 'I'm opening that bottle.'

India grabs her phone from her bag. 'I wish you'd told me about Charlie, Han.'

'I met him just after Dad died, and you'd gone off backpacking. I was hardly going to call you back here.'

Carrie pours a glass of wine. 'Sure you won't change your mind?' The glug of the yellow liquid makes me want to join her.

'Pour me one,' India says. 'I can't believe what you're saying. Dean seemed so nice. We FaceTimed regularly. I had feelings for him.'

'The same as I did for Charlie when I first met him. Then he moved me in with him, and he turned.'

India slams her hand over her mouth. Her eyes dart between Carrie and me. She drops her hand. 'Was Charlie Lucas's dad?'

TWELVE

I nod.

'Dean's his uncle?' India cries.

I nod again.

'Why have you never told me this?'

A knock at the door echoes around the room.

Johnny!

I rush to answer it with repeated anticipation.

But it's my loving boy who grabs me, clinging tightly to my legs.

Alan stands on the doorstep, still dressed in his wedding suit minus his bow tie and the red rose that decorated his button hole.

My pulse races at the expression on his face. A look displaying he has news for me.

Lucas releases his grip from my legs. He's lost his bow tie, too, and he has ketchup down his shirt. 'I hurt my knee, Mum.' He rolls up his trouser leg. 'Look.' Blood trickles down his leg from a gash on his knee. 'Oh, no. It's bleeding again.'

I wince and close my eyes. Nausea overcomes me. I can't

stand the sight of blood. Ever since Charlie's death. The blood. Oh, so much blood.

'It's all right, Mum. It doesn't hurt.' He rolls his trouser leg back down when I open my eyes.

'Alan said I can still stay with them. What do you think, Mum?'

I open the door wide. 'Come in.'

'Can I go back with Alan, Mum? I still want to go and see Santa tomorrow.'

Alan steps inside and closes the door. 'Aunty Carrie and Aunty India are in the kitchen.' I pat my son's shoulder. 'Why don't you go and say hello.'

Lucas kicks off his shoes and runs to the kitchen.

I turn to Alan. 'You've heard from him, haven't you?'

He nods.

My pulse races at the wistful look on his face, telling me he isn't here as the bearer of good news. 'Let's go in the living room.'

Laughter filters through from the kitchen. One of my sisters is tickling Lucas. At least someone is happy.

I perch on the edge of the sofa, trying to stay composed. 'What did he say?'

Alan taps the screen of his phone and hands it to me. 'He sent this text. I didn't want to tell you over the phone, so I came straight here.'

I grab the phone and read the message as he stands beside the sofa, head down, staring at the floor.

Hi Dad. I've been a coward, I know. You must be so ashamed of me. But I just couldn't go through with it. The same feelings I had about Alison came over me. I shouldn't have waited until the last minute. It was wrong of me. But it's happened. I'm going away for a bit to get my head straight. Don't worry about me. Look after Hannah. I love you. I hope you still love me. Johnny.

That's it, then.

The message is clear.

He's not coming back to me.

But something is amiss. I reread Johnny's words before returning the phone. 'It's not from him.'

Alan frowns. 'What do you mean?'

'He never sent that message.' I shake my head. 'He didn't write it, anyway.'

He rereads it. 'What makes you say that?'

'Allison is spelt wrong. She spelt it with two ls. Someone else wrote that message.'

He sucks his lips into his mouth. His eyes scan the message another time. 'That must be a typo, Hannah.'

'It doesn't sound like him.' I lift my shoulders to my ears and drop them with a deep sigh. 'Does it sound like him to you?'

'I don't know what to say.'

'Do you think I'm kidding myself?' The words are leaving my mouth faster and faster.

'No... but, I—'

'You do, don't you?' I'm sounding desperate. 'I think we should go to the police.'

Perhaps he doesn't mean to, but he looks at me as if I'm mad. 'What're they going to do about it?'

I want to tell him about Dean, but I can't drag him back to those dark days of my life. Alan likes me. I'd even go as far as to say he loves me. The thought hurts. How can we carry on our relationship after what his son has done to me?

He continues. 'Johnny's a grown man of sound mind. He's spoken to his brother and messaged me, his dad. The police will laugh us all the way out of the door.'

I pause, taking a deep breath before replying. 'You're right. I need to accept it. Johnny's not coming back to me, is he?'

He slowly shakes his head. 'I'm sorry, Hannah. So dreadfully sorry for my son's behaviour.'

But as we hug, my eyes are dry.

He might think I'm in denial. But I know Johnny didn't write that message.

THIRTEEN

Alan offers to take Lucas for the night and continue their plans for tomorrow.

I don't want my boy to go. A sudden urge to keep him safe tells me not to let him go. But it would be selfish of me to stop him.

He'll have a much better time with them with the mood I'm in. Despite Angela's brusqueness in the workplace, she's good with Lucas. And Alan treats him the same as Johnny does – as if he were his own. So when they willingly offered to look after Lucas at the wedding, and for the rest of the weekend, I happily agreed. Weather permitting, they plan to take him to see Santa at the local zoo tomorrow.

After hugging my boy tightly and sending him off with Alan, I return to the kitchen.

India grunts, shaking her phone in the air. 'I can't understand why Dean's not answering his phone. This is so frustrating.'

'I know how you feel.'

'Sorry, that was insensitive.' India momentarily closes her

eyes and shakes her head. 'I've sent him a couple of messages, as well.'

'He's sent Alan a text.' I relay Johnny's message to his father.

'Too right, he's a coward,' Carrie says.

'Go over it,' I say to India.

She drinks her wine. 'Go over what?'

'How you and Dean met to how you ended up bringing him to the wedding.'

India takes another sip of wine. 'It started out seemingly platonic. You know – friendly messages backwards and forwards. He's got a good sense of humour. But it kind of—' She pauses and shrugs. 'It kind of developed, especially over the past few weeks when I told him I was coming back to the UK for my sisters' weddings. Now I think back, he was pretty insistent about us meeting yesterday.'

'Didn't that ring alarm bells for you?'

'Not really. I wanted to meet up with him as well. I'd kind of...' Another pause. Another shrug. '...I'd kind of grown fond of him. Then the whole issue with the mole arose, and he supported me. I know it was all online, but I had feelings for him.'

'Perhaps he set out to stalk you, but ended up falling in love with you,' Carrie suggests.

The thought of that beast going after my baby sister fills me with rage.

'So how did he end up coming to the wedding?' I ask.

'We arranged to meet last night before Pippa's evening reception in a pub in Stanfield.'

I'd been upset when she'd first mentioned about going to her friend's evening wedding reception. I thought she'd join Carrie, Lucas and me for an early dinner. But it felt selfish to stop her going. She was meeting a large group of friends who hadn't all met up together since school, and in all honesty, I wanted an early night, so I'd told her to go. How I'm regretting that decision now.

'He said that's where he lived, so it would be easy to meet up. He was nervous to start with. With hindsight, I'd say he was a little shaken up, but I put it down to nerves. Hell, I was nervous, too. We chatted and got on so well, it was like we'd known each other forever. I guess that's what led me to inviting him to the party. I did have a plus-one invitation. Then, yes, I invited him back to the Airbnb where I was staying. There. I've said it.'

Carrie raises her eyebrows.

India holds up her hands. 'Don't judge me.'

'I'm not,' Carrie says.

'He's very attentive,' India says.

Carrie squirms. 'We don't need the details.'

'I don't mean like that.' India pauses. 'Actually, I do. But he also seemed very kind. When we woke up this morning, he went out to get milk to make me a coffee. Then later he went back out for food to make me breakfast.'

She frowns and shakes her head. 'Then when the time came to leave, my car wouldn't start. He took a look but couldn't tell what was wrong with it. He called the hire company for me. They said they'd send someone out, but we waited and waited and no one showed. I was really getting stressed out. I knew I wouldn't make it to the hotel to join you, but I was scared I wouldn't make it to the service. But he offered to drive me to the church. If I'm honest, I wanted to spend more time with him.' Her eyes fix on mine. 'I really liked him, Han.' She shivers. 'That's when I called you to tell you what'd happened. And I asked if you'd mind if he joined me at the evening reception tonight, and you said to invite him to the whole day.'

I recall the conversation when I was getting ready at the hotel. I was upset India wouldn't be joining Carrie and me for the pre-wedding preparations. It was bad enough that she wasn't a bridesmaid because she thought she wouldn't make it to the wedding because of her operation. She'd sounded tearful that she'd let me down, but she was on her way thanks to this kind man who had come to the rescue. I couldn't have been thinking straight.

Being caught up in all the excitement had obviously clouded my judgement.

A thought occurs to me. 'Do you think he was planning this all along?'

Despite her healthy tan, India is pale. 'What do you mean?'

'He could've had something to do with your hire car not starting?' I say. 'And the hire company not showing?'

'That's a bit far-fetched, don't you think?'

'Let me tell you, India! If Dean Ferguson is anything like his brother, he could effortlessly manipulate any situation to his advantage. He managed to worm an invite to my wedding out of me through you, for heaven's sake.'

'Do you think he did something to the car so it wouldn't start, then faked a call to the hire company, all so he could come to the church to haunt me?'

'But to what end?' Carrie says.

'I don't know,' I cry.

India rubs her forehead. 'Have I been taken for a fool?'

'Who knows,' I say. 'Have you got a photo of him?'

'Funny that. I tried to take a selfie of us at the party last night. But he said he didn't do photos.'

'We need to find a way of contacting him,' I say.

'How?' She lifts her phone. 'He's not answering my calls.'

'How about I call him? Maybe he'd answer a call from a different number.'

'Do you really want him knowing your number?'

I succumb. 'You're right. No. I don't.'

As the day has rolled into the evening, my anxiety levels have spiralled. What started out as extreme excitement at dawn has progressed to a deep fear that danger and uncertainty are lurking around every corner.

Carrie pours herself another glass of wine. She holds up the bottle, offering it to India.

India pushes her glass forward for a refill. 'Do you want me to stay the night with you?' India asks me. 'I could sleep in Lucas's bed as he's not going to be here. Or I could go back to the hotel. Use that room that's been paid for.' She shivers. 'On second thought, I don't want to go back there. Not if that stalker's going to turn up.'

'Stay here,' I say. 'It'll be good to have the company. But don't tell Dean where you are. I don't want him knowing where I live.'

She looks at me in horror. 'But he knows. He dropped me off here.'

FOURTEEN

The reality of the situation I'm in hits hard. Not only has Dean Ferguson turned up in my life, but he now knows where I live. I lace my hands on top of my head. 'This is hell,' I cry.

Carrie lays a hand on my shoulder. 'Calm down, Han.'

'I can't calm down. That psycho now knows where I live.'

'I really liked him, you know,' India says. 'We've grown close. Albeit, online. And then last night!' She shudders again.

Carrie pours herself another glass of wine. 'What was his plan, do you think?'

'He must've known who you were, Han,' India says. 'It can't have been a coincidence.'

'Maybe he just wanted to freak you out on your wedding day?' Carrie says.

'But to what end?' I say.

Carrie glares at me. I stare back.

'Why are you two looking at each other like that?' India asks.

'We're not,' Carrie says, rubbing her hands together. She always does that when she's lying.

I continue pacing the kitchen.

Carrie turns to India. 'You should know by now not to trust people you meet online.'

'That's not fair.' India crosses her arms. 'I've made some wonderful friends online. There has to be some explanation. Let me try him again.' She reaches for her phone and stabs the call button. The ringtone belts out before morphing into a muffled voicemail message. She huffs and puffs and cuts off the call.

I stop pacing to check the back door, ensuring it's locked. Did I already do that? I can't remember.

'I'll stay here tonight,' India says. 'But don't forget I need to leave early in the morning for the christening.'

A knock at the front door startles us all. The thought of answering it to Dean intensifies the pool of nausea swimming in my stomach.

'That'll be Tom.' Carrie gets up. 'Listen, India. Tom doesn't know about Dean, or Charlie, so let's not discuss this in front of him.' She goes to let him in.

India frowns. 'Why doesn't he know about them?'

I don't know how to answer her without spilling the truth. 'Because... because, I just didn't want anyone knowing about that part of my life.'

She looks at me aghast. She's got a right to. 'But...'

Tom is a robust guy, tall, broad and muscular. His body is his temple, and he works out practically daily at the local gym. Johnny joins him after work a couple of times a week. His shoes click along the hallway. He must still be dressed in his wedding gear.

He squeezes my shoulder. I look up at another washed-out face, pale and drawn from the stress of the day. The sight of his tuxedo is another reminder of what I've lost. 'I'm so sorry, Hannah.'

Carrie stands by his side, leaning into his broadness.

My bottom lip trembles. 'I don't understand it.'

'He's done this before, though, hasn't he?' Carrie says.

Tom draws away and glares at her.

'Well, he has, hasn't he?' Carrie demands. 'With that Allison woman.'

'Let's not go there,' Tom says. 'This isn't the time. You'll only torture yourself more. Anyway, he and Allison happened years ago, and he ended the relationship way before their wedding day.'

My head throbs. I get up and fetch a packet of paracetamol from the kitchen drawer. I take two tablets. It's too soon after the previous dose, but I can't risk one of my debilitating migraines just now. 'I want to know his movements. When did you last see him?'

Tom strokes his full beard. 'Oh, Hannah. Really.'

'Yes!' I shout. My voice wavers. 'Really.'

'He was meant to meet the lads for a drink at The Bell last night, but he called to say he wasn't going to make it.'

'I never knew that. I mean, I knew the plan was to meet for a drink, but not that he didn't turn up,' I say. 'Why not?'

'He said he wasn't up for it. He was going to the gym and then home.'

'Wasn't up for it? It was the night before his wedding, for heaven's sake.'

'He said he'd had a hell of a day. He was knackered and was going to have a quiet one.'

A quiet one? Johnny is usually a sociable person, especially where his friends are concerned. He is always *up* for meeting them. 'That doesn't sound like Johnny, especially on the night before his wedding. It's tradition, surely?'

'I thought it was strange, as well. I told him he had to come for at least one drink. Everyone wanted to see him, but he said he had a headache yesterday when he got back to the office after seeing a client. So I just put it down to that and didn't think anything more of it.'

'Did he speak to any of the other lads?' I ask.

'Not that I know of.'

I feel more and more sick as the evening progresses. 'And today, what happened?'

'I was meant to go and help him get ready, as we agreed, but he texted to say something had come up, and he'd meet me at the pub at two o'clock with the other ushers, as planned.'

'What came up?'

'I don't know. But you know Johnny, he's always *busy*.'

He's right. Johnny is always rushing here, there and everywhere. He's popular. He knows a lot of people. He's the type of person who keeps in contact with almost everyone he meets and has over three thousand friends on Facebook to prove it.

I used to be the same. I had friends galore and an active social media presence... until I moved in with Charlie, and, eventually, they all became part of my past. He manipulated me. At first by seemingly having alternative plans for us every time I was due to meet up with one of them. But as time crept on, he outright forbade me from seeing them.

'Then what happened when he didn't turn up at the pub today?' I ask.

'I called him a few more times but got his voicemail. That's when I really started to worry. I kept texting him. Then, when we left the pub, he sent a text.' His voice cracks mid-sentence. 'To... to say he wasn't coming.'

'Show me,' I say.

He frowns.

'Show me your phone.'

'Are you sure you want to do this, Hannah? It'll only torment you.'

I hold out my hand. 'Give me your phone.'

He hesitates.

I raise my voice, detesting the desperation ringing out loud and clear. 'Give it to me.'

He pulls his phone out of his pocket. Tapping the screen, he goes to give it to me but pulls back. He glances from me to my sisters as if seeking their agreement. 'I'm not sure this is a good idea.'

I snatch the phone from him, my fingers shaking as I click on the recent message conversation he had with Johnny.

1.30 p.m. Where are you? T

1.45 p.m. Just call me. T

2.02 p.m. What the hell is going on, Johnny? Just call me, will you? I'm getting pissed off now. T

2.30 p.m. We're leaving the pub now. Will have to meet you at the church. T

2.38 p.m. I'm not coming. J

2.39 p.m. WTF is that meant to mean? T

2.40 p.m. What I said. I'm not getting married. J

2.41 p.m. You can't leave that kind of message and just disappear. Call me! T

2.45 p.m. Answer your bloody phone. This is your wedding day, for fuck's sake. Think of Hannah. Just call me. T

My finger swipes further along the conversation to the last message Johnny sent. Ten minutes before I was due to join him at the altar.

2.50 p.m. I just can't go through with it. I need time away. Look after Hannah. J.

FIFTEEN

I lie in bed circling my engagement ring around my finger, a sapphire square surrounded by a cluster of diamonds that sparkle even in the dimmest of lights. I wonder what happens to it now. Do I give it back to him? All I know is, I can't bring myself to remove it. Not just yet. Not until I've spoken to him.

A noise makes me sit bolt upright. I grab handfuls of duvet.

Johnny!

I swing my legs over the side of the bed, pausing to quell the flurry of nausea at the thought of how I'm going to face him.

At least I'm going to get some answers now.

I grab my bathrobe and rush to the stairs. I can't get to the bottom fast enough.

I run along the hallway, my bare feet cold on the wooden floor. There's another knock. I stop, wondering why he hasn't used his key. Just like I have a set of keys to his apartment, he has a key to this house. But after what he's done, he doesn't deserve to let himself in anymore. He wouldn't have been able to get in anyway, because I bolted the door.

My hands tremble as I unbolt the locks.

'You've got some talking to do,' I say as I swing the door open.

But it isn't Johnny.

Standing on my doorstep, his large frame dominating the entrance, is Dean Ferguson.

I must be imagining it. Johnny says I sometimes do that... imagine things that aren't there. But this isn't one of those times. I know what I'm seeing.

The sight of him returns all the dark memories from years ago. Charlie's death. The inquest. The threatening words he whispered in my ear, *You'd better be looking over your shoulder, because I'll get you one day.*

His lips part in a form of smile. But I can't work out what form that smile is taking – if it's evil or genuine.

I can't bear it. I panic. 'Get the hell away from me.' I slam the door shut. The noise echoes along the dark hallway. In my haste, I didn't even bother to turn on the light.

'Hannah! Hannah! I need to talk to you,' comes his cool, calculated voice through the frosted glass door panels.

I stand with my back against the wall. I don't believe it. My pulse thuds in my ears. I don't know what to do. India. I need to get India.

I race upstairs to Lucas's room, surprised she didn't hear him knock. I prod her shoulder. 'India! Wake up.'

'What the hell?'

'Dean's here.'

She sits upright, her long dark hair shaggy from sleep. 'Where?' The fear in her voice is as palpable as the fear in mine.

'At the front door.'

She discards the duvet and swings her legs over the side of the bed. 'For goodness' sake.'

I pull her up. 'Hurry. We need to speak to him. Find out what's going on. But I can't do it alone. Please come with me.'

She grabs a jumper.

'I'm going to get a knife.'

'Jeez, Han. Really?' She glares at me in horror – like I'm mad. The same way Carrie does sometimes. And so does Johnny. 'Don't be silly.' She takes my arm. 'Come on, let's just talk to him.'

'But you don't know what he's like.'

'Han, you're overreacting!'

She leads me back downstairs and along the hallway. I haven't felt so full of fear since Charlie was alive. I walk two footsteps behind her as we approach the front door.

I breathe in deeply and open the door, only to be greeted by the blackness of the night. 'Where the hell has he gone?' I march outside into the coldness of the night air.

India follows me, clutching my arm. We peer up and down the street. The sharp wind whips through our pyjamas. She raises her voice to be heard. 'Are you sure you didn't dream it?'

'I know what I saw.' I pull her back inside. 'He was there. I swear he was.'

I don't like her expression. The one Carrie often gives me. She closes the front door.

'Bolt it,' I say. 'Here, let me.' I push her out the way.

She stumbles. Her shoulder hits the wall. 'Good grief, Han!'

'I'm sorry. I'm sorry. I didn't mean to push you so hard.'

She stares at me. 'What happened?'

'He said he needed to talk to me.'

'Are you absolutely sure?'

She doesn't believe me.

'Yes!' I cry. I repeat what happened. 'He said my name!'

'Perhaps he'll come back. You get back to bed. I'll keep a listen out.'

'But you've got to be up early in the morning.'

'I can sleep on the train.'

My throat is dry. I fetch a glass of water, the fear deep inside of me churning my stomach. I return to bed. But I can't sleep. I'm too angry with myself. I could've had it out with Dean. Learn why he has turned up in my life again.

I should've learnt my lesson by now.

Never panic!

I'm wide awake, tormented by images of Dean standing on my doorstep and the last time I saw Johnny.

Tears pour down my face.

Johnny has broken me. Destroyed everything I've believed in since we got together.

The wind outside is hammering the windows like the mix of feelings thrashing through my soul: anger, sadness, confusion, and fear, all mixed into a bitter blend of emotions.

I wipe my eyes and pick up my phone, checking for the hundredth time of news from him. I'm still perplexed that he contacted his dad, and his brother, but not me. I click on Facebook. I have an account but keep it private, only using it to follow what people are up to. I find Johnny's page. He's an active user, mainly sharing funny jokes.

He last posted a photo of the traffic jam he was stuck in on the way back from seeing a client on Friday afternoon. He was meant to have the day off, but he was due to see that new client last Wednesday and the meeting had to be rescheduled due to staff sickness. The only day the company could do this side of Christmas was Friday. Angela was adamant he couldn't leave it. They'd lose the deal. So Johnny reluctantly agreed to it. The photo shows a line of traffic at a standstill over a mile long on the northbound carriageway of the M11. I read his message accompanying the post.

> Help! I've got a bride-to-be to meet. I hope I get back in time!

Followed by several head-exploding emojis.

Around fifty people have commented on the post, mostly wishing him luck for our big day. Several mention the weather being a burden, to which he replied saying it has nothing to do with the weather. There are far too many damn cars on the road.

I scroll through earlier posts, but nothing appears out of the ordinary that could explain his actions.

I reread the latest post.

So, on Friday afternoon, he had every intention of marrying me.

And I want to know what changed his mind.

My thoughts return to Dean and what he wanted to tell me.

That smile of his.

It haunts me.

I can't work out if it was genuine or provoking.

Did he turn up to taunt me, or did he come to bear news of Johnny?

Eventually, I fall into fragmented sleep, unable to settle into a comfortable position. My dreams are unsettling and disjointed, starring Dean and Johnny in a full-blown fist fight on the patio where Charlie died. The blood. So much blood.

On Sunday morning, I wake with a start. For a few seconds, I wonder where I am. Something isn't right. And then I remember, and the pain returns, stabbing my heart like a knife.

I'm in my own bed.

And I'm not the wife I thought I would now be.

I grab my phone and gasp.

Johnny sent a text at seven minutes past five this morning.

SIXTEEN

My shaking hands fumble with the phone. I read the message, my heart in my mouth.

I'm so sorry, Han. You don't deserve this, but better now than later. Let's meet when the dust has settled. For now, I need to be alone to get my head together. Look after yourself. You'll find someone better than me. Johnny.

No I won't.

I'll never find someone better than him.

The briefness of the message stings. I deserve more than a couple of pathetic cliché lines.

The way he has left me with no prior warning or reason is unforgivable, which makes it even more confusing. It isn't Johnny's style. He is the kindest, most considerate person. If he decided he didn't want to go through with the wedding, he would've told me to my face. Which is why I can't help believing Dean has something to do with this.

I check my inbox. Perhaps he's sent an email explaining himself some more, but I only find messages from people expressing their deepest sympathy for what I must be going through and other emails from wedding-related companies reminding me I should be a bride by now.

The phone beeps with a text from Angela. Lucas is fine. They are happy to have him for the day. But she wants to know what I want her to do with all the wedding presents she brought home from the hotel that are currently in her car.

I groan at yet another layer of mess Johnny has left me to wade through: the aftermath of the wedding, our house purchase, and my house sale. Let alone my and Lucas's feelings. His actions have far-reaching consequences.

I reply to Angela, saying I can't think about the presents at the moment. Anyway, I'd rather think that's something Johnny can deal with.

It's just after nine o'clock. The day stretches long and lonely ahead. I'm exhausted, but I can't bear to stay in bed anymore. I crawl out, my eyes as heavy as my heart.

The stillness of Sunday morning presses down on me. Johnny always lets me sleep in on a Sunday. If we stay at his place, I'll find him and Lucas under Lucas's duvet, playing on the PlayStation. If we stay here, they'll be in Lucas's room, building a train track, or their heads bent over one of Lucas's many books about the solar system. My whole body aches for my son. I don't think it's fully hit him yet, but Johnny will have left a hole in my boy's heart as big as the one he's left in mine.

Sunday mornings are never going to be the same.

No morning is.

I pause as I pass Lucas's room and stick my head around the door. India has already made his bed. His absence deepens the weight of sadness crushing my heart. Apart from the odd occasion when he stays at Carrie and Tom's place or the couple of times he's been on a sleepover with his best friend, he's always here, brightening my day.

It's so quiet downstairs. I miss it all: the thunder of the two of them bolting down the stairs on a Sunday morning, discussing why the planets move anticlockwise around the sun. Johnny whistling as he cooks us bacon sandwiches, and Lucas's excitement as Johnny embellishes a story from his youth.

I trudge along the hallway, where photos of Lucas from birth and through the years adorn the walls like precious gems. On the end wall hangs a blown-up print of Johnny and me from the summer when we were hiking in the Peak District. We were standing at the top of Kinder Scout, the highest point, arm in arm, our free hands splayed out horizontally to show off our achievement. I've always thought the shining sun half-hidden behind Johnny's head looks like a halo.

I stop and clutch my belly and bang my head against the wall. The pain is unbearable. I have no idea how I'm going to survive the coming days.

India has left a note on the back of an envelope on the kitchen worktop.

Sorry I missed you, but you were sleeping soundly, and I heard you up in the night, so I thought it best to leave you. I'll call later. Call me with any news. I've had nothing from Dean. Stay strong. I love you so much.
India X

I fill the kettle and search in the middle drawer of the dresser. It's full of rubbish, but I planned to have a good sort-out this coming week before the move. I should've already made a start, but the wedding has taken over my life these past few weeks.

At the back of the drawer, I find my old clutch bag and remove a half-empty packet of cigarettes and a lighter. I used to be a heavy smoker until I met Johnny. I started when I moved in with Charlie. When I found out I was pregnant with Lucas, I stopped, but stupidly started again after he was born. But

Johnny was so anti-smoking I gave up... almost. No one knows about the sneaky cigarettes I have when I'm alone and Lucas is in bed asleep.

I make a cup of coffee, throw on my coat and step outside into the narrow back garden. I shiver. The air is cold and sharp, but at least the sun is out. I look across the garden, fully expecting to be confronted by Dean.

I place my cup of coffee on the round bistro table where Johnny and I often shared dinner on the warm summer evenings this year. Brushing the condensation off the metal chair with the sleeve of my coat, I perch on the edge and light a cigarette, desperate for the nicotine hit, wincing as the smoke mixes with the cold air and hits my lungs. I thump my fist on the table. Coffee spills over the side of the cup and onto my leg. I jump up, swearing.

'Damn you, Johnny.' I double over, the pain too much to bear. I clutch my belly. The loss is immense. My baby, and now her father. It's too much.

My breathing quickens.

I can't stand this.

I stub out the cigarette.

I have to see him.

I'm going to his apartment.

SEVENTEEN

I start the engine and drive to Johnny's apartment. It's unbelievable that less than twenty-four hours ago I thought my future was as rosy as the show of affection Johnny left on that hotel bed. It feels like a lifetime away.

At the busiest of times, it's a ten-minute drive across Ditton Morton, a medieval town that dates back to the twelfth century. But with the roads still so quiet, I arrive in less than six minutes. I've rehearsed a script of what I'm going to say to him when he answers the door: a vague barrage of abuse followed by 'Why?'

If he answers the door.

He could be anywhere.

The double yellow lines don't allow me to stop outside the apartment, so I drive to the side street where I usually park. The road is packed with the cars of normal people who are still in bed at this time on a Sunday morning, or at least having breakfast. I find a space at the end of the road and walk to his block.

Standing outside, I stare up at the sash windows. Johnny's apartment is in darkness, unlike the others where light shines through the blinds, shutters and curtains.

I step into the small alcove where a main door leads to the

six apartments in the building. My trembling hand, blue from the cold, presses the buzzer to apartment six on the top floor. There's no answer. He could be in bed. If he's here at all. He must be. I can't think where else he would've gone. I try again in vain, before digging my keys out of my pocket. He gave me a set of keys when I was coming over one day, and he knew he was going to be late. 'Keep them,' he said when I went to give them back. 'You can come and go as you please.'

I falter. It's wrong. I feel like a crazy girlfriend snooping on her boyfriend. But we're not loved-up teenagers anymore. We're mature adults who willingly agreed they wanted to spend the rest of their lives together.

A nauseating bitterness rises in my throat as I envisage him in bed with another woman. I shake it away. I'm being silly. Johnny isn't that type of guy. But then, what do I know? I never would've believed that he would've jilted me.

Another horrible thought torments me.

What if I find him dead?

My relentless anxiety and overthinking fuels me onwards. I just need to get this over and done with.

I fumble with the key and place it in the lock. It won't go in.

Johnny has changed the locks.

I can't understand why the hell he would've done that.

It's the ultimate betrayal.

I jangle the keys, staring at them, then realise the key I'm trying to use is the one to his individual apartment, not to the block.

I sigh with relief and search for the correct one. The door clicks. Ignoring the warning signs swirling around in the pit of my stomach, I push open the heavy door to the faint smell of dampness and grease from the two bicycles leaning against the wall. The mountain bike is Johnny's. He uses it to cycle to work in the summer months. The other, an upright Dutch-style bike, belongs to Betsy, an older lady from Ireland who occupies one of the two apartments on this floor.

I glance behind me before entering the communal hallway, half expecting Dean to be there. I berate myself for letting my paranoia take hold. But then again, given he was standing on my doorstep in the middle of the night, I wouldn't put it past him.

Stepping over a pile of post, I quietly close the main door, picking up the envelopes and leaflets and placing them on the window ledge.

My heart pounds as I climb the carpeted staircase to the top floor. I shiver, my breath fogging the air. I pass the three smaller apartments on the first floor, continuing to the second floor to Johnny's penthouse suite, as the estate agent described it when preparing the sale. He's meant to exchange on this property next week, in sync with us purchasing our dream home. I wonder what his plans are now.

The thought of him making plans without me wrenches my heart. He's given me so much hope.

The hope that I can fight my demons and lead a normal life.

I never thought I'd be making plans alone again.

My heart grows heavier with each step until I reach Johnny's door. A burning sensation throbs in my thighs. It always does when I climb these stairs. I need to get fitter. I grab the railing, hauling myself to climb the final step.

I take a deep breath. The thought of him answering the door is sickening. But so is the idea of him not answering it.

I knock. The hollow sound reverberates around the empty hallway. I wait. There's no answer. I knock again, this time harder. Unease races through me. Still no one comes to the door. After the third attempt, I slot the key in the lock and turn it. The door opens.

I'm in.

EIGHTEEN

The earthy smell of sandalwood from Johnny's aftershave, which I usually find comforting, hits me.

It's eerily silent. But not in an empty house way. The atmosphere is heavy, as though there's a presence.

I call out, 'Johnny, are you here?' I pause, bracing myself, before closing the door. An odd sensation overcomes me. This apartment is no longer my territory. I feel like an intruder. But, equally, I feel I have a right to be here. He damn well owes me an explanation.

A chill of dejection and emptiness mingles in the air. The morning heating turned off hours ago, but a vacant coolness makes it seem as if no one has been here for a few days.

It's a large, two-bedroom apartment with en suites to both. One of the bedrooms is on this floor along with an open-plan living area. The master bedroom occupies the floor above, leading to a roof terrace overlooking the town.

I step out of my wet boots. Johnny doesn't like people wearing shoes in the apartment. I walk along the hallway, passing the bedroom that he uses as a study and doubles as a room for Lucas when he stays. I pause and step backwards, checking in case he's in there. But he would've heard me call his name. The room is tidy, how he'd normally leave it. There's a breeze. I shiver. The window is open. How strange. Johnny is typically more security-conscious, even bordering on obsessive at times, double-checking all the windows and doors are closed before leaving the apartment. I stall, not knowing whether to shut it or not.

I continue to the living space, a heaviness in each step. A grey L-shaped sofa facing a giant flatscreen TV and a glass dining table with eight chairs occupies half the space. Johnny loves to entertain and often invites friends to dinner. A generous-sized kitchen with a large centre island that doubles as a breakfast bar fills the area behind the sofa.

'Johnny,' I call, louder this time. I wonder if he's upstairs. But he isn't one to lie in. He's a morning bird, always up at the crack of dawn to catch the worm of opportunity – his words, not mine.

I stroke the smooth, soft surface of the velvet sofa. The room appears frozen in time. A half-empty cup of coffee and a plate with toast crumbs rest on the kitchen counter beside a knife balanced on the butter dish. That's odd. It's exactly how I left it when I rushed out on Friday morning.

I stayed here on Thursday because it was Lucas's friend's birthday, and his mum had invited him for a sleepover. I was reluctant to let him go at first. It was a school night and I'm still not comfortable with the whole sleepover arrangement. His friend has stayed a few times, and it felt an enormous responsibility to have another child that wasn't mine to look after. But I still had so much to do for the wedding, and Lucas was so keen to go. He begged me with his beautiful big brown eyes until he wore me down, and I ended up giving in. That boy. He always manages to melt my heart.

I was running late and remember thinking Johnny would tick me off for not tidying up after myself. He's a stickler for neatness. But it's as if he hasn't been back here since. My gloves that I forgot to take with me that morning as I left in a rush rest on the curved arm of the sofa.

'Johnny,' I call again, my voice hauntingly echoing around the empty room.

Something's wrong. I know this apartment well. I've spent many happy nights here, evenings packed with love, laughter and passion. Never have I been so comfortable in someone else's space. But now it's as if I've entered a ghost town.

I pick up my gloves and leave the room on the opposite side into the small passage with a narrow half-turn staircase that leads to Johnny's bedroom. Clutching the bannister, I peer upwards and call his name again, my voice trailing off to a whisper. Perhaps he tucked into a bottle of whiskey last night to drown his guilt and fell into a deep sleep.

But, no, that's not Johnny. He likes a drink, but he's not a binge-drinker. But what do I know? It's as if the man I thought I was going to spend the rest of my life with is now a stranger.

I creep up the stairs. The third and fifth ones creak. I've never noticed that before. When I reach the top, the bedroom door is shut. I grab the handle but pause, unsure if I really want to go in there. The sour thought from earlier returns. What if he's in bed with another woman? I knock. There's no answer. Gingerly, I open the door. It creaks like those stairs. I step inside and glance around. The room is empty and appears as I left it on Friday morning, the window shutters open, the bed made.

The smell of Johnny's eucalyptus shower gel wafts from the en suite. All kinds of questioning thoughts flash through my mind. I stride across the room to the en suite, half expecting to find him passed out on the floor, or slumped dead in the corner of the walk-in shower.

I push open the door and frown. He isn't here.

Where are you, Johnny?

NINETEEN

My thoughts turn ugly.

He must be at someone else's place.

Another woman's house.

The image of him in bed with someone else tortures me.

I guess he could be at a mate's place. He has enough friends to hang out with for a couple of days. A couple of weeks, even, if he wanted to. But why not tell me that? If not me, at least he could've told his mum and dad, or Tom, even.

I replay our conversation from when he drove back from the Midlands on Friday afternoon. The one I recounted in my mind during the endless hours I lay awake in the night. He was stuck in traffic and was worried he'd be late picking Lucas up to take him to his mum and dad's. He'd sounded stressed, an undertone of panic in his voice, but I put it down to him running late. It was the eve of the biggest day of our lives. Anyone would've been stressed. He said he still needed to drop into the office and was concerned he wouldn't fit it all in.

I walk to the double doors that lead to the roof terrace, confused and doubting myself. The bottom tier of the door shutters is closed, but the top tier is open. I can't remember if I left them like that on Friday. I peer outside, but I can only see ahead, not around the side to the larger area.

The keys are in the lock. I open the door and step outside to a rush of cold air. I step to the edge of the terrace and, at arm's length, I grab the slippery railing that's dripping with condensation.

A flashback haunts me. Memories from seven years ago when I witnessed Charlie's body splattered on the ground after falling from his bedroom balcony. My hand grips the railing tighter. I can't bear to look over the side. I'm too terrified I'm going to find Johnny's body in the same mangled state on the ground below.

Summoning the courage, I edge closer to the railings. The fear inside me delivers another surge of nausea. I stop and take deep breaths before peering over the side to the small, private car park below. There are no broken bodies in sight, and Johnny's car is there. I do a double-take. It's not parked in his dedicated space. That's strange. I can only think someone must have been parked in his spot when he returned.

I wonder where he is now. I can only think he's gone out to pick up a coffee. He often does that on a Sunday morning. But then, that doesn't explain why the apartment appears as if no one's been here since I was last here on Friday. The first thing he would have done is clear away my breakfast things.

I glimpse at the panoramic view of the town and the green fields beyond. During the long summer nights and even into early autumn, we sat out here and enjoyed bottles of cold beer. But now it feels odd as if I've never been here in my life. My bottom lip trembles. I tighten my hold around the railings, yearning for Johnny to hold me gently in that special way he does.

I give my head a shake.

Johnny isn't here.

I need to grab my stuff and go.

I walk into the dressing area comprising of two wardrobes either side of a small dressing table. My heart jolts. Johnny's wedding suit hangs in a bag from the top of the wardrobe. His patent shoes rest on the floor beneath. I well up. He got everything out on Thursday night, saying he wanted to clean the shoes again. He'd planned to get ready here with Tom. It caused an argument because Angela had wanted him to get ready at the house. I overheard them arguing about it in her office at work. I couldn't make out the whole conversation because it started with something about money. She got quite angry. It was one of the first times I've heard him stand up to her.

I slide open one set of mirrored doors, gather my clothing and shove the items into my bag: a spare dress, jeans, and a couple of tops. As I claim my toiletries from the en suite, a sudden noise from downstairs stops me in my tracks.

I stand rigid.

My heart skips a beat. It sounded like the front door opening.

Johnny is back!

Stuffing the toothbrush and skin care products in my bag, I run to the bedroom door. 'Johnny?' I call out.

There's no answer. I make for the stairs, calling out his name again, my heart in my throat. At the bottom, I stop suddenly at another noise. That was the front door banging closed. I'm sure of it. I dash through the living area and into the hallway. There's no one there. I check the spare bedroom. It's empty. I hurry to the front door and open it as the main door to the block two floors below slams shut.

I leave the apartment and race down the stairs for the exit. I don't deserve this. I've never put Johnny down as a coward. But now he's showing his true colours, which are wholly unappealing.

I pull open the heavy door, glancing left and right along the street. The faintest glimpse of a figure turns the corner. It could be anyone in the misty morning air. I rush after them. But when I turn the corner, the street is quiet and empty.

I return to the apartment, the feeling of unease growing heavier by the minute. If that was Johnny, he must've heard me call his name. So he clearly didn't want to see me.

If it was him?

With a heavy heart, I grab a few items of mine from the living area: a book I lent Johnny, a lipstick, the throw neatly folded over the side of the sofa he bought for me because I feel the cold. On my way out, I stop in his study and grab a few toys and books of Lucas's. I spy the PlayStation console on the bottom shelf of the bookcase. My heart pangs for my son. He's going to miss his gaming sessions with Johnny.

I scan the room, my anxiety growing. My eyes fix on the desk in the corner. A gleam of light from the window illuminates the glossy surface, on which rests a computer, a table lamp and a desk tidy full of pens and highlighters. Johnny's favourite grey hoodie is draped over the back of the chair.

I walk to the desk, swallowing hard to see a book titled *A Father's Guide To Loss* propped up against the side of the filing tray. I rest my hand across the middle of my body, remembering the severe cramps and intense fear on the night Johnny drove me to hospital. Memories that haunt me daily... and will for the rest of my life.

I pick up the book and flick through the pages. A folded down corner catches my attention. It's the start of a chapter on supporting your partner through the profound sense of loss in the early days. Another dog-ear highlights another chapter about grappling with the distressing days post loss for dads.

An intense pain stabs at my heart. It's crippling. I drop the book. My breaths come hard and fast as I try to control the tears bursting for release. The profound sense of loss is overwhelming. Johnny must have felt it too, although he hid it well. Perhaps it all got too much for him. After we lost the baby, perhaps he realised he didn't love me as much as he thought he did. Trapped. That's what he said to Tom.

Trapped.

That word hurts like no other at this moment.

Three red rose petals at the foot of the desk catch my attention. Similar to the petals that Johnny took to our hotel suite for the staff to decorate the bed. I pick them up, reflecting on the romantic gesture he arranged for our arrival back to the hotel as husband and wife.

Another surge of suffocating pain crashes through me.

A knock at the front door makes me jump. My stomach churns. Something's not right. When visitors come here they have to press the buzzer at the main door to be let into the building.

Another knock springs me into action.

I head to the front door.

I go to open it but stop.

No one ever comes here so early on a Sunday morning.

TWENTY

Visions of opening the door to Dean shoot through my mind.

He knows where I live. He could've followed me here.

I can't answer it.

Another knock. 'Who's there?' I call out.

'Hannah! It's Betsy.'

I sigh with relief and open the door to the owner of the ground-floor apartment. Betsy is a pale-skinned woman, with whom Johnny has grown close. When her husband was diagnosed with cancer around Easter time, Johnny helped her keep him at home until he passed away. Now she makes him dinner every Monday, and he spends an hour or so with her. Lucas and I have joined them on a few occasions in the school holidays.

'Hannah, dear. I didn't expect to see you here,' Betsy says. 'I heard about what happened. I'm so sorry. When I arrived at the evening reception on Saturday, the hotel manager told me. You poor thing. After everything you've been through as well.' She glances at my stomach. 'You know, what with the baby...' She prattles on about the weather and the extortionate price of the block of butter she had to buy from the express supermarket this morning. I can't get a word in. 'Anyway, I won't keep you. It's just Johnny has parked in my parking space, and my daughter is coming to see me this afternoon. A bit odd, I thought. He's never done that before. Could he possibly move it?'

'He's not here. But I'll do it for you.'

'That would be most helpful.'

'Consider it done.' I excuse myself, and she leaves.

I grab Johnny's spare set of car keys he keeps in the kitchen drawer. I'm about to rush out of the front door but stop. I twirl his car keys around my finger. Perhaps I'm being too presumptuous. He has made it clear he no longer wants me to be a part of his life. He might not want me to move his car. Too late. He's not here to do it, and I've promised Betsy now.

I head to the car park situated at the rear of the apartment block. Standing by his Mercedes jolts my heart. He loves this car – the comfy heated seats, the spacious leg room, the satisfying gentle thud and the subsequent crisp click as the door closes and locks. I do, too. But he'll never take me anywhere in it again.

I climb inside and move the car into the correct parking space. When I switch off the engine, another wave of grief hits me for the loss of my fiancé and my baby. It's excruciating. I hug my belly and rest my head on the steering wheel. I need to get used to this. The pain is going nowhere for a very long time to come.

I reach over and open the glove compartment, where I keep a pair of sunglasses Johnny bought for me to keep in this car. A book slips out. It's a brand-new copy of *Wuthering Heights*. That's strange. We were discussing this book only last week. I mentioned I've always wanted to read it but have never got around to it. I pick it up and open the front cover. A white envelope addressed to me and Lucas drops out.

I open it, astounded at what I find inside.

TWENTY-ONE

I stare at the three tickets.

Tickets to Disneyland Paris for after Carrie and Tom's wedding.

Paris! I've never been there, but taking Lucas has been on my bucket list. Johnny promised he'd take us one day. My heart sinks. Just like he promised to take me to many places. We didn't plan a honeymoon. Because of the expense of the wedding and our house purchase, we ran out of money. I didn't care. All I wanted was to get married and move into our new home. I had visions of feeling safe there. The plan was to get settled and then arrange a getaway early springtime. But it appears he had other plans.

I read the message written inside the cover of the book in the same sprawling handwriting as on the card left beside the vase of flowers in the hotel room:

To my darling Hannah,

By the time you read this, you'll be my wife. I can't wait!

Never have I wanted something so badly in my life. Here's a little something for you to read while you relax in Paris, and I whizz Lucas around the rides.

All my love.

Yours forever,

Johnny. X

I grab the steering wheel, the sickly sensation in my stomach intensifying.

He went to all these lengths only to pull out at the ungodly eleventh hour. It doesn't add up. Visions of Dean flash in my thoughts. The fair hair he now wears to his shoulders. The wiry moustache and patchy beard. And the same brown eyes as his brother... and my son.

My phone rings. The sound is deafening in the quietness of the car. It's Angela trying to FaceTime, most likely because Lucas wants to speak to me. I join the call.

'Mum, Mum, look, I'm with the giraffes.' His voice reverberates around the car, bouncing off the leather seats. 'I'm allowed to feed them later.' He pauses. 'Where are you?' He's so astute for a six-year-old.

I can't lie to him. 'I'm at Johnny's.'

'Is he there? Can I speak to him?' The hope and enthusiasm in his voice deflates me.

'He's not, darling.' I hopelessly try to control the emotion in my voice. 'I just came here to pick up a few of our things.'

'Can you bring the PlayStation home?'

'We'll see.'

'Please, Mum, please.'

'What else do you have planned?'

He reels off the animals he wants to see and his twelve-thirty slot to visit Santa. I smile, wholly grateful I have him in my life.

A chilling thought occurs to me. I grab the steering wheel.

Perhaps, somewhere along the line, as the months have rolled into years, Dean cottoned on that he is Lucas's uncle.

TWENTY-TWO

The thought terrifies me. Dean may be Charlie's brother, but, still, I don't want that man anywhere near my son.

I've worked so damn hard to keep him away from him.

Lucas is too pure to have such evil in his life.

'Wow! You're going to be busy,' I say when Lucas pauses for breath. Although I love chatting with him, I want to get away from here. 'I'll see you later when I pick you up. Tell Angela and Alan I said hi.'

I end the call and shove the book and tickets back in the glove compartment. They're no longer mine.

I return to the apartment and put Johnny's car keys back in the kitchen drawer. On the way out, I stop in the study to close the window.

I spot the PlayStation on the bookcase. I step towards it and pause. 'Damn you, Johnny Caxton! It's the least we can do for Lucas after what you've done.' I grab the console and controllers. I'll buy Lucas his own PlayStation, but Johnny won't mind if I borrow this for the week. My bag is full, so I shove them under my arm and hurry out of the apartment.

I sit in my car, deciding what to do with myself. I consider going for a walk, shopping or going home, getting in my PJs, dragging my duvet down to the sofa, and watching a film. There's a new series on Apple TV, *Slow Horses*. Johnny and I watched the first series, so I could do that. But nothing appeals. My enthusiasm is as dead as my heart.

I cry out in pain.

All I want is to see him. Talk to him. Find out why he's done this to me.

The not knowing is killing me as much as the hurt and disappointment.

This is my fault. I should've come clean with him. Told him everything about me.

Everything.

Full of misery, I decide to leave my car and walk to the café in the town centre Johnny and I sometimes go to on a Sunday morning.

It's a cosy place, tucked away in a side street off the main market square. A trail of fairy lights circles the low ceiling beams that Johnny has to duck when he passes beneath them. He always chooses a flat white and me a hot chocolate. Today, I order a double espresso and an Americano.

It's still early. Only one other customer is here. An elderly gentleman with sagging jowls and square, black-framed glasses sitting in the corner who I've seen before. He appears as sad and lonely as me. I pass the table for two in the alcove that was once a fireplace where Johnny and I usually sit, and settle at a small table in the window bay.

I fish in my bag for my phone and answer all the texts that have come in since yesterday afternoon with a blanket message:

> *Thanks for your thoughts. I'm slowly coming to terms with what's happened. I just need time to process it. I'll be in touch soon. Much love. Hannah. X*

Carrie has replied to the screenshot of Johnny's text that I sent her this morning.

Coward! He could've at least called you. You deserve better than this. I hate him at this moment. What are you up to today? Do you want to come over? Or I could come to you? Love you. Cx

I hunt through my phone, wondering if I can find someone Johnny is close to whom I can speak to, but I don't search for long. I refuse to come across as desperate. To everyone, I'm the poor woman who has been left at the altar. People must feel desperately sorry for me. But I don't need or want their pity. I may have lost my fiancé, but I haven't lost my dignity.

Dean gatecrashes my thoughts again. I don't know what's worse. The ideas that he may have sought me out to warn Johnny off marrying me, or to worm his way into Lucas's life, are equally as sickening.

I won't let him.

I won't.

I need to speak to him. I don't care that he'll then have my contact details. He knows where I live, after all. I call India to ask for his phone number but get her voicemail. She's probably at the christening by now.

I type *Dean Ferguson* into Google. Hundreds of men appear. I add *oil rig worker* to narrow it down. I scroll through possible articles about him. I must be able to find something on him. But all I come across are the articles I've read several times before about Charlie Ferguson, the man who fell from the makeshift balcony on the roof of his house.

I flick through the stories about the tragic accident where the thirty-two-year-old builder died from his injuries. I was mentioned in a few of them. The poor girlfriend who discovered his body lying in a pool of blood.

No one resembling the Dean I'm hunting for appears. I open Facebook and search for him. Hundreds of Dean Fergusons are listed. I try to whittle it down to UK people only, but each time I try, the screen freezes. So I scroll through all the possibilities until I find the guy I'm looking for. I click on his profile, but annoyingly it's set to private. I find India's Facebook page and click on her friends, not surprised to see Dean's name listed. I need to view his page through hers. I try other social media platforms, but apart from Facebook, he doesn't appear to have any digital footprint.

I cup my hands around my mug of coffee, staring out of the window at the carefree Sunday morning shoppers strolling by. I don't know how long I've been sitting here, but when I look around, the place is almost full. A young fresh-faced waitress appears with cropped hair and wrists full of jangling bangles. 'Can I get you another drink?'

'Sure.' I hand her my empty mug. I'm shivering, even though it's warm in here and I still have my coat on.

'What would you like?' she asks.

'Sorry?' A strange airiness overcomes me as if I'm having an out-of-body experience. The waitress down there, me above, unable to connect to what she's saying.

Her eyebrows rise in a questioning arc. 'What can I get you to drink? Another coffee? We do great festive hot chocolates: gingerbread. Terry's Chocolate Orange.'

I nod.

'Which one?'

I shrug. 'I'll have another Americano, please.'

'Anything to eat?'

A bell rings. A young couple, my age, walk into the café. The woman is laughing at something the guy is saying. He ducks under the ceiling beam and places his hand on the small of his partner's back, steering her towards an empty table. Johnny does that... places his hand in the small of my back. I recall the tingles in my spine from his gentle touch. The woman removes her coat. Tears prick my eyes. The swell of her belly so full of promise is how mine should look right now.

But it's not. It's empty and hollow from the loss that has plagued me every day since that dreadful night when I awoke to a bed of blood. I blink, stifling tears, remembering the intense cramps, the narrow bed, and the coldness of the ultrasound probe sweeping across my body. The doctor's tense words, 'I'm so sorry, Ms Young. We can't find a heartbeat,' ring daily in my ears as if it only happened yesterday.

I drop my head. I'll never get to experience my angel baby growing up. She was a girl. Victoria, Johnny and I called her before they took her tiny body away.

The shrill of the waitress's voice snaps me back to the moment. 'Food. Would you like some food?'

'Sorry?'

The waitress frowns. 'Can I get you something to eat?'

I shake my head. 'No. Nothing to eat, thanks.'

The way I feel, I can't imagine ever wanting to eat again.

TWENTY-THREE

The thought of going home to an empty house is deeply depressing. Seeing that pregnant lady has twisted the knife that Johnny has savagely plunged deep into my heart.

The sky has darkened, the sun now playing peek-a-boo from behind the granite-grey clouds. I drive aimlessly around town, the wipers scraping robotically across the steamed-up windscreen. I pass the common where kids are playing on the swings and slides, and the Chinese restaurant where Johnny and I sometimes take Lucas for their all-you-can-eat Sunday buffet.

I find myself sitting outside Carrie and Tom's place. It's only then that I realise that the wipers are still screeching across the windscreen, but there's no reason to have them on.

The five-bedroom detached house they bought earlier this year sits in prime position backing onto open farmland on a brand-new executive housing development on the edge of town. Double-fronted and set over three floors, the house is large enough to accommodate the four children they plan to have. Carrie has wanted kids since forever, the first of which will arrive next year if I know my sister.

While Johnny and I had a brief engagement because of the

imminent arrival of our baby, Carrie and Tom got engaged two years ago and have been planning their wedding since. Carrie even gave up work in the summer to prepare for pregnancy. Although she never admitted it, I could tell. She started going to the gym, joined Slimming World, and lost the excess two stone she'd been carrying since our mum died.

I call her. Not that she'd mind me turning up unannounced. I just don't want to intrude if she and Tom have made plans.

She answers immediately. 'What are you doing out there? Get in here straight away.'

The door is already open when I walk up the path. She's still in her pyjamas and a pale cream designer hooded bathrobe that reaches her feet. 'I've been trying to call you.' She beckons me with a waving hand. 'Hurry up, it's freezing.'

I step inside to a rush of warmth. It's always hot in this house, while I brave the cold at home and only turn the heating on in the mornings and late afternoon for a few hours. It's one of the downsides of being a single mum. Although I earn good money, I have a budget to stick to. I took on a large mortgage when I bought my house.

Tom has a share in his mum and dad's company, as does Johnny, and earns a good salary, enough for Carrie to have given up work. It was one of the many things I was looking forward to when Johnny and I got married – sharing the burden of daily living. Life has been challenging the past few years, what with the cost of living crisis and the food and heating bills spiralling out of control. He said I could give up work, as well, but, however much I love him, I will never be beholden to a man ever again.

Carrie closes the door. 'Coffee? Tea?'

'I'd better have tea. I've drunk a ton of coffee already this morning.' I point to a pile of gifts at the bottom of the stairs. 'Are they the wedding gifts?' It's a stupid question. The presents are wrapped in paper plastered with *bride and groom*. Someone has even gone to the lengths of getting the paper personalised: *Mr and Mrs Caxton*. I turn away.

She screws up her face. 'I'm sorry, I would've moved them had I known you were coming. Paulo dropped them off from the hotel this morning.'

'Send them back.' My tone is cutting. 'I'm sorry, I didn't mean to sound so aggressive. It's the way it came out. I mean it. I'm going to contact The Wedding Shop and cancel all the presents. See if I can get everyone their money back. I don't want any of it.' My voice catches in my throat. 'How come I get left with all this crap to sort out?'

Her lips turn downwards.

I slip out of my coat and pull off my boots, my feet sinking into the lush, thick carpet. 'Do it for me, will you? Coordinate it with Angela. She's got presents in her car from the hotel as well. Try and get everyone their money back. If not, sell it all on eBay. Or better still, give it all to charity – every single present. I don't want any of it.'

She briefly hugs me. I'm taken aback. Unlike India, Carrie isn't a hugger. 'Let's leave it for a few days for things to calm down.' She gently pushes me towards the kitchen. 'Let's get that tea.'

'Where's Tom?' I enter her large kitchen that doubles as a breakfast room. I can just imagine a brood of kids sitting there scoffing homemade muffins in ten years' time.

She flicks the kettle switch and prepares two cups. 'He went to the gym to destress and then to the hotel to meet the guests who stayed for breakfast.'

I cringe. I can just imagine everyone talking about me.

'He should be back soon.'

I sit on the bench at the wooden table by the patio doors and look out onto the landscaped garden. It's very pretty but also very modular. A bit like my sister. 'Why didn't you go with him?' I ask.

'I was waiting to hear from you.'

I reach out to touch the smooth glass of the vase in the centre of the table holding Carrie's bouquet from yesterday. I peer around the room. She must've brought back my bouquet, as well. Three vases filled with red and white roses and stems of foliage line the window ledge.

My voice wobbles. 'I don't want you to hide your excitement about your wedding.'

She sighs loudly. 'Oh, Han! I'm not going to lie. It's going to be difficult. I'm going to feel guilty mentioning anything wedding-related around you now. Frickin' hell, Johnny Caxton. He's got a lot to answer for.'

I raise my hand, pointing my forefinger to emphasise my message. 'I mean it. Carry on talking about your wedding. What's happening next?'

'The marquee went up yesterday.'

I gulp. As they are holding the wedding in the grounds of Angela and Alan's house, that marquee will be in my field of vision every day while I'm at work.

Johnny suggested using the same marquee for our wedding. He wanted a much bigger event than we ended up planning. 'I want to show you off,' he said. 'Show everyone I got the most beautiful bride in the world.' Those were his exact words. But it isn't me. I'm not like my sister. I wanted a quieter affair. Something more subtle, intimate, more discreet.

'That's good,' I say. 'Then we can start decorating it.'

'You don't have to if you don't want to.'

I fake a smile. It isn't easy, but I plaster it on my face like another layer of make-up. I refuse to let Johnny ruin her big day like he has mine. 'I'll be fine. I've just been to his apartment. It was odd.'

She's about to open the fridge door but stops. 'Odd, how?'

'It was as if he hasn't been back there since he left for work on Friday morning. And get this...' I shake my head, still in disbelief, and tell her about the tickets to Paris.

Her head juts forward. 'Oh, Han. It's all so confusing.'

I continue. 'And then, when I was fetching my stuff from his bedroom, I thought I heard him come in the front door, but when I went to look, no one was there. But I saw someone turn the corner into Berry Street.'

'Are you sure it was the same person who came into the apartment?' She pulls a carton of organic milk out of the fridge. Since giving up work and going on her health kick, she buys organic everything. It's at odds with how much wine she drinks.

'Don't look like that,' I say, irritated. It's the same expression that India gave me in the early hours when she questioned if Dean had really been at my front door.

'Like what?'

'Like I'm losing my mind.'

She fills the two cups with steaming water and a dash of milk. 'Are you sure you didn't imagine it? You know what you can be like sometimes.'

'No!' I don't mean to shout. But her comment hurts. I've got better lately. Ever since I met Johnny.

A hurt look appears on her face. She shrugs, wordlessly speaking volumes.

Maybe she's right.

Maybe I am losing my mind again.

TWENTY-FOUR

I stare out of the patio door onto the rattan table and chairs packed into a square and hibernating under a waterproof cover. I wish someone would wrap me up and let me hibernate until spring.

'Have you heard from India?' I ask.

'Nope.'

'She left before I woke up, and I haven't been able to get hold of her. I still can't believe Dean turned up. What the hell was that all about?'

She shrugs. 'I don't understand either.'

'You didn't say anything to Tom, did you?'

'About what?'

'About Dean. And Charlie.'

She frowns at me. 'You know I wouldn't. What happened is our secret.'

Our eyes lock, and we briefly nod.

She pours the milk into two cups. 'What've you got planned for the rest of the day? Want to hang out here with us?'

'I'm going to try to get myself together.' I let out a deep sigh. 'I need to pull out of my house sale and the house purchase.'

'I wondered about that.'

'I need to contact the solicitor. Preferably before she gets into the office in the morning. I'll be stuffed if she goes ahead with the exchange of contracts now. I'll send some emails and make some calls when I get home. Those poor people in the chain. All the money they've paid out.'

'Johnny must've thought about all this, surely?'

'You would've thought so but evidently not. But I can't leave it up to him, can I? He obviously can't be trusted.'

She picks up two mats from a metal holder in the centre of the table and places a cup of steaming tea on each one. 'Do you want something to eat?'

I shake my head.

'You've got to eat, Han.'

'I can't. I feel sick to the core. As if what Johnny did wasn't enough, now I'm stressed out about Dean's motives for hunting down India and turning up at the church. What if he's found out about Lucas, Carrie? What if he wants to be a part of his life? I couldn't stand it.'

'Calm down. You don't know that yet.'

I drop my head in my hands.

'Just forget Johnny. He's not worth it.'

I raise my head, taken aback at the harsh tone of her words.

'I mean it. Tom said Johnny was—'

The front door opens and closes. Tom strides into the kitchen. He kisses my sister's cheek. I look away. Johnny greets me in exactly the same way when he comes home.

Tom slips out of his coat, throws it on the kitchen worktop and sits beside me. He's agitated. I can't blame him. This must be hell for him as well.

'How's things?' he asks in a sullen voice.

'So-so. How was breakfast?'

Carrie gets up. 'I'll make you a cup of tea.' She picks up his coat and takes it out into the hallway to hang up.

'It was...' Tom strokes his beard. 'It was OK. Only a handful stayed in the end.'

'Who?'

'Your aunt and uncle. They said they'd be in touch soon. Then a couple of Mum and Dad's friends who came from up north. And the lads. They said he's an idiot if that's any consolation. I'm ashamed to call him my brother at this moment.'

I'm quietly pleased he's sticking up for me. In the year I've known him, Tom's become the brother I've never had. I can see why Carrie fell in love with him. Like Johnny – or so I thought – he's kind, honest and reliable.

'What did Tom say?' I ask when Carrie hands Tom a cup of tea.

She gives me a puzzled look. So does Tom. He laughs. 'What did I say?'

I stare at my sister. 'You said, just as Tom got back, that Tom said Johnny was...' I glance from her to Tom. 'You didn't finish. Johnny was what?'

If looks could kill my sister would be on her way to her coffin with the expression on Tom's face.

'What are you keeping from me?'

'Tell her, Tom. Tell her what you said to me last night. Be honest with her,' Carrie says. 'She needs to know.'

Tom looks at Carrie sternly. 'This isn't the right time.' He gives a disapproving click of his tongue.

'Tell me,' I demand.

Tom rolls his eyes. 'Look, Han. I don't want to upset you, but perhaps it's best you forget Johnny.'

'Forget him? Why?' I'm bordering on shouting. I can't believe he's saying this about his brother. He and Johnny are close. There's only an eighteen-month gap between them, and they might only be half-brothers, but they've practically grown up together. 'Why would you, his brother, say that?'

He blushes as if the conversation is embarrassing him. 'I'll be honest with you.' He hesitates as if he's considering how to phrase his next words. 'Before you came along, Johnny could be unreliable.'

'In what way?'

Tom shifts uncomfortably on the bench. He struggles out of his hoodie.

'Tell me.'

'Mum will tell you. He often didn't show up for work and he was...'

I push his arm. 'He was what?'

'He was a bit of a womaniser. He played the field. Upset a few people along the way.'

'You never told me that bit,' Carrie says.

I feel like he's just slapped me around the face. This is the first time I've ever heard a bad word said against Johnny. I've never once doubted him. I glare at my sister and back at Tom. I struggle to breathe. I need to get out of here. Everything I've believed in over the past year is slowly being torn away from me, strand by painful strand. I stand. Tom tries to pull me back down. I resist, tugging my arm from his grasp. 'I need to go.'

'Stay, Han.' Carrie sounds as if she's about to cry. 'Tell her, Tom.'

'Come on, Han.' Tom sounds as if he's about to shed a tear as well. 'Please don't go. Stay with us.'

I'm angry for what he said, but it was my sister who pushed him. My voice cracks. 'I can't stay. I've got stuff to do.'

'At least finish your drink,' Carrie says.

'I'm sorry, Han. You probably didn't need to hear that right now.' Tom glares at my sister.

'It's fine. Perhaps it'll help me come to terms with what he's done.'

TWENTY-FIVE

Womaniser!

That's a ridiculous notion. But I don't know what to believe anymore.

I spend all afternoon under the duvet, flicking through TV channels, but it's as good as watching white noise. I can't stop tormenting myself with Tom's unwelcome words. They've given me a dull headache that's at risk of turning into a migraine.

The fear Dean might turn up has made me lock all the doors and windows. But still, I jump at every sound. I recall the beady-eyed powerhouse of a man from six years ago when I sat in that freezing cold courtroom during the inquest into Charlie's death. He was a monster then, and, whatever India says, he's a monster now.

But despite my fears, if he does turn up again, I'll swallow a cup of bravery and listen to what he has to say. Because I can't carry on like this.

Womaniser!

Johnny and I didn't have lengthy discussions about our exes.

There was very little to tell him from my side. Before Charlie, I'd only had a few short relationships, nothing serious.

And between Charlie's death and meeting Johnny, I didn't date anyone. He asked about Charlie but soon learnt that it was a topic off-limits. The less he knew about that man, the better.

Womaniser! It sounds like an ugly swear word I never want to hear again.

Does it matter what he was like before I met him? Until now, he's given me no reason to distrust him. Besides, everyone has a past. Some more chequered than others.

He told me about Allison, his first serious relationship. The hotel manager, who he was engaged to for a year. They had a good relationship, he admitted, until, out of the blue, she told him she no longer wanted kids. She'd been promoted to the management team of the small but prestigious hotel chain she'd worked for since leaving school and was working long hours and travelling more than she was at home. One weekend, she told Johnny she'd decided the world was no longer a place she wanted to bring a child into and she was going to concentrate on her career. She changed, and he fell out of love with her, which is when he ended it. A few relationships followed, but nothing that lasted more than a few months.

I send Johnny a WhatsApp message, telling him I've been to his apartment to collect my things and borrowed his PlayStation to placate Lucas, who's distraught and wants to know when he'll see him again. I lay it on thick, but he deserves it. It's the truth. And he needs to know how his actions have affected my beautiful, innocent son.

My phone rings. It's India. A baby is crying in the background. She tells me about the christening and how seeing her friend's baby had made her broody, until it cried incessantly for over an hour, and the feeling quickly disappeared.

What I'd do to hear my Victoria crying right now. I wouldn't care if she screamed all day and all night.

'Have you heard from Dean?' I ask.

'Nothing. I've tried to call him loads as well. It's really creeping me out.'

'You're not the only one.'

'I'm coming back this evening.'

'I thought you were staying there tonight?'

'It's fine. I want to be with you.'

After the call ends, I check the WhatsApp message I sent to Johnny to see if he has replied. Only one tick has appeared to the right of the message indicating the message has been sent but not delivered.

He must've turned his phone off.

TWENTY-SIX

I drive to pick up Lucas, my head in a mess. There are so many questions, but I have no way of contacting the two people who can answer them.

I pull into the driveway of Highland Hall, an elegant Elizabethan property dating back to the sixteenth century, set in mature, secluded grounds of two acres. Angela and Alan purchased the property partly as an investment and partly for the barns lining the right-hand side of the estate that they converted into a large office space from where they run their growing business empire.

I should say *her* business empire, because although they jointly own it, Caxton Events is Angela's baby. She's the beating heart of the company. Alan had a successful career in IT security that he gave up because he had a heart attack and subsequent surgery. He'd earnt enough to retire and wanted to lead a less stressful life on the golf course. But Angela had other plans and dragged him in to help run Caxton Events part-time.

The shingle driveway sweeps up to a turning circle in front of the property. The sight of the grand marquee for Carrie and Tom's wedding dominating the front lawn stirs the pool of sickness in the pit of my stomach. I park my car beside Angela's Mercedes and sit for a minute, preparing myself. Facing Angela and Alan is going to be difficult. I feel awkward. They probably do, too. I guess in normal circumstances, we'd go our separate ways. It must be challenging, if not impossible, to remain friends with the parents of the man who left you stranded at the altar.

But my sister is marrying their other son and Angela is my boss. And I can't afford to leave Caxton Events. She gave me a significant pay rise in the summer, taking my base salary well over the market rate. He wouldn't admit it, but I'm sure Johnny helped secure the salary I'd find impossible to achieve elsewhere. Not with six weeks' annual leave, two half-yearly profit-related bonuses, and most importantly, the flexibility that Caxton Events affords me. Because Lucas always comes first. Always. I work from home if he is sick, or his school has an inset day. And on the rare occasions that breakfast and afterschool clubs aren't running, I can arrive at work late or leave early. I give back, mind you, granting the role one hundred per cent commitment which involves often working late into the evenings after Lucas has gone to bed and at weekends.

Alan answers the door with Lucas bouncing around him like a ball. His cute face is bright red, and mud covers the knees of his jeans. I grab him and hold him tightly, not realising how much I've missed him. I've adored him since the day he was born. Sometimes, I wonder if Johnny is envious of how close we are. Not that he's ever said anything, but there have been a couple of occasions when I spotted him studying us together with a curious look.

The family dog, Ruby, a regal red setter, the queen of the house, nudges Lucas with her nose.

Lucas wriggles out of my hold. 'I've had an epic day, Mum.'

Epic. That's a word Johnny uses.

Lucas hands a bag to me. 'Look at what Father Christmas

gave me.' His enthusiasm among the chaos of the past twenty-four hours manages to fill my heart with love. Never a day passes when I regret having him, despite how Charlie treated me and the trepidation of raising a child alone.

I open the gift bag to find a golden football embossed with his name and a chocolate selection pack.

'Alan played football with me in the garden when we got home. I won, didn't I, Alan?'

Alan nods and smiles. 'I'm sorry about the mud.' He looks weary as if he has the weight of the world on his hunched shoulders. 'Do you want to come in for a drink? Angela's in her office, but I've just put the kettle on.'

'Thanks for the offer.' I ruffle Lucas's blond curls. 'But I need to get this one home.' My voice is strained from the effort of the brave face I'm struggling to wear. Being here, with so many reminders of Johnny, is harder than I thought it'd be. 'School in the morning.'

'Do I have to go tomorrow?' Lucas cries.

I give his curls another ruffle. 'You know the answer to that. Now get your shoes on.'

Alan opens the door wider. 'At least come in out of the cold.'

I step inside the reception hall, dominated by a Tudor oak staircase with elaborately carved balustrades and a giant moose's head that protrudes from above the kitchen door. That thing always gives me the creeps.

Lucas crouches to slip on his trainers.

I mouth to Alan, 'Have you heard anything more?'

Alan shakes his head. 'I'm sorry,' he mouths back.

Lucas jumps up.

I hand his bag back to him. 'Go and get in the car, darling. I'll be there in a minute.'

Lucas hugs Alan's legs. I don't know who is more moved by

the loving gesture, Alan or me. 'Thanks for having me, Alan. See you soon.' He scutters off to the car.

'He's such a polite boy. You've raised him well,' Alan says. 'Don't stop him coming here, will you? I've grown fond of the child since...' He gives a straight-lipped smile. 'Since you and...' He doesn't need to finish his sentence. He takes a deep breath. 'Angela said you should take the week off work.'

'I don't want to. I need to keep busy.'

'Fair enough. Just know the offer's there.'

I tell him about what happened at Johnny's apartment this morning.

'Are you sure?' The doubt in his voice sounds like the cynicism in my sister's earlier.

'Someone came in, Alan.' I slam my hand on my chest. 'I can't say for sure it was Johnny. But someone definitely came in.'

'What are you implying?'

I shrug. 'I'm angry with him. Angrier than I ever thought I could be, but I'm also a little scared.'

He places his hands on his hips. 'Scared of what?' he asks curiously.

'Scared that something could've happened to him. And I don't know what to do for the best.'

'Go home and get some rest, Hannah.'

He gives me that look.

The one Carrie gave me.

A look of pity.

Or is it one portraying he knows more than he's letting on?

I can't stand this.

TWENTY-SEVEN

Lucas doesn't mention Johnny again until I'm reading him a bedtime story. He is fidgeting and wriggling like a worm, unable to settle. I'm the same, constantly on edge, waiting for India to come home.

Or for Dean to make another appearance.

'Can I still go to Johnny's place and play on his PlayStation with him?' he asks.

I close my eyes, silently swearing at my ex.

Ex – it's so damn difficult thinking of the man I thought I'd be collecting my pension with in these terms. The person who told me he couldn't wait to make it official that we'd be together in sickness and in health until the day one of us died.

'Can I, Mum?'

The knot of tension in my stomach tightens. Johnny didn't consider the effect of his actions on Lucas. He should've at least spoken to him and explained what was happening.

His bottom lip quivers. 'Or does he never want to see me again?'

My boy doesn't deserve this.

I don't deserve this.

'I'm sure he'd love for you to still go around and for you to play your usual games together.' I don't know why I said that. It's a cop-out. I don't want the two of them to have a relationship going forward. But I want to protect my beautiful, innocent boy, save him from the hurt and pain that's suffocating me. 'I have a surprise for you.'

He pushes the book away. 'What?'

'When I went to Johnny's apartment today, I brought back the PlayStation.'

His eyes widen. 'Where is it?' He tries to get out of bed.

I grab his arm. 'Not now. You've had a busy day. You need to get some sleep. I'll set it up and you can play with it when I pick you up from school tomorrow.'

'Isn't that stealing, Mum?'

He always manages to slip questions into our conversations I find impossible to answer. I bet I'd never find a response to this one in any books on parenting. But, the situation justified my actions, and I know Johnny wouldn't mind. He's got to feel some remorse about what he's done to us. 'I've sent him a message and told him I've borrowed it for you. Can I ask you a question?'

'Fire away.'

My heart jolts. Fire away. That's another of Johnny's sayings. It's uncomfortable hearing it coming from a six-year-old. But over recent months, I've noticed Lucas adopting little sayings of Johnny's. 'When Johnny picked you up on Friday to take you to Angela and Alan's house, where did you go?'

'To the hotel.'

'Why?'

'He wanted to drop off a surprise for you. But he wouldn't tell me what it was.'

'Why?'

'It was something special for you. What was it?'

I shrug. I don't want to confuse him any more. 'How was he?'

'When?'

'When he picked you up?'

'OK.'

'He was just OK? Did he seem happy?'

'He didn't want you to see us at the hotel, so he was hurrying. When's he coming back?'

'I don't know.'

'He said he loved me. He said he was going to be my dad.'

My head turns sharply. 'He said that! When?'

'On Friday. He said he couldn't wait to be my dad.'

I can't believe what I'm hearing.

'Why didn't he want to marry you anymore, Mum?'

'I don't know, darling.' My voice trails off. 'Come on, let's finish this book.'

I continue reading. Usually, I love story time. It's one of my favourite parts of the day. But my mind is elsewhere. The words escape my mouth. I'm turning the pages. But I couldn't relay what the story I'm reading is about. My mind is too fixed on Johnny.

He told Lucas he wanted to be his dad.

The taste of bile shoots into my throat.

He's found out what I did.

There can be no other explanation.

TWENTY-EIGHT

With each passing hour, the anger that consumed me after leaving Carrie and Tom's house has morphed into fear. The fear that Dean has got to Johnny, or that something untoward could have happened to him. Because, unless everything I've thought to be true about my life is a lie, I can't believe he would've done this to me. Especially not after telling Lucas he couldn't wait to be his dad.

My body is heavy as I go downstairs. Lucas took ages to get to sleep, even though he was exhausted after the weekend. Every time he was about to drop off, his eyes opened wide, and he asked another question about Johnny I couldn't answer.

I head to the kitchen and open the fridge, only to find it as sad and as empty as me. I sit at the kitchen table and pull out my MacBook from my leather laptop bag. The bag Johnny bought me for my birthday in the summer. Before that, I'd used a tatty old one that was falling apart. I can hear his voice when he gave it to me as if he were sitting beside me. 'You deserve only the best.'

The computer is a top-of-the-range model that Angela bought for me so I could work from home whenever I needed to.

I'm sure Johnny encouraged the purchase. While waiting for it to charge, I answer texts that have filtered in during the day. More people sending their condolences as if someone is dead.

To me, it feels as if they are.

My go-to person has died.

I take a sip of tea. The fear of the unknown, a path that's now my destiny, makes me well up. But I haven't got time for any more tears. I've done it before. When I left Charlie's place with only a suitcase, a holdall and a growing baby to my name, I turned my life around. I can do it again.

But it's different now. I'm older. I want security. I want to be settled. Lucas needs a family unit. *I* need a family unit. And I want another child. I glide my hand over my belly. Perhaps what's happened is my punishment. I don't deserve another child.

I answer every text, expressing my need to have time to get my head together and carve a way forward for Lucas and me. I compose an email to my solicitor, telling her I'm pulling out of my house sale and the purchase of my and Johnny's dream home, and send her a text to confirm my request, cringing at how angry and upset the six parties in the purchase chain are going to be. Lots of people are about to lose a lot of money and the homes they'd set their hearts on.

A thud and a clicking noise sound from the direction of the front door. The hairs on my arms stand on end. A low tapping sound follows, exactly how Johnny knocks to let me know he's here when he comes around at this time of the evening so as not to disturb Lucas.

I slowly stand. My heart thumps in my chest as I leave the kitchen and creep along the hallway. I'm being irrational. India is due back any moment. But I can't help my heart pump even faster at the sound of another knock. 'Who is it?' I call out, half expecting Johnny's voice asking me to let him in, or Dean's, asking to speak to me again.

But it's India who replies.

I breathe a sigh of relief and quickly unbolt the door.

'Sorry, Han. I left my key here.' She looks shattered. Her long dark hair is dishevelled and her face make-up free. She kisses me and dumps her holdall on the floor. 'Heard anything?'

I shake my head, cringing at how many times people are going to ask me that question in the coming days. I lock the door behind her and bolt it at the top and bottom. 'Have you?'

'Nothing.' She follows me into the living room.

I tell her about my day.

She frowns. 'So a guy arranges for your bed to be decorated in rose petals, buys you *and* your son, who isn't even his real kid, tickets to Disney. Tells your kid he can't wait to be his dad and then buggers off without a trace.'

'Exactly,' I say. 'Dean's got something to do with this. I know he has. I tried to look at his Facebook account, but it's set to private. But you're his friend, so you can. Let's look through his account and see if there's a way of contacting him.'

'I already have on the train this morning. There's nothing on his account suggesting where he lives. All I know is that he said he lived in Stanfield, which is why it was convenient to meet up when I was there on Friday. We originally arranged to meet late afternoon, but he got held up and we didn't meet until early evening.'

'Let me take another look in case you missed something.'

Removing her phone from her pocket, she taps the screen and frowns. 'That's weird.'

'What?'

'He's blocked me.'

We both look at each other, mouths agape.

'He's trouble,' I say. 'He's got something to do with why Johnny did this to me. I'm telling you.'

TWENTY-NINE

I run my hand through my hair. It's coarse and matted from the hairspray yesterday. 'We have to speak to him.'

'I don't know if I ever want to see him again.' India gathers her long dark hair and twists it into a knot. 'This has given me the creeps.'

The unease deepens inside of me. 'It's all very weird. My ex's brother suddenly turns up at my wedding with my sister, and then my fiancé disappears. And now we can't get hold of either of them.'

'I can't disagree.' She studies her phone. Her hand is shaking. It takes a lot to unnerve my sister. Our mum always said she'd been born with bones of boldness. But this has disturbed her almost as much as it has me.

'What were his plans?' I ask.

'What do you mean?'

'Did he say when he's going back to the oil rig?'

'He has a month's annual leave,' she says uneasily. 'He isn't going back until the twentieth of December. He had the whole of Christmas off last year, so he has to work this year.'

'I can't wait to see whether he comes back here. I want to find him and confront him,' I say.

'Hang on a minute. Are you crazy? Why would you want to stick your neck out like that? When he came here, you wanted to get hold of a knife to face him.'

'Things have moved on from then.'

'In any case, how are you going to confront him when he's not answering his phone, and you don't know where he lives?'

I pause, staring my sister in the eye. 'Wait there.' I go to the kitchen and return with my MacBook. 'Think, India. Did he say anything that could lead us to where he lives?'

She puffs out a large breath, shaking her head. 'Like I already said – only that he lives in Stanfield.'

'That's strange. I remember Charlie telling me that Dean owned a flat near to his house. He kept having to go around there to repair the boiler for the tenants Dean rented it to while he was away on the oil rig. He must've moved after Charlie died.'

'So you have a name and a town. How do you find him, then?'

'Data Protection laws make it virtually impossible these days, but I might know a way.' I turn to my MacBook and type *Electoral Register* into Google and search for Dean's name in Stanfield. 'Mmn... There's no Dean Ferguson in Stanfield.'

'But that's where he said he lived.'

I wonder if he still owns his flat near to Charlie's old house. I type *Fletton* into the search bar. 'I don't believe it.' I do a double-take. This has proved easier than I thought it would. I shudder. Memories come flooding back like a bad dream I can't wake up from.

'What?' India muscles her way in to look at the screen.

'He doesn't live in Stanfield.' I point to the screen. 'He lives in Charlie's old house. Dean must've sold his flat – or continued renting it – and moved into Charlie's place.'

'Come to think of it, he did talk about a house, not a flat, because he mentioned a garden. So why did he lie and say he lived in Stanfield, then?'

'To persuade you to meet him.'

Her hand covers her mouth. She lets out a low groan. 'This is getting creepier by the minute.'

'Look, India. Johnny hasn't contacted me. Dean has now done a disappearing act. I can't live like this. I need to find out what the hell is going on.' The thought of returning to where I lived with Charlie and where he died is unbearable, but I don't see that I have a choice. I must face this man and find out why he's wormed his way back into my life via my sister. 'You'll need to come with me. I can't go there alone.'

'No way! Not you. Not me. Are you insane?'

'What's the alternative?'

'We go to the police.'

The police! I can't afford to involve the police.

No way!

'What are the police going to do?'

India falls silent.

'Come on. Please. I need you. I think he warned Johnny off marrying me. And I have to know if he's found out about Lucas.'

She relents with a heavy sigh. 'Perhaps when I get back from Dorset. Let me think about it.' She has meticulously planned her days back in the UK to catch up with all her friends and is going to the beach tomorrow. She shakes her head. 'I don't know, Han. This is really scaring me now. Don't you think you should go to the police?'

I shake my head, steadfast. 'No. No police. Absolutely not.'

If only I could tell her the real reason why I can't involve the police. But Carrie would kill me.

'What do you propose then?' she asks.

'If neither of them has been in touch by the time you get

back from Dorset, then we're going to go and have a chat with Dean Ferguson. Because I need to determine what the hell he's up to.'

THIRTY

'Where are the games?' Lucas fiddles with the PlayStation controller.

'Games?' I fold up the duvet scrunched up on the sofa from where India slept last night.

I can't rid my mind of what I'd be doing now if things had gone to plan. Johnny and I would've probably just woken up after our second night at the hotel. We were going to leave there after breakfast and return here to continue packing ready for the move. The finger of sadness gives me another dig in the ribs. The move to our dream home.

'Mum! Didn't you bring the games back as well?' Lucas points to the PlayStation.

I wince at the throbbing pain in my head. I squeeze my eyes shut tightly.

'Mum!'

I open my eyes.

'Where are the games?'

Games! They hadn't even crossed my mind. 'I'm sorry, my darling. I'll get you some later.'

'But I wanted to play before school.'

'There isn't time.' I glance at my watch. 'We need to leave in five minutes, and you haven't even brushed your teeth.' I shoo him out of the room. 'Go. Go.'

'Will you get them while I'm at school today? Please, Mum!'

'I'll see what I can do.'

'The *Astro Bot* one. That's the best. Make sure you get that one.'

I swear at myself for bringing the PlayStation back here. I should've just left it at Johnny's apartment.

India appears. 'I'm almost ready. Are you sure you don't mind giving me a lift to the station? I could always get an Uber.'

'It's fine.'

'Are you sure it's a good idea for you to go back to work?'

I nod. Despite everyone's insistence that I take some time off, a day moping around and smoking far too many cigarettes was enough. I need to find a way of picking up the broken pieces of my shattered life and work out a way to move forward.

She walks to the door and pauses, clinging to the side. 'Look, Han. You promise me you won't go and see Dean on your own. He could be dangerous.' She hits the door. 'He *is* dangerous, for Christ's sake. He sure manipulated me.'

She's right. If Dean is anything like his brother, he's a person you don't want to mess with.

'I'll come with you when I get back.'

I can hear the reluctance in her voice.

I don't hurry Lucas along like I normally do, purposefully making him late for school. It occurred to me in the night that I'll be the talk of the town in the coming days until people have something else to feed their hungry appetites of gossip. The poor, poor bride who was jilted at the altar. No! I can't face other school mums yet. I need the wheel of gossip to stop turning first. Let them have a chinwag at my expense and get it out of their system while I'm not around.

When I pull up at the school, a group of mums who always

hang around after drop-off on a Monday morning, catching up on their weekends, are hobnobbing at the school gates. I turn to Lucas. 'Aunty India will take you in today.'

India doesn't even question my request. 'Sure, come on, buddy,' she says willingly.

Lucas unbuckles his seatbelt. 'Don't forget to get that game, Mum, will you?'

I nod and kiss him goodbye.

'You won't forget the game, will you, Mum?'

'I'll try my best. Now come on, just go.'

I watch them walk hand in hand towards the school gates. Something tells me I shouldn't be letting my boy go. I should be keeping him close to me. I climb out of the car. 'Lucas,' I call out. My voice emerges as a faint whisper caught in the wind whirling around me. They've merged with the sea of kids cruising into the playground. I go to call him again but stop. I'm being irrational. He's safe here.

The engine is running, the heater humming on maximum, but I still can't get warm. I drop my head that's swimming with visions of Charlie and Dean. It's Charlie's eyes that attracted me to him in the first place, but ironically they are what has haunted me the most since he died. Shiny balls of brown moonstone that glistened black in moments of anger. I often wonder if they were open or closed when he plunged to his death, and what was going through his mind.

THIRTY-ONE

The car door opens. I jump, constantly on edge.

India climbs in. 'Sorry,' she says. 'He got a little upset.' She rests her hand on my arm. 'Don't worry. He's fine.'

'Was he crying?'

'No. Just asking what has happened to Johnny. He's worried about you.'

'Do you think it's a good idea to leave him? I thought he was being pretty brave about the whole situation. Perhaps I should keep him at home for the day. I don't like it. What if Dean is after him?' I thrust open the car door. 'I'm going to get him.'

She grabs my arm. 'Han, Han. Chill. You're being completely irrational. I had a word with his teacher and told her what's happened. She said she'll keep an eye on him and contact you if there are any problems. He's safe here and occupied for the day. It's the best place for him.'

Reluctantly I close the door.

'Anyway, whatever we think about Dean, he'd never do anything to harm Lucas.'

I'm not so sure. Maybe I am being illogical, but the fear is real. 'Ever since Lucas was conceived I've had an unhealthy obsession with keeping him safe. It's the fear that Dean, at some point, would somehow learn about him and click on that he's his uncle,' I say as I drive her to the station.

'How, though?' she asks. 'You're not on social media. Lucas's father is not mentioned on his birth certificate.'

I shrug.

'Oh, Han. You've been through so much. What with the loss of the baby, and now Johnny. Do you think perhaps some therapy would be beneficial for you?'

'I'm not insane,' I snap. 'You don't know the Dean I know.'

She bites her lip. 'Do you think there's a chance Johnny could turn up at work today?'

Another shrug. 'I've been thinking that, but I doubt it. Surely, he'd have contacted me first?'

'You'd have thought so.'

'I know there's no way forward for us as a couple, but he at least needs to give me answers before expecting us to carrying on working together. Do you remember Dad used to say, never mix business with pleasure!'

'After his friend stole from him.'

I nod. 'I should've heeded his advice.'

* * *

After I've dropped her at the station, I drive to work. Snow is falling, and the sky has darkened, affecting visibility.

The sight of Carrie and Tom's marquee turns my stomach when I pull into Highland House. A sprinkle of snow covers the surrounding grass. If the weather holds until the weekend, it will make for an idyllic setting for the fairytale wedding my sister has always envisioned, like a dream scene from *Frozen*.

I pull into the small car park and freeze.

I do a double-take.

It can't be.

Johnny's Mercedes is parked in the far right-hand corner.

My heart races. He's here. The anger I felt on Saturday returns. Finally, I'm going to get some answers.

My car skids along the gravel as I come to a stop. My whole body is shaking. I ram on the handbrake and quickly check my face in the mirror. Dark circles ring my eyes, and I'm deathly pale. At least Johnny will be able to see what he's done to me.

I grab my bag and hurry out of the car.

Tom is getting out of the Mercedes. Johnny must've given him a lift. But as I look over to the car through the falling snow, I realise it's Tom's car, not Johnny's. The company leases a fleet of Mercedes for company use and all the family have one. Waves of continuous frustration pass through me. I thought I was finally going to get some answers.

He jogs towards me. 'Hey, Han, how're you doing? Can I have a word?'

I lean against my car. The confusion has left me dizzy.

'I need to tell you something. Johnny messaged me. He's in Wales.'

'Oh!'

The knife of betrayal lodged in my heart twists another forty-five degrees.

He told his family this but not me.

'I'm sorry. I guess that's not what you want to hear. He said he needed time to clear his head. He plans to be back for the wedding, though.'

Damn him! Anger, disappointment and sadness fight for the top spot of my emotions. Unless he gets in contact beforehand, I'll have no choice but to wait until Tom and Carrie's wedding before we speak. That'll be awkward with him as best man and me as a bridesmaid. Surely, he won't do that to me. 'Where in Wales?'

'He hasn't been specific.'

I study his face, wondering if he's telling me the truth. But there's no reason for him to lie. Unless he's covering up for Johnny. 'At least we know he's safe,' I say.

He raises his eyebrows. 'Why wouldn't he be safe?'

I want to tell him about Dean. But I can't. Because then I'd have to involve Carrie.

And she'd kill me if I let on about our secret.

THIRTY-TWO

Wales? Johnny doesn't know anyone in Wales.

At least I know he's safe.

Despite what he's done to me, I don't want him to come to any harm. No one could wish harm to a man like Johnny. Even with my anger at what he's done to me, to Lucas, I still love him. Feelings aren't like a tap. You can't turn them on and off at will.

Tom heads to the marquee, and I walk into the offices. I've been bracing myself for facing the fifteen staff members who work for the company. I sent an email to Angela and Tom early this morning and asked them to tell people not to talk about what's happened. Business is business, and I want to move forward. I can't afford to lose this job.

When I couldn't sleep last night, I surfed the internet looking for alternative job opportunities. I found a possible opening in a start-up organisation. The pay was on par with what I earn at Caxton Events, and the role sounded interesting, but the company is based north of Manchester, over two hundred miles away. If it was just me, I'd move again. Get the hell away from here. But I have Lucas now. He comes first. He's settled at school. He's made good friends. It isn't fair to uproot him.

I enter the main office where the large workstations are generously spaced and the specifications high-end. Staff are already at their desks. A few lift their heads with a muted acknowledgement before returning to their work. Others keep their heads down; either they haven't seen me, or they're ignoring me. I can't blame them. They were all invited to the wedding, mostly to the evening reception, so they probably feel embarrassed not knowing how to face me, or what to say to me.

Out of habit, Johnny's empty desk that is partially in view of mine catches my eye. He isn't in the office all the time. He spends three-quarters of his working week out on the road doing site checks, meeting clients and drumming up new business. But on the days he is here, he always arrives before me. I drop Lucas at school so I'm always the last one in. When I arrive, he gives me a minute to get settled before turning around and winking at me.

I stifle tears. I miss my morning wink.

Now I think about it, he hasn't been particularly happy here lately. We were having a heart-to-heart one evening, and he admitted to not really enjoying his job anymore, which had surprised me as I thought he was happy here. He said things had changed. He wanted out, but he felt trapped. The money was good; like for me – more than he could earn elsewhere. He didn't want to let his mum and dad down. But when I pressed him on why, he brushed my questions off.

My desk is situated by a window with a blissful outlook of the manicured lawn and year-round colour thanks to Angela and Alan's gardener, an older man with fingers as green as the perfect lawn. I think he adores the garden more than they do. Usually, I love this view, but with my sister's wedding marquee stuck in sight, the constant reminder of what I've lost doesn't afford me pretty viewing.

This week is one to get through.

Hundreds of emails fill my inbox that I can't find the inclination to deal with. Perhaps everyone was right. Maybe I need more time off to deal with the trauma of what has happened. Sandwiched between Johnny's absence and the marquee for my sister's wedding isn't the ideal place to heal the scars still so blood raw.

I sigh heavily. But neither is a cold, empty house that I should've been packing into boxes to move into my dream home.

A lorry pulls into the driveway. Three sturdy men jump out and unload the rest of the flooring for the marquee. As they are finishing up, another lorry arrives. The driver unpacks two hundred chairs and twenty tables, helped by a guy who is barely old enough to smoke the cigarettes he has constantly hanging out of his mouth, who obviously doesn't want to be there.

Carrie turns up and heads straight to the marquee. Tom meets her outside. They appear to bicker, which is surprising. They rarely argue. Tom's pretty laid back and generally goes along with Carrie's wishes. But now I think about it, tension levels have been high within the whole family this past few weeks. Tom has been stressed out trying to complete a work project before the wedding, and Angela seems to have been on everyone's case more than usual.

Even Johnny hadn't been his usually smiley self. It's been like driving around London in rush hour at times. I put it down to pre-wedding nerves, but now I wonder if Johnny was having second thoughts way before Saturday.

Tom storms off into the house, leaving Carrie in her glory, instructing the men on the exact placement of each table.

I phone her. 'Did you know Johnny's gone to Wales?' I ask before she has the chance to speak.

'Yep. Tom told me.'

'Didn't you think to tell me?'

'Calm down, Han. I've only just found out myself. Can you spare me a minute? Tom and I are having a domestic. He says we—' She continues, but I'm not listening.

My ears have pricked up to the question Jenna has shouted across the office, 'Has anyone heard of a Dean Ferguson?'

THIRTY-THREE

I stare at my computer in shock. My chest tightens. I choke on my breath.

'Dean Ferguson, anyone?' Jenna calls out, louder this time. 'Is he a client? Supplier?'

People either ignore her or stop what they're doing and shake their heads before resuming their work. She returns to her screen.

A foreboding races through me, wondering if she could mean Charlie's brother, Dean. Of course she does; it's too much of a coincidence if she doesn't. But I can't think of one reason why the name Dean Ferguson would've crept into the workplace. Unless Dean is playing games. Or he somehow had his claws into Johnny.

I reach for my phone and call India. She doesn't pick up. I send her a message asking her to call me urgently.

I wait for my chance. Jenna is the biggest tea drinker in the office. At least once an hour she totters upstairs to the staff kitchen to refill her cup. I don't need to wait long. Only minutes after asking about Dean Ferguson, she stands and picks up her oversized mug with *I'm never too busy for tea* written over the side. I give it a minute before following her.

On the way, annoyingly, Angela calls me into her goldfish bowl of an office, a large space decorated in the company's brand colours: turquoise and hot pink. It always smells of lemon in here from the fragrance mist she sprays around every morning. Apparently, it's meant to reduce stress, not that I think it does any good. Angela is often pretty stressed around here.

I consider telling her I need to speak to Jenna first, but Angela's not the type of person one keeps waiting. 'You really didn't need to come in today, you know.' Strands of hair that haven't made it into the bun on the top of her head frame her attractive and perfectly, but subtly, made-up face. She looks more tired than usual, the effects of Johnny's actions affecting so many people. 'I would've understood.' Her voice is clipped and professional, as it usually is. Even how she treats Tom and Johnny in the workplace, you'd never know they are her sons.

'I need to keep busy.' I rub my shaking hands together. 'I hear Johnny's gone to Wales.'

She nods. 'He's taking some time away from the office.'

I still can't believe he spoke to her but not me.

'Look, Angela. I just want to say. What's happened has happened. When Johnny comes back, we'll remain professional.' I'm unsure how true that is. Who knows how I'll feel seeing him again and conversing over business matters after what he's done. But until I can find another job that pays as well as this one, I have to give it my very best shot.

Angela and Alan have probably discussed whether I'll stay at the company. I can envisage Angela believing it'll be too disruptive to the workforce. I need to assure her that won't be the case. We all have little choice other than to make the best of a bad situation. My sister is marrying their other son, after all. Like it or not, Lucas and I are going to be a part of the Caxton family.

'You have my word that what's happened will not affect my work,' I say.

She gives a sharp nod. 'Understood.'

I go to leave. I have to speak to Jenna. But Angela carries on. 'Now then.' She picks up a file from the side of her highly organised desk. Johnny's is the same. I inwardly sigh. How long will it to take for me to stop comparing everything to Johnny?

'We've had a possible last-minute contract come in.' She waves the file at me. 'And it's a big deal – a new client we can't possibly turn away. Red Glow Engineering; they've been let down on an exhibition on the twelfth of January. It'll be tight... very tight, what with Johnny out and Tom and Carrie's wedding, but it'll open doors for us in the future if we can pull this one off. Big doors. I'm snowed under at the moment, so I want you to work with Tom and Jenna on this one.' She hands the file to me. 'Make sure it happens, can you, please?'

She's testing me. I know how she operates. She wants to see if I can still perform to her standards. I'll be out of the door if I don't. I've seen it happen before to other staff members.

I nod at my boss. My ex-future-mother-in-law is a self-confessed workaholic, and a control freak. But she has her positives. Being forthright means you know where you stand with Angela, which many find an unnerving characteristic, but one I've always appreciated. And she is generous to a fault, supporting many local charities and dishing out a good chunk of the company profits in the form of healthy bonuses to staff members who do their job well.

'For what it's worth, Hannah, I want you to know that I'm extremely disappointed in my stepson.'

I'm taken aback. I've never heard her refer to Johnny as her stepson. The same as I've never heard Johnny and Tom talk in halves as far as their relationship is concerned. And Johnny has always called her his mum, never his stepmum.

She continues. 'And ashamed. Very ashamed indeed. I

didn't raise him to behave in this manner. He should've been a man about it and faced you, not just traipsed off. When I next see him. I'll be having words. But let's crack on. As you say, we can't have this whole unsavoury affair affect business.'

THIRTY-FOUR

The staff kitchen is small, but modern and well equipped with a microwave, a toaster and a dishwasher. Jenna has boiled the kettle by the time I get there and has her head in the fridge. She's a large woman, late thirties, and is a serial dieter, always starting one new diet plan or another on a Monday, only to be raiding the biscuit tin by Wednesday lunchtime.

I make her jump as if I've caught her doing something she shouldn't be doing. She turns. 'Hannah!' She throws her hand to her chest. 'How are you?' She pauses. Her jaw tenses. 'I'm so sorry. I can't believe what's happened. I know you don't want to talk about it.' She talks faster and faster. 'Angela made that perfectly clear to us all. But I can't not say how terribly sorry I am.'

I'm fond of Jenna. She's a talker, which is what makes her so good at her job. She brings in more business than anyone else, which is great for the company, but not so good when you aren't in the mood for conversation.

She continues, not pausing for breath, asking about the wedding that never happened and relaying what she would've done if her husband had never turned up to marry her. Her spiel is insensitive, but it's her. She means well. 'Sorry, I'm rabbiting. You probably don't want to hear all this, do you?' The kettle finishes boiling. She fills her cup with water. 'Anyway, how are you? Want some tea?'

I hand her my cup. 'I've had better days.' I cut to the chase. 'I was wondering why you asked about that Dean Ferguson guy.'

'You know him?'

'The name rings a bell. I can't remember where I've heard it before,' I lie.

'There was a meeting in Johnny's diary to meet this Dean fella last Friday.'

My breath catches in my throat. 'What time?' I try my best to sound nonplussed. But that's hard to do when your pulse is racing as if you've taken some kind of illegal drug.

'Three o'clock. I don't know if they did meet, but Angela asked me to follow up on all Johnny's appointments from last week and rearrange any for this week and next. Did Johnny ever mention a Dean to you? I can't find any details for him. No number. No company. I thought it might be something personal.'

Johnny couldn't have met this Dean at three o'clock because he was stuck in that traffic jam. Perhaps he rearranged to meet him later but never rescheduled the meeting in his calendar. 'No, sorry. I don't.' I hope she can't detect the panic in my voice. 'If you find out a company name, let me know. It might trigger a thought.'

'I'll leave it until Johnny comes back.' She continues talking about the diet she's currently following. Something about fasting until midday.

I take my cup of tea back to my desk. The adrenaline racing through me makes me feel sick. It's got to be the biggest coincidence if this guy wasn't *the* Dean Ferguson, my ex's brother, who Johnny arranged to meet last Friday.

THIRTY-FIVE

I'm scared. Really scared that after dropping Lucas off with his parents on Friday, Johnny met Dean. And hell only knows what Dean said to him. And that's why Johnny has run off to Wales.

I sit at my desk, question after question flying through my mind.

Tom appears and asks me a question about a client. I find him the information he needs. 'Have you got a minute?' I say.

'Sure.'

'What time did Johnny come back here on Friday?'

He shrugs. 'I can't remember exactly.'

'Apparently, there was a meeting in his diary with a Dean Ferguson. Do you know if Johnny met him?'

He frowns. 'Who's he?'

'So Johnny never mentioned the meeting?'

He shakes his head. 'Sorry.' He walks off.

I have to trace Johnny's steps after he picked up Lucas from me on Friday evening.

I turn to the window. Carrie waves at me from the entrance to the marquee, beckoning me to join her.

Reluctantly, I slip into my coat and head outside. One set of workmen have finished laying the floor. The furniture suppliers are arranging the tables and chairs. Carrie is ordering the guy with the cigarette hanging out of his mouth to move one of the tables to the left a bit.

She's always been a perfectionist. When we were kids, she was the one who tore up pieces of school work because they hadn't gone exactly to plan. And she drove me and India crazy when playing with our Lego by her obsession of organising the bricks by size and colour before we were allowed to start building anything.

She makes a beeline for me. She's on the brink of tears. 'Tom and I've had a big argument about Johnny.'

'Why?'

'Don't say anything, will you? But I don't want him to be the best man anymore.'

'Oh.'

'Part of Tom agrees with me. Johnny is unreliable. Who knows if he'll even make it back from Wales. But Tom thinks it'll cause a family rift that we don't need before the wedding if he chooses someone else. What do you think?'

'I haven't thought about it.' I mull over the word she used. Unreliable. Before the weekend, unreliable wasn't an adjective I'd have used to describe Johnny. Womaniser. Unreliable. Have I just had my head in the clouds this past year?

'Well, think now!' My sister can be so demanding at times. Whereas India is laid back like Tom, Carrie's a stress bomb constantly on the brink of explosion.

'It's up to Tom, I guess.'

'I knew you'd take his side.' She's getting worked up. She wants this wedding to be perfect. 'You always do.'

'I'm not taking sides. You asked me what I thought, and I told you what came to mind. Johnny's his brother. I guess it's like Tom saying he no longer wants me to be your bridesmaid, because it might upset his brother. How would that make you feel?'

Her face reddens. She taps the tips of fingers together. 'I was thinking of you.'

'Where do you want this one, Miss?' the guy with the cigarette bobbing out of the corner of his mouth asks, straining under the weight of the table he and a colleague are holding.

'Over there.' Carrie points to the right of the marquee. She lowers her voice. 'Honestly, these guys are useless. How difficult is it to follow a table plan?'

Tom walks into the marquee. Carrie has her back to the entrance so she doesn't see him.

'Wouldn't you prefer it if Johnny wasn't best man anymore?' she says.

'Carrie!' Tom joins us. 'That was a conversation between us.' They start arguing.

I hold up my hands. 'Chill, you two. It's your wedding. Do what you want. I'm fine either way.'

The marquee walls are closing in on me. The roof and ground too, as if all four sides are seeking to crush me to a pulp. It was the same feeling I had in Charlie's house on the night he died.

And just like then, I need to get away from here.

THIRTY-SIX

On the way into town, I stop at the gym on the outskirts. It's a small outfit, a private business run by two ex-military personnel, Peter and Paul, who ended up marrying each other when they left the forces. Johnny invited them over to dinner in the summer.

I switch off the engine. Something's not adding up. I know Johnny went to the hotel before dropping Lucas off at Angela and Alan's house on Friday. Then he was meant to meet the lads at the pub for a drink, but he told Tom he'd changed his mind. He wanted a quiet one and was going to stop at the gym on his way home. I want to know if he did actually come here.

I hold the door open for a group of rosy-faced people with damp hair exiting the building. People who have either worked out in the gym or completed Peter's Monday lunchtime Body Blast Circuits Class that Johnny and Tom sometimes attend.

The building is warm compared to the outside. A musty, sweat-fuelled smell catches in my throat, making me cough. Peter, fit and muscular, stands by the reception desk wearing Lycra shorts and a singlet. He waves, surprised to see me. 'Hello, Hannah. I, erm—' He pauses, awkward.

I need to get used to this – seeing people for the first time since the wedding that never happened.

He tries to continue. 'I'm sorry to hear—'

I save his embarrassment. 'It's OK.' I find the fake smile I need to get used to wearing. 'But I need to ask you a question.'

His eyes dart from me to his fitness watch. 'Sure, but I have another class starting in a few minutes.'

'I'll be quick. Did Johnny come here on Friday evening?'

He shrugs. 'I don't know. I wasn't here. I was on a training day.'

I point to the computer behind the desk. 'Can you check?'

I can tell what's coming – some spiel about client confidentiality.

His voice is soft, a contrast to his usual loud, lively tone. 'Why do you want to know?' He feels sorry for me. It's degrading.

'I don't want your pity, Peter. I'll be honest with you.' I know I can trust him. He's that sort of person. I need to be careful. I thought Johnny was *that* sort of person. 'I can't get hold of Johnny. Between you and me, I'm concerned something might have happened to him. And I'm trying to find out what. Apparently, he planned to come here on Friday evening. I want to know if he did.'

Peter draws a deep breath and heads around to the other side of the desk. The chair squeaks as he sits down. 'You know I'm not really allowed to give out that information.'

'I know. But in the circumstances... please, Peter. Please!'

He holds my gaze for a second before tapping the keyboard. It seems to take ages before he says, 'I can't tell you.'

'Why?' I sidestep along the matted floor to try and get a glimpse of what he's looking at.

His finger jabs the screen. 'The system seems to be down. It's not showing any data since Thursday evening.'

I grunt in frustration.

'Paul might know. I'll ask him when I see him later.'

The door opens. A group of women dressed ready to put their bodies through torture enter.

'I need to get to my class now,' he says.

'I'll leave you my number.' I snatch a pen from the desk, looking for something to write on.

He hands me a leaflet advertising some type of body-building formula. 'Again, I'm sorry, Hannah. I understand what you're going through. Something similar happened to me before I met Paul. Not quite as bad, but the guy I was planning to marry jumped ship two weeks before the wedding.' He squeezes my shoulder. 'It hurt like hell. I feel for you. I never thought I'd love again.'

My bottom lip quivers.

'These things happen for a reason. I ended up meeting Paul, and I'm far far happier than I was with Jason. My advice would be to move on.' He taps his watch. 'Must dash. Speak later.'

Move on!

How can I?

I thought I could trust Peter, but he's keeping something from me. I'm sure of it. Or perhaps it's my paranoia that has multiplied tenfold since Alan announced those humiliating, devastating words, 'Johnny's not coming.'

Johnny often said I could be paranoid. I overreacted to situations. Overthought conversations.

'Stop worrying,' he'd say. 'You need to chill more, darling. What're you worried about anyway? You can always talk to me.'

But if I'd revealed the reason why I was so guarded, he would never have proposed to me.

THIRTY-SEVEN

I head into town and park at the supermarket. I thought it would be empty, but the weather seems to have brought people out in force as if they feel the need to stock their cupboards for the severe weather warning ahead.

When I leave the car park, I glance around. I could swear someone called my name. But no one's around.

The constant anxiety is playing games with my mind.

The supermarket is packed. I grit my teeth and fill a basket for the empty days ahead. As I trudge the aisles, everything reminds me of Johnny. The packet of bacon I pick up; the special block of butter I drop in my basket that he insists on buying because it's made from grass-fed cows and free from artificial additives; the sushi bar where he often buys a platter for the weekend.

As I turn the corner into the bakery aisle, my stomach somersaults. A man is studying the bread on offer. He's wearing the same coat as Johnny's. Without thinking, I march over to him. But, of course, it isn't Johnny. He's two hundred miles away in Wales. And the guy looks nothing like him. Taken aback, I drop my head and grab a shelf until the shudders of disappointment and nausea subside.

After the supermarket, I head to the games shop at the end of the shopping arcade. Halfway there, I look around with an odd sensation that someone is following me. This is exactly what happened after Charlie died. For months and months, I thought I saw him everywhere, often turning to him calling my name as if his spirit had returned to haunt me. But there was never anyone there. It was merely the demon of guilt messing with my head. I press my palms into my eyes. I've got to hold myself together.

I've been to this shop a few times when Johnny took Lucas to buy a new game.

Johnny. Johnny. Johnny.

I head to the PlayStation section and scan row upon row searching for the *Astro Bot* game Lucas wants. I've been given strict instructions. 'Don't get it wrong, Mum. It's got a blue cover.'

I head to the shop assistant at the till, a tall, lanky guy dressed in black with shoulder-length dark hair and several ear piercings. 'I'm looking for a game called *Astro Bot*.'

'Sorry! We've sold out.'

The last thing I want to do is upset Lucas any more. 'When's your next order due in?'

The guy unloads a stack of games from a large box. 'Try again on Friday.'

The thought of Lucas's disappointed face if I go home empty-handed is too much. I never spoil him. Johnny does. But not me. But there are times when kids deserve to have what they want. And this is one of those times. 'Which game can I take home for my six-year-old son that will make him as happy as *Astro Bot*?'

'Has he got *Spyro*?'

I stare at him blankly. 'I haven't got a clue.' I've never taken an interest in the games Johnny and Lucas play.

I grab the counter. Used to play, I should now say.

'Kids love it.' He leaves the till and returns holding a game with a purple-faced dragon on the front. He hands it to me. 'Keep the receipt. If he's already got it, just bring it back, and I'll give you a refund.'

After paying, I stop outside the store and pull up the Amazon app on my phone to order a copy of the highly sought-after game. I shiver. It's cold. I zip my coat up to my neck, groaning to learn Amazon doesn't have any in stock either. I select the alert box for them to email me when the item is back in stock.

My phone buzzes. No Caller ID flashes across the screen. I answer it.

It's Peter from the gym. 'Hi, Hannah. I just wanted to let you know. Johnny didn't come here on Friday night.'

THIRTY-EIGHT

I stare blankly at my computer screen. I'm raw, inside and out. The job I usually adore has turned into the biggest chore. While the time usually passes in a flash, it has dragged since I returned yesterday. A minute feels like an hour. An hour feels like a day. I'm constantly on edge.

Having endured another sleepless night waiting for Dean to knock on the door again isn't helping. Neither is the marquee for Carrie and Tom's wedding staring me in the face every time I look out of the window. I can't stop thinking back to Friday night, wondering why Johnny lied to Tom about going to the gym, when he clearly didn't go. But I can't think of a reason. Unless he met Dean, and then his mind was made up. Not only was he not going to the gym. He wasn't going to the church, either.

Mid-afternoon, Tom approaches me. 'Are you ready, Han?'

'Sorry?'

'We've got a meeting to discuss this new client. I put it in your diary yesterday.'

Did he? When a meeting is added to my calendar, I usually

receive an email. I don't recall seeing one. 'Sure. Give me a minute, and I'll join you.'

'I'll get the coffees.'

As he walks away, I view my calendar. The meeting is there. I check my emails. The message is there too. I'm too distracted.

I leave my desk to join him upstairs in the large meeting room with luxurious décor. I take the chair beside him. 'Before we start, I wanted to let you know' – Tom jabs his pen on a brown file – 'I've decided to ask Roddy to be my best man.'

Roddy is one of his best friends from school. I met him briefly at a party Johnny took me to, but I can't remember much about him other than his beautiful dark skin and the mass of dreadlocks that reached his waist.

'I hope that's not because of me,' I say.

'Partly. Carrie's getting stressed out about it. It'll make things too awkward with you as chief bridesmaid and Johnny as best man.'

He doesn't say it, but I know what Carrie has probably said. She doesn't want the day to turn into 'Hannah and Johnny's drama'. Understandably.

'Have you told Johnny yet?' I ask.

'No. He's not returning my calls. Have you heard from him?'

I shake my head. 'Nothing since the text he sent me on Saturday night.'

'I'm sorry, Han. This must be hell for you.'

'Why, Tom? I can't understand it. Everything was fine between us when he picked up Lucas on Friday.' My voice breaks. 'He told Lucas he couldn't wait to be his dad.'

'He's a dick. You know, Mum would understand if you wanted to take time off. We all would.'

I tap my forefinger on the brown file. 'Let's just get on with it.'

But I'm not fine. Being here is proving harder than I thought it would be.

* * *

After the meeting, I return to my desk to see Jenna has sent an email, titled *Dean Ferguson*. My stomach flips. *I asked around yesterday, but you weren't all here,* she wrote, *but if anyone knows if Johnny was in contact with someone called Dean Ferguson, please let me know. I'm trying to tie up any loose ends Johnny left before he went on holiday.*

Went on holiday! How tactful.

The noise of the office grates on me. People chatting to clients, phones ringing, chairs scraping all morph into a grating hum. I look out of the window and clench my jaw. I can't get Johnny, or the fact he most likely met with Dean, out of my mind.

Resolute, I push back my chair, stand and march to Angela's office. 'Can I have a quick word?' I say.

She straightens her back. 'Of course.'

'I know it's short notice, but I need to take a day's leave tomorrow.'

She remains silent and tight-lipped.

'Something personal has come up that I need to deal with.'

She continues staring at me as if she's wondering if I'm still cut out for this job. 'Fine. Is everything OK, Hannah?'

'Never been better,' I say mockingly. 'I'll make up the hours over the next few evenings.'

She nods.

'Thanks for your understanding. I'll see you on Thursday.'

I have to know what Dean is playing at – what he's doing with my sister, and what he said to Johnny about me when they met on Friday.

I know where he lives.

I'm going to pay him a visit.

Because now the fear of never knowing what he had to tell me is way stronger than the fear of facing him.

THIRTY-NINE

'Can we go to Johnny's place, Mum?' Lucas looks up at me, his brown eyes full of hope. 'I want to play *Astro Bot*.'

'No, darling.' I wince as I pick up the piece of dinosaur truck I've just trodden on.

'Why not?' Lucas asks.

I'm unusually irritated with him, which adds another layer to my anxiety. He is the sweetest of kids. None of this is his fault. But I'm exhausted from a lack of sleep and the apprehension of facing Dean today. 'We've discussed this, darling. Johnny and I are no longer together.'

His bottom lip quivers.

'I told you, as soon as *Astro Bot* comes back in stock, I'll get it for you. I promise.'

'What if you forget?'

'I've set up an alert on my phone. Now go and get your shoes on. You'll be late for school.' I clap my hands. 'Come on. Let's go.'

'Are we still going to see Santa tonight?' he asks.

'Santa? What do you mean?'

'At Angela and Alan's house.'

Damn. I inwardly groan. I forgot about the small gathering this evening that Johnny and I were meant to be joining. Carrie initially arranged the pre-wedding get-together for the ushers and her bridesmaids at a local wine bar, but Angela suggested holding it at the house to include her sister, Diane, and her American family, the Taylors, who flew in from New York last night.

'I really want to go, Mum.'

'Let's see how we feel tonight, darling. I'm very tired.'

He's trying his best not to cry. 'OK, Mum. I love you.'

My poor sweet boy. My heart goes out to him. I hug him. 'I love you more.'

'I'm having second thoughts about this,' India says when I collect her from the station.

'I'm not exactly happy about it myself. But we need to find what he's playing at and what his intentions are.'

'It's not that he appeared dangerous or anything. In fact, I'd say he was the exact opposite. He was more of a gentle giant.' India reaches into her bag and pulls out her iPad. 'It's just...' She twists her lips to the side. 'I'm not sure I want to see him again knowing what I know.'

I glare at my sister, incredulous. It's like we know two different people. 'That's not how I'd describe him. A giant, yes. But certainly not gentle.'

'Maybe he's changed.'

I scoff.

'People do change, you know, Han.'

'Do they?'

'Yes!'

I think back to when I was with Charlie, and she's right. I'm not the same person I was when I was with him. He changed me. And so did Dean. Between them, they stole my innocence and threw it to the wind.

The tail of rush-hour traffic is making slow progress. Even in the outside lane, I can't get above sixty miles per hour. It's frustrating and only prolonging the agony.

'So how do you think is the best way to play this?' India says. 'Do we start with you or me?'

'I've been thinking the same.' I breathe deeply. 'I don't think we say anything. We let him start the conversation, but whatever happens, I'm not walking away from this without an explanation of what he said to Johnny that made him have such a drastic change of heart.'

'What if he denies meeting him? What if it's a pure coincidence, and he genuinely didn't know you and I were connected?'

I scoff. 'Come on, India!'

The ringtone of my phone reverberates around the car. We're that far on edge, we both flinch. 'It's Carrie.'

'Answer it,' India says.

'I can't. I'll only end up lying about what we're up to.' I send the call to voicemail. 'I'll call her later.'

'What does she think you're doing today?'

'I said I need to sort out the house and paperwork.' I hate lying to my sisters, but I can't tell Carrie where we're really going. I don't want to burst her wedding bubble. 'I can't tell you how glad I am that you're here.'

She drops her head to the side. 'I'll cancel some of my plans and spend more time with you.' She opens her iPad. 'I need to send a quick email. The wi-fi was dreadful on the train.'

'I thought you were on holiday.'

'I am, but I still need to answer emails and keep on top of my blog and social media.'

'What a story you have for this one! *My Sister was Dumped*

at the Altar, I bet that'll get you a few clicks.' Sarcasm drips from my voice like blood – thick and heavy.

The traffic slows to a standstill, elongating the dread swirling around my stomach. In less than an hour, I could be facing the man who, I believe, scared my fiancé off marrying me.

And who accused me of murdering his brother.

And I hope to discover what he plans next for me.

Because until I find out, I'm never going to sleep again at night.

This man has the ability to tear my life apart.

Further than it already has been.

FORTY

'Why do you think Dean didn't stay to face me at the wedding?' I say. 'I just can't understand why he went to all that trouble to hunt me down by fostering a relationship with you but didn't stay around to confront me, or at least jeer at me? Can you imagine if Johnny had turned up and the wedding had gone ahead? What then? What had he planned to do? Taunt me on my big day?'

Or worse still. Expose what he believed to be the truth behind his brother's death to the whole congregation.

India glances up from her iPad. 'Unless he knew Johnny wasn't going to turn up.'

'That's what I've been thinking. It's why I must speak to him.' The muscles in my neck tighten. 'And what's with him turning up at mine only to disappear?'

'It makes no sense. How could I've got him so wrong?'

'I'm sorry, sis, but he's played you. I've seen firsthand the venom that can come from the guy.' The unimaginable thought of him confronting Johnny consumes me.

'He ghosted me. But he told me he loved me.'

I shake my head, incredulous.

'I'm ashamed I let him get to me. I really liked him, Han. He seemed a decent guy. Don't tell Carrie I told you that. I feel she judges me a lot of the time.'

I turn into the long, unkept lane leading to the house. Brambles line each side, encroaching the route. I slow the car to a crawl. The engine ticks over, a mere murmur that barely disrupts the surroundings. I don't want to draw attention to ourselves.

I check the rearview mirror. 'Oh, no.' I speed up, turning a bend. 'I think someone's behind us.'

India twists around, staring out the back windscreen. 'Is it Dean?'

I panic and slam on the brakes.

India jolts forwards. 'Good grief, Han! Careful.'

I turn around and wait, but the car doesn't appear. 'Where've they gone?'

India frowns at me. 'Are you sure you didn't imagine it?'

I blink several times. My nerves are getting the better of me. 'Perhaps it was the swaying branches.'

An icky sensation burns in my throat. I take a deep breath, summoning all my inner resolve to tackle this brute of a man, but I can't deny part of me wants to turn around and go back home. But I refuse to leave here without knowing what he has done to ruin my one chance at happiness. And what his plans are for me going forward.

I take the familiar blind bend where the tree branches hang low. A few scrape the windscreen. It's like only yesterday I was driving here, to the place I called home. I shudder at the thought.

Charlie's old house comes into view, and I stop. My stomach turns full circle, and the perspiration on my palms turns the steering wheel slippery.

Pulling up outside Charlie's old house is like taking a trip down memory lane. A very bleak, dark memory lane. The feelings of persecution, the mind games, the outright physical abuse come flooding back.

Apart from the laurel trees surrounding the house that have grown out of control at varying heights, and the chipping paintwork on the windows, little has changed. Charlie planted those trees during the short time I lived here. They were only knee height at the time, but they now shadow the house like a thunder cloud, making it even more secluded. I always thought this was a bleak place. A miserable existence. And little has changed.

'That's his car.' India points to the black, older-style Porsche parked at the side of the property. I can just make it out from the covering of snow.

'Good. So he's here then,' I say, trying to convey confidence and assertiveness. Who am I kidding? I'm as scared as the day I saw Dean here when I came to collect my stuff after Charlie died.

She recoils in the seat. 'This is freaking me out.'

'Me too. But there's no going back. Come on, let's get this over and done with.' I switch off the engine.

An eerie silence hangs in the air. The heating fades. The coldness bites, even though a faint beam of sun now filters through the windscreen. I reach into my bag and dig out my beanie and gloves.

India grabs my arm. 'This morning, I was all up for facing him. I wanted answers. But now we're here, I don't think I can do this.'

'If we wait, he might appear.' I accidently beep the horn. The noise makes us both jump.

'Good grief, Han!'

I wait, fully expecting Dean to fling open the front door and his large frame to come marching towards us.

But nothing.

After a few anxious minutes, I give up. 'You stay here.' I

pull on my beanie and slip my hands into my gloves. 'I'll go on my own.'

I open the car door. A stillness hangs in the air that's incredibly unsettling.

India opens her door. 'Don't be silly. I'm coming with you.'

A sinister silence greets us as we leave the car. I glance around the desolate surroundings. Our feet crunch along the snow-covered path to the front door.

'My heart is thumping.' Her voice is a whisper lost in the freezing breeze.

We stand before the ugly front door with a cat flap carved into the bottom. It's the same door as when I lived here with Charlie. He was about to replace it before he died.

I take a deep breath and peer behind us again before knocking on the door. I promptly step back. My hand trembles. We glance at each other and wait. Nothing – no movement outside and no movement from within, only an eerie air of emptiness.

Resisting the urge to turn and get the hell away, I knock again, louder this time. It sounds like a gun going off against the silent surroundings.

India bounces from one foot to another. 'He's not in.'

'His car is here. He has to be in. Unless he's playing games with us. He could've seen us and is ignoring us.' I knock again. 'He might still be in bed.'

She twists her lips to the side. 'I guess so.'

We wait for what seems like an age, knocking intermittently. I keep peering around the grounds with an uneasy feeling that Dean could be hiding in one of the bushes spying on us, waiting to jump out.

'How about I leave him a note to call me?' India says uneasily.

I shrug off her suggestion. 'No. We're here now. We're speaking to him.'

I step backwards and glance at the upper floor. Then I make my way slowly, deliberately, to the side of the property, where the snow is thicker. India follows me. I peer into the oh so familiar kitchen window. The sink is full of dirty dishes. An overflowing ashtray on the worktop makes me long for a cigarette. I'm surprised my sister got together with someone who smokes. Ever since Dad died, she's advocated anti-smoking. I turn to her standing shivering beside me.

'Does he smoke?' I ask.

She nods. 'Not much. Not when he was with me, anyway.' She must have really liked this guy.

I return my gaze to the kitchen, beyond the mess in the forefront of my vision. As my eyes adjust to the darkness, I gasp and blink, trying to process what they are telling me, but what my brain demands can't be possible.

My eyes must be deceiving me.

I blink again. 'Oh, no!' My stomach recoils. 'No, no.'

As the full horror comes into focus, I can't stop the bloodcurdling, throaty rasp that escapes me.

I turn away and bend over double.

FORTY-ONE

I retch. My eyes water from the gag reflex and the terrorising sight I've just witnessed.

I instinctively throw my arm out as India approaches the window. 'No. No. Don't look.'

But I'm too late.

She glimpses inside and turns to me. Panic flares in her eyes. Her hands shoot to her mouth. She steps backwards and slides down on her haunches, glaring at me and shaking her head in disbelief.

I stand upright and return to the window. It's morbid, but I take another look as if I need to make sure.

India appears beside me, mirroring my actions.

'Don't touch anything,' I say urgently. The sharpness of my voice slices through the stillness of the air like the blade of a knife. 'You haven't got gloves on.'

She glares at me, her eyes wide.

'Let's not look anymore.' I drop my hands and try to guide her away.

She shakes me away and peers through the glass. 'My God!' She steps backwards again. 'Is he dead?'

I can't help but take another look. 'I can't believe you've just asked me that.'

The sight is sickening. Dean's head lies on the kitchen table, a dead weight that has succumbed to gravity. What looks like dried blood covers his face and has pooled around the kitchen table. His eyes stare ahead, boring into me as if they are searching for my soul.

Redness splatters the kitchen units, and blood on the floor surrounds the dead figure. He must've taken several blows to the head with a devasting force. 'Without a doubt he's dead,' I whisper.

Time stands still. Memories, graphic and unrelenting, from the night I found Charlie's body on the patio return to haunt me like a nefarious ghost from the past. Two brothers who have met untimely and tragic ends. I lift my hand to my face, shading my eyes from the sun to gain a better view. His vision appears fixated on me. I shiver. It's like one of those works of art in a museum where the artist has cleverly painted their subject so that their gaze follows you from whatever aspect you look at them.

I point downwards. 'Look at that!'

India's face touches mine as we stare into the room. 'What?'

'Can you see that club hammer on the floor? It looks as if someone has smashed it over his head. It's covered in blood.'

'What do we do?' Her voice is drenched in panic.

I steal myself from the scene. 'We get the hell out of here.'

'We can't just leave him,' she cries.

'We have to.' I tug the sleeve of her coat. 'Let's go.'

It starts to snow. Flakes flutter in the air. I drag a speechless India back to the car. Her eyes are full of questions. When we get into the car, she says, 'Don't you think we should at least call the police?'

I start the engine but turn it off. My mind is in pieces. My hands clench the steering wheel as I consider our options. I don't know what to do for the best. I'm shaking more than when I learnt Johnny wasn't coming to the church.

'Stay here.' Climbing out of the car, I cling to the door and glance around the property and the surrounding area.

India leans over the driver's seat. 'What are you doing?'

'I want to make sure there're no security cameras fitted anywhere.' When I lived here with Charlie, he was too tight to install any form of security. He said no one was interested in a rundown, desolate house. But Dean could've since he moved in.

'I never thought of that.' India gets out of the car and joins me. 'We must call the police, Han.'

'We can't,' I repeat. 'I can't be associated with this man. He was trouble.'

It's time to tell her the truth.

'What about footprints?' she asks. 'When the body is found, won't the police be able to tell someone has been here?'

She'll understand.

I kick the concrete driveway. 'I doubt it. The ground is rock hard. And it's started to snow, which is a godsend. If it comes to it, we say we came here to speak to him. We don't have to say we found him.'

She'll support me.

'Han, that's dreadful.'

'I'm more worried that he has a video doorbell.'

She frowns. 'What's that?'

'You've been away far too long. They're a camera fitted in the doorbell that records who's at your door.'

'I've never heard of them.'

'Johnny was going to get one for our new house.'

'You knocked on the door, though.'

I vigorously rub my forehead. Nausea overcomes me. I feel sick to my toes. 'Yes. Yes, I did.' I lace my hands over my head and study the front door, wondering if I missed any type of camera when we arrived. 'I doubt Dean's the type to have one.

But, then again, given he works away, he could've had one installed.'

'Don't you think whoever did this to him would've removed it if he did have one?'

'It's not that easy. They're linked to your phone, where you can view footage, so you can't just remove the physical device. Get in the car. I'll be back in a second.'

I run to the front door. My legs are so weak, they can barely carry my weight. Every noise is so loud in the quietness. But there's no sign of any doorbell. I walk the length of the house. There are no security cameras either. Not that I can see. I run back to the car and start the engine, breathless. 'Let's get out of here.'

She grabs my arm with the hand of reason. 'It doesn't feel right to just leave him.'

I ignore her and reverse out of the driveway, my stomach in my throat. 'I don't want to be dragged into his drama, India.'

'But the guy's dead, Han.'

'I don't care. We're not going to the police.'

I can't. If the police link me to this death, they'll revisit Charlie's case. And then I could lose everything.

Everything.

I won't do that to my boy. I won't.

It's time to tell her the truth about the night Charlie died.

The version I shared with Carrie, not the police.

FORTY-TWO
SEVEN YEARS AGO

I peered over the edge of the makeshift balcony. Bile shot up into my throat. I closed my eyes as I drew away, heaving.

I must've been dreaming.

But I knew I wasn't.

I opened my eyes, catching sight of the plastic table smudged with scatterings of white powder. On top was a half-smoked joint balancing on the edge of an old chipped bowl he used as an ashtray. Two crumpled cans of lager lay beside a half-empty pint glass, a lighter and a packet of cigarettes.

Slowly, I edged forward, leaning over the metal railing to see Charlie, the man I'd loved with a passion when I first met him, lying face down, crumpled on the concrete patio below. His arms and legs were splayed at all angles, and a pool of darkness spread beneath him like an expanding puddle of muddy water. I glanced around, my breathing laboured. But I could see very little beyond the garden. Not that there was much to see other than fields.

I tried to scream. Nothing came out of my mouth. My voice was trapped in the cage of my troubled thoughts. The police. I needed to call the police. But the streak of raw panic shuddering through me told me not to.

A weird peacefulness washed over me – like the calm before a beastly storm. But I could ride any storm now.

I was free.

I clutched my belly. It was my chance.

But first I had to get away from here.

I scrambled to find my keys in my handbag which was as cluttered as my life, and raced to my car as fast as I could. Light rain teased the windscreen, followed by harder heavy droplets that pounded the roof as I sped away along the country lanes. A car flashed me as I nearly clipped it on a bend, startling me. I carried on regardless.

When I approached the road to the restaurant on the edge of town, where I was meeting Carrie and a group of her friends for a birthday celebration, I slowed down. But only because of the warning signs of the cameras ahead. Getting caught speeding was a no-go.

I found a parking space, but I couldn't get out of the car. My body was shaking too much. I needed to calm down. I was going to lose my baby at this rate. That couldn't happen. No way. Switching off the engine, I closed my eyes to steady my nerves. As I opened them, a flash of light bolted in my vision. Nausea gripped my stomach. I groaned. One of the incapacitating migraines that had marred my life so much since moving in with Charlie was the last thing I needed. The ones that tormented me as much as he did and forced me to bed for hours at a time.

I touched my scalp. It was tender. Not a good sign. I reached into my bag and rummaged around for the packet of ibuprofen I kept stocked for those occasions. Popping two from the silver foil, I went to take them but stopped. I held my belly. I was on new territory and didn't even know if it was safe to take them. There was so much for me to learn. I checked the packet, reading the small print. No. I would have to suffer.

A car pulled up beside me. I rubbed the steamed-up window, relieved to see Carrie's car. She got out and opened her umbrella, sheltering her body as she hurried to me. She knocked on the window hard. I wound it down. She bent over until her head was level with mine, wafting her cloying perfume into the car. 'You didn't need to wait for me. You—'

I cut her short. 'Something terrible has happened.'

'What?'

'Get in.' I raised the window before she could ask again and unlocked the passenger door. I picked up our friend's birthday cake from the passenger seat and placed it on her lap when she climbed in.

She turned on the light and squinted at me. 'You look like you've seen a ghost.'

Oh, the irony of her words!

I thumped my head. 'Charlie's dead.'

'Did you kill him?' She giggled. 'About time too.'

I slapped her shoulder. 'I'm serious, Carrie. He's dead.'

Her jaw dropped. The smile left her pretty face. 'You *are* serious, aren't you.' Her big blue eyes, heavily made up for the evening ahead, widened. 'Whatever has happened?'

'I got home and didn't expect him to be there, but when I went to the bedroom, the door to the balcony was open.' My voice was a whisper as I relived the evening. 'I went to shut it but noticed he'd left some stuff on the table. Something... I can't put my finger on it... but something didn't feel right. It was spitting with rain, so I went to get the stuff in. I don't know what made me look over the bal... balcony.' I panted, my breathing ragged. 'But he was there, splattered on the ground. He was a mess. He must've fallen off. He'd been smoking weed. There was a half-smoked joint on the table. And some coke.'

'Hell, Han. What did you do?'

'I panicked. And... and... I came straight here.'

'You left him.' Her face screwed up into a ball of incredulity. 'Why?'

Panic grew in my voice. 'I was scared.'

'Of what?'

'That I was going to pass out. The blood, Carrie. There was so much blood.'

The way she stared at me was disconcerting. 'Was he dead at that point?'

I nodded my head vigorously. 'His limbs were all mangled,' I said in a pathetic wail. I clutched my head. 'I feel sick to the core. I think I've got one of my migraines coming on.'

'Take some tablets.'

'I can't. I've only got ibuprofen.'

'Why can't you take them?'

I hesitated before saying, 'I'm pregnant.'

'Blimmin' hell, Han. You're full of surprises tonight.'

'That's why I couldn't stay. I'd have passed out. Who would've found us? I would've lost the baby.'

'This isn't good. None of it. Oh, hell, Han. What have you got yourself messed up in!'

'I'm done for.'

'I've got some paracetamol. You can take them, can't you?' She fished in her bag, withdrew a packet of tablets and scanned the instructions. 'These are safe to take during pregnancy.' She popped two white pills out of the silver foil and handed them to me with a bottle of water. 'Here you go.'

I swallowed them with a gulp of water.

'We can discuss this more later, but for now, you need to go back there,' she said. 'Straight away.'

'I can't.'

'You've got no choice. Go back and act as if you've just found him. Call the police. Don't admit you left him for dead. God, Han. As much as I hate that bastard, he could still be alive.'

'I'll end up in prison for leaving him.'

'You won't. No one will ever know.'

'*You* do.'

'But I'm your sister, Han. I'm not going to say anything to anyone. It'll be our secret. Deep breaths. You need to control your emotions.'

'But what are you going to say to the girls? They will ask where I am.'

'Forget about them. You need to cover your tracks.' Carrie paused. The air in the car stank of deceit. 'I'll say you had one of your migraines coming on, so you came to drop off the cake and decided to go home.' She took a deep breath. 'You need to think this through.' She took another deep breath and glanced at my jeans. 'You need to get changed. What were you going to wear tonight?'

'My black skirt and boots.'

'Go home and put them on. And some make-up. As you would've if this never happened and you were coming out with us all. Then call the police.'

FORTY-THREE

All the way home, I kept to the speed limit along the country lanes, voicing my plan for when I got home, and what I'd say when the police turned up. The rain had morphed to light snow, and the roads proved slippery around the bends.

As soon as I arrived back, I followed Carrie's instructions. My legs were weak as I ran upstairs to the bedroom and pulled the curtains to the balcony. Otherwise, the police were going to ask why I didn't look outside. I needed to be careful. There was so much to think about.

In a hurry, I changed, carefully following the order in which I would normally act and throwing my clothes in the laundry basket. I selected a Taylor Swift song from my iTunes, cranked up the volume and croakily sang along as I applied my make-up. After three attempts with the eyeliner, I gave up. My hands were shaking too much to perfect a straight line. So I went with a pasting of gold shadow and plenty of rouge to disguise the ghostliness of my cheeks, finishing with a dab of gloss on my lips.

Downstairs, I turned on the patio lights and screamed. I

didn't even need to pretend. Now all I needed to do was act as I would've if I'd just found him. I screamed again, louder. Not that anyone would've heard. The remote rundown cottage that Charlie was in the process of renovating seemed like the dream place to live when he first took me back there. It was perfect. He was perfect... until he moved me in.

I opened the patio doors and ran outside into the snow. *Don't look at the blood*, I kept telling myself. But it was impossible. Kneeling beside my boyfriend's dead body, I grabbed his limp wrist to feel for a pulse, confident I wouldn't find one. I was right. He was gone. The side of his face exposed to the elements was deathly pale, as white as the falling snow. His mouth was open as if he was about to speak. It was gruesome. I gently laid down his wrist and rested back on my haunches, my hands covered with blood. My head spun. I closed my eyes, willing myself not to faint. I had to get through this.

Flakes of snowdrops hit my face and dissolved. I slowly stood, my legs an ungainly wobble as I hurried inside.

This was a nightmare.

And it had only just begun.

Grabbing my phone from my bag, I called the police and ran back outside.

'Accident and Emergency, which service do you require?' the calm voice asked.

'Erm... erm. Accident,' I said with my eyes closed.

'Do you mean ambulance?'

'Yes. Yes.'

'Is the patient breathing?'

'No.'

'Do they have a pulse?'

'No.'

'What's happened?'

'I think he's fallen off the balcony. There's blood everywhere. I need help.' The desperation in my voice was real. 'Please send help.'

'Are you with him?'

What a stupid question. Of course I was with him. 'Yes.' There was no denying the panic in my voice. A panic I wasn't faking. It was as real as the dead body at my feet.

'Is the phone you're calling from registered at the same address?'

'Yes.'

The snow intensified, heightening the drama that was playing out around me.

'OK, love. Try to stay as calm as possible. Help is on its way. Don't try to move him. I'll stay on the line until help arrives. Can you tell me your name, please.'

Events unfolded in a blur. I stood frozen to the spot, my eyes closed, until an ambulance arrived with a police car. It took a while given the declining weather conditions. Two paramedics saw to Charlie while two police officers dealt with my lies. I couldn't even remember afterwards if they were male or female.

I was hysterical. One of the officers found me a towel to dry myself, while the other made me a cup of sweet tea and tried to calm me down. They grabbed the blanket that was thrown over the sofa and placed it across my shoulders. 'When you're ready, we need you to go over what happened, please?' they said.

I nodded vigorously.

'You say you arrived home at what time?'

'Around six.' My teeth were chattering. 'I didn't think Charlie was home. I usually get back before him.' I didn't recognise my own voice. It was as if I was listening to someone else relaying my lies to the police. 'I was going to a friend's birthday dinner, so I went upstairs to get changed. I was hurrying because I was already late. I shouldn't have gone. I wasn't feeling great.'

'But you did, why?'

'I had the birthday cake. One of the other girls had ordered it, but the cake shop is near my work, so I picked it up. But when I got there, I knew I couldn't stay as I had the beginning of a migraine. I get them now and again. They knock me for six, so I came home. And that's when...' My teeth were chattering so badly, the police officer could barely make out what I was saying. They kept asking me to repeat myself. 'That's when I found Charlie.'

While relaying my account, I repeatedly glanced outside. In the beam from the light they had set up, I watched the paramedics manoeuvre Charlie's body onto a yellow stretcher.

One of the officers stepped outside while the other made notes and asked me further questions. The officer returned inside. 'He's still alive.'

No way!

He couldn't still be alive. Not in the state I'd found him in.

'But he didn't have a pulse!'

'There was a faint one. It would've been hard to detect. They're taking him to St. Margaret's. ICU is my guess.'

I jumped up and cried, 'Can I go with him?'

'It's going to be busy in the ambulance, my love. We can drive you there.'

'But I want to be with him. Please, he's my fiancé.'

'And your fiancé is in a bad way. I doubt the paramedics will allow it. We'll take you.'

'No, it's OK. I can drive myself.'

'Do you think that's a good idea?'

There was no way I was getting in their car. I didn't want to speak to them any more than I had to. 'I'll go now. I want to be there when he arrives.'

'We'd rather take you, but if that's what you want. I'll need you to come to the station to make a statement at some point, but can I just ask you.' They pointed to my arm. 'What happened to your hand?'

I glanced down at the fresh burn wound. Damn, my hand. I had forgotten about that. 'Oh, that. I did it on the cooker. It was a silly accident. I did it a while back, and it just won't heal.'

The officer held my gaze and frowned. 'Nasty. You should get that seen to.'

FORTY-FOUR
PRESENT DAY

Relaying the evening of Charlie's accident, and the subsequent weeks where I lost myself in guilt and shame while dealing with the morning sickness that hit me like a brick, brings back dark memories as I drive home. The panic, the fear, but also the relief. The relief that he eventually died, and he would never hurt me again.

'So you see why I can't involve the police? I can't have them digging up my past with him.'

'So Dean thought you killed him.'

I nod.

'Why?'

'He never liked me. From the moment I met him. He was jealous of my and Charlie's relationship. Before we met, when Dean came off the oil rig, he used to live with Charlie. Then I came along and Charlie said that arrangement wouldn't work anymore. It pissed Dean off.'

India is pale. Seeing the state of Dean, coupled with my account of what happened to his brother has taken its toll.

'I'm not proud of what I did. You know, leaving him when maybe I could've helped him.'

'But you didn't do anything to Charlie. He did it to himself.' She takes a tissue from her bag and hands it to me. 'You couldn't have done anything.'

'I lied to the police. I should've stayed there and helped him. There was a chance he could've lived. That's what the coroner said.'

I'm panicking, remembering that fateful night and the coroner's report that followed. 'If someone had found him earlier, there was a small possibility he could've survived. Instead, he lived another six days until Dean agreed with the medical team that the kindest thing was to turn off his life support.'

She stares blankly at me.

'Please don't judge me. Charlie treated me like hell. He abused me, physically as well as verbally. I can't even begin to tell you what I went through that night. I panicked. I didn't know what to do.'

'Like you're panicking now.'

'But I paid the price. All these years I've lived with the fear that Dean would come after me.'

'We should just call the police.'

'No!' I scream.

'Calm down, Han. We'll have an accident. You should've told me all of this sooner.'

'I've already said. You were away. What was the point? There was nothing to gain apart from worrying you.'

'Yes, but...'

'No buts. The world is a better place without Charlie Ferguson. Maybe Dean Ferguson, as well.'

'And this is why he stalked me – to get to you.'

I shrug. 'Who knows.'

My hands grip the steering wheel. 'That's why I can't go to the police. I can't be seen to be involved with this guy. It'll drag up the past. Dean made a song and dance about seeing me in my car driving to meet Carrie that night. He claimed I was there when Charlie died. The timings didn't match, he said. He claimed I murdered him.'

I suppress a shiver. How I hate that word. Murder. It sounds so brutal. So final. 'Of course, when the police investigated his allegations, they couldn't find any evidence. But when they find Dean's body, they'll investigate it all again. I can't cope with going through all that again. I need to think things through. I could lose Lucas. I'm not going there.'

'Good God, Han. You should've told me all this.'

'I'm sorry.'

India opens the window. 'He stalked me to get to you. I'm sure of it. And now Dean's dead. Not just dead. He's been brutally murdered. Won't the police check CCTV of the surrounding area when they find the body?' she asks.

'It could be days, weeks before he's found.'

'That's awful, Han.' She smacks her hand on the dashboard. 'Stop!' she shouts. 'Stop the car.'

'Why?'

'We can't just leave him. Go back.'

'That can't happen. Just chill out.'

I turn on the radio and raise the volume high.

India turns it down. 'I'm creeped out that I slept with a guy who'd been stalking me to get to you. And your husband-to-be may have met him. And now he's dead. It can't be a coincidence.' She runs her hand through her hair. 'This is a frickin' nightmare.'

'Perhaps he stalked you to get to me but ended up falling in love with you.'

'He must've royally pissed someone off to end up like that.' The panic in her voice intensifies. 'What do you think he did?'

We hypothesise – drugs, jealous husband, money. A few minutes of silence ensue, both of us deep in shock. I think about Lucas. And Johnny, wondering if he's involved, but for the life of me, I can't think how.

'He didn't seem the type of guy to be mixed up in that kind of trouble. Do you think it's got something to do with Johnny?'

I glance at her. 'That's what I've been thinking. But what's the connection? I can't get my head around it. Since seeing Dean with you at the church, I've wondered if he was somehow connected to Johnny disappearing. But I just can't work out how.' A sea of red lights swims before my eyes. I hit the brakes and slam my hand on the steering wheel. 'Hell! Look at this.'

'Good grief. There must've been an accident.'

'That's all we need.'

She taps the screen of the sat nav. 'Yep. You're best getting off at the next junction. It's three miles away.'

We crawl along the road at a snail's pace, discussing theories about Dean's demise. 'I need to get back in time to pick Lucas up at three fifteen,' I say.

'Isn't he in afterschool club today?'

'Not on Wednesdays.' My fingers vigorously tap the steering wheel.

'Sat nav says we should be OK,' she says. 'When the body is eventually found, won't they trace his movements? Won't the police find out he spent the night with me?'

'Yes. But you have nothing to hide. You just tell them you came here to see him, but there was no answer.'

'Hell! I hate lying.' She sighs heavily.

I look at my baby sister and shudder. She doesn't deserve to have been dragged into all of this.

'When do you think the body will be found?'

I shrug. 'As far as I'm aware, Charlie didn't have any other family besides an aunt in Canada.'

'Dean told me the same.'

'You know, I've been hoping the potential Dean and Johnny connection would lead me to the man who unceremoniously dumped me at the altar. Now, more than anything, I hope the two never laid eyes on each other.'

'Now I think about it, throughout our weeks of communication, Dean struck me as a bit of a loner.'

'Didn't that ring alarm bells?'

'Not really. I felt a bit sorry for him, actually. His social media interaction was kinda... lame. You know, like he was a bit of an underdog. He talked about his brother a lot.' She shudders. 'He was so nice to me, Han.'

'Perhaps he genuinely liked you.'

'He used me.'

Eventually, the traffic starts moving at a decent pace. Snow falls as we join the country road home. A salt truck is preparing the roads for the forecasted snow in the coming days. 'I'm going to stop at Johnny's apartment and pick up that PlayStation game Lucas wants. It'll keep him entertained for a while. I need time to think. What else did Dean say about Charlie?' I ask.

'Just how much he loved him and missed him. And what I told you before – that he believed he'd been murdered.'

'That's ludicrous.' I sigh deeply. 'This is torture. I need to know if Johnny met him.'

'You don't think Johnny did this, do you?'

I look at her in horror. 'India! Whatever Johnny did to me, he's not a murderer.'

'But I thought Dean was the sweetest man, Han. I'd never have believed he would've got close to me to get to you. I just thought he was a shy, lonely guy. It just goes to show. You never know anyone, not really. Not truly.'

'No. Johnny wouldn't have anything to do with this.'

But the words leave my mouth peppered with a sliver of doubt. I battle a rising panic. Did Johnny somehow get messed up with Dean and this is the result?

This could be all my fault.

FORTY-FIVE

'If he was that much of a loner, he might not be found until he doesn't turn up for work.' My throat is dry with fear. 'When did you say he was due back on the oil rig?'

Her voice still shakes, each word a wobble of terror. 'The twentieth of December. Won't the body decompose in that time?' She recoils in the chair. 'It'll be covered in all those horrible flies.'

'The twentieth of December. That's over two weeks away,' I say. 'And all the while, there's a murderer out there.'

'And the police need to know about them.'

'No!' I lower my voice. 'Not from us.'

More snow falls as I approach the road to Johnny's apartment. A light coating covers the streets. I park up and turn to India. A look passes between us. A look that, without either of us uttering a word, says: can you believe what's happened?

'I won't be long,' I say.

'I still think we should call the police.'

During the drive, I've wondered the same. I've now got the added stress of the police discovering we were at the property. But as quickly as the thought entered my mind, I banished it.

No good can come from becoming embroiled in Dean Ferguson's demise.

'Do you want me to come with you?' she asks.

'No. I'll just pick up the game and be right back.'

I get out of the car. The snow deadens the town's usual sounds, dulling the bang of the closing door. I find the key to Johnny's apartment and pause. Perhaps I should just leave it now. But I promised Lucas I'd get that game. And I need something to entertain him for the rest of the afternoon, while I work out what to do for the best with the fresh barrel of trauma the day has thrown my way.

I enter Johnny's apartment and hurry along the hallway, past the shoe rack neatly stacked with his shoes, trainers and boots. That's odd. He loves those tan boots. He wears them all the time. It's strange that he hasn't taken them to Wales with him.

A ripple of sadness trickles through me. It usually smells so good in here. The welcoming, earthy smell of Johnny. Now, a dampness hangs in the air. It's a distinct lack of freshness from the apartment having been uninhabited with the heating off in the depths of winter.

I head to the bedroom Johnny uses as a study, stopping suddenly in the doorway and drawing a sharp breath. The air is musty, confirming what I thought when I was last here. Johnny hasn't been back.

But I'm wrong.

He has.

Or someone has.

The room is a mess, at least by Johnny's standards. The top drawer of the desk is open slightly, and the paperwork in the faux leather filing tray is crooked. I scan the room. Items are out of place on the bookcase. Again, only someone who knows Johnny well would understand this is not his usual level of tidiness. My heart pounds in my chest. It has all the hallmarks of someone looking for something in a hurry.

Or perhaps my thoughts are a gear too high in overdrive. Maybe Johnny's been back here to collect some of his belongings and left in a mad rush, not caring about tidiness in the circumstances. It would make sense if he left in a hurry for Wales.

I creep along the hallway to the living room, where the same musty smell lingers, but everything appears the same as it did when I came here on Sunday. An inner sense draws me to the staircase to Johnny's bedroom, but I stop at the bottom, clinging to the handrail. A noise from the street startles me, reminding me I shouldn't be here. It's not my place anymore.

I should get out of here. I return to the study and head straight to the bookcase. On the bottom shelf sits the pile of PlayStation games where Lucas told me I'd find the *Astro Bot* one he desperately wants. All the boxes are neatly stacked, except the end three, which have fallen over. I crouch down and search among them, finding the *Astro Bot* one in the middle. I pull out the box. A banging sound echoes through the apartment. Every unexpected noise rings with danger. Dean's mangled face enters my thoughts, merging with the fate his brother met seven years ago. And I was the person to find them both.

I jump up and dash to the window. That's odd. It's open. I shut it the other day when I came here. Perhaps I'm mistaken. I think back. I'm sure I did. I can't remember. I'm losing my mind. I dip the slats of the Venetian blind and peer out of the window. I'm confident the noise came from outside, but I can't see much in the fading light. Johnny's car is still parked there. It's odd that he didn't take it to Wales.

I open the box, checking it contains the correct game. The last thing I need is to go home with the wrong one or an empty box. Another bang sounds from outside. I peer out the window again. Betsy from the downstairs apartment is emptying rubbish bags into one of the wheely bins. She lets the lid drop with another crash. I consider knocking at her door on my way out to ask if she has seen Johnny. But I can't stomach someone else asking how I'm coping.

The box is empty. Damn! I turn to the door, suddenly feeling vulnerable that someone could come in and find me here. I'm being irrational. Alan is the only other person I know of who has a key, and I shouldn't be scared of seeing him. I could easily explain my rationale for being here.

Kneeling on the floor, I search through the dozen or so boxes, discarding each one that doesn't contain the disc I'm looking for. I have to leave here with the right one. When I reach the last box, I swear out loud. With a deep sense of unease, I recheck each box, but none contain the *Astro Bot* disc I'm looking for.

My phone rings, scaring the hell out of me. It's Carrie. I let it ring out, cringing with every buzz that grates on my nerves that are now shot to pieces.

I search the shelves above, tapping along the pile of books. Perhaps Lucas discarded it after he changed games rather than putting it back in its box. But it isn't there, either. I hunt around, reaching my hand underneath the bottom shelf. Patting the carpet, my hand touches a disc. I pull it out, dragging a newspaper with it. The disc is the size and colour I'm expecting. I read the inscription, sighing with relief that it's the *Astro Bot* game Lucas wants.

After securing it back in the correct box and placing it in my bag, I pick up the newspaper. Pink highlighter pen circles an article on the front page. I take a cursory look, when a knock at the door disturbs me. I aimlessly stuff the paper in my bag and step into the hallway.

I falter, wondering if I should answer the door. I shouldn't be here. A fleeting thought passes through my mind: it's Johnny, and he's lost his keys. It's as if I can't allow myself to lose hope that he'll return, and we'll somehow manage to navigate some kind of route back to normal.

I creep to the door and pause.

My heart beats in my ears. What if someone followed us here from Dean's place? Or perhaps someone was waiting for me to return here.

I dither. I don't know what to do.

All I know is, there's a fear inside that I've never felt before.

FORTY-SIX

I bend down and pick up a small piece of mud from the doormat that would be invisible unless you were looking for it. The tension in my chest tightens. I pick up another one. These clumps of mud weren't here when I came on Sunday. Johnny was a stickler for keeping the place clean and tidy. He would've noticed the mess and cleaned it up. But perhaps he was so keen to get away that he just left it.

Or maybe Alan has been here. I could ask him. But I'd be too embarrassed to admit I let myself in. Given Johnny has made it clear that I'm no longer a feature in his life, it's wrong. And I'll only come across as desperate.

Another knock startles me.

With trembling hands, I slide the end of the chain into the latch and push the door until it opens slightly.

'Hannah, dear, is that you?'

I sigh with relief and disengage the chain.

Betsy from the ground-floor apartment stands on the doormat, her silvery white hair shimmering in the hallway light. She's holding a plant pot with a green bow wrapped around the rim. A small envelope is tucked inside the foliage. 'I didn't mean to frighten you, but I saw movement through the window when I was putting out the bins and thought it was Johnny.'

'He's in Wales.' I cling to the door, anxious to get away. 'I just dropped by to pick up my stuff.'

'How are things?' She delivers the same straight-smile, boundless look of pity that I've detected on everyone I've met since the weekend.

Engaging in a conversation about Johnny is the last thing I need right now. I just want to get out of this apartment. I adopt a brave face. 'I'm OK, thanks, Betsy. I don't want to appear rude, but I need to go. My sister is waiting in the car for me.'

'I took this in.' She passes me the rubber plant. 'It was delivered yesterday. I've watered it, so it should be OK in this weather for a week or so.'

'Thank you. That's very kind of you.' I take the plant, wondering who it's from and what to do with it.

'This one needs plenty of sunlight.' She turns to leave. 'Indirect, though.'

'I'll put it in the kitchen.' I hesitate. 'I guess you haven't seen Johnny since the weekend?'

'No, I can't say I have. I'm sorry.' Her pale blue eyes radiate kindness. 'I'll leave you be. Take care, sweetie. Pop in any time. I'd love to see you and your gorgeous boy.' She turns and heads to the stairs, waving her hand without looking back.

I return to the kitchen and place the plant on the breakfast bar, curious who would send Johnny a plant. Not that it's any of my business. But I can't help sneaking a peep. I pick out the small envelope accompanying the gift. It's not sealed, so I remove the card and read the typed message.

Dear Johnny,

It was so nice to meet you. Thank you for your keen

interest in the foundation. Your generous donation is very much appreciated.
I hope your wedding went well. I look forward to catching up soon. Enjoy the plant.

Best wishes,

Rachel Radcliff

I take my phone out of my pocket and snap a photo before carefully replacing the card, wondering who the hell Rachel Radcliff is. Johnny never mentioned anyone called Rachel before. I'm good with names. I would've remembered if he had.

My head pounds as I walk to the front door, filled with an overwhelming sense of foreboding. The fear inside is growing by the hour. I open the front door and glance behind me. An oppressive pain fills my heart knowing I'll never step inside this place again. It's unbearable.

FORTY-SEVEN

A mother struggles to manoeuvre her buggy out the main door of the apartment block. The wheel has jammed on the metal threshold. Her baby is crying. It's stressing her out. The shrill sound makes me well up. Although it's piercing and grating to her, at least her baby is alive. What I would do to hear my darling Victoria cry now. I think of the moment the nurse handed me my dead baby. The moment Johnny broke down.

I help the mother unjam the wheel. She nods her thanks, mute, as if she's trying to bury her tears in her silence, and walks away. I hug my arms around my body. It's crippling to watch her, knowing I won't be pushing a baby in a pushchair ever again. Not one of my own, anyway. I couldn't risk the potential loss.

I hurry back to my car. I'm breathless when I climb inside. 'Someone's been there. And it wasn't Johnny.'

India looks up from her phone. Her eyes are red. 'What makes you say that?'

'There was mud on the doormat, and someone has been in his study. The bookcase is a mess and the paperwork out of place. He never leaves it like that.'

'I thought he was in Wales.' She frowns. 'Perhaps he came back for some stuff.'

'It wasn't him, I said.' Desperation coats my words. 'You only met Johnny a couple of times, but you must understand, he's a very tidy person.' If I had to say anything negative about Johnny, it would be this: his tidiness is sometimes over the top. Although he tries to hide it, I annoy him with the way I leave clothes over the chair in my bedroom or the breakfast dishes in the sink to deal with when I get home from work. 'He'd never leave it like that.'

'How does he cope with Lucas being there?'

I remember when Lucas first stayed at the apartment. Although he tried to hide it, Johnny was a little on edge about the trail of destruction Lucas left in his wake. He admitted that it was difficult for him. I understood. It can't be easy if you're not used to having a child around. 'He got used to it. He always had a big tidy-up when we left.'

'If it wasn't him, then who was it?'

I fasten my seatbelt. 'I haven't a clue. And also, his car is still there. He must've caught a train to Wales. But that doesn't sound like Johnny. He rarely takes the train anywhere. Unless... unless he went with someone else.'

'Come on. I know what you're thinking. Don't jump to those kinds of conclusions. It's not good for your mental health.'

'Too late. My mental health is shot to pieces.'

'He must've got a cab to the station and then caught the train. What took you so long in there? I thought you were just nipping in there to pick up a game.'

'It took me ages to find it.' I delve into my bag, dig out the newspaper and hand it to her. 'I eventually found the game underneath the bookshelf, along with this. It looks like Johnny's highlighted the article on the front page.'

'It's a local paper from Peterborough,' India says. 'That's a little weird. That's not far from where we've just come from. I mean, from Fletton, where Dean lives. Peterborough is the local city. Is that a coincidence?'

I look at her, perplexed.

I jab my finger on the front page. 'Read that article. Tell me what it says.' I start the engine and pull into the road, staring at Johnny's apartment block as we pass. 'Thinking about it, I've never seen Johnny read a newspaper. He hates reading the news. He says it's depressing. What does it say?'

'It's about a lorry driver charged for dangerous driving. Vince Pooley. You heard that name before?'

'Not off the top of my head.' I pull over to the side of the road and stop the car. 'Let me look.' I scan the article, but there's nothing to suggest why Johnny would've drawn attention to it. I slip my phone out of my pocket. 'Before I left, the lady from the ground-floor apartment knocked on the door with a plant that was delivered for Johnny yesterday.' I show her the photo of the card.

'Who's Rachel Radcliff?' she asks.

I shrug. 'I've never heard of her, either. Johnny's never mentioned a Rachel.'

I reach into the glove compartment and search for the packet of paracetamol I keep in there. My head is pounding. I pop a couple of tablets into my mouth and swallow them dry.

She holds out a hand. 'Look, I can't stop shaking.'

'Me neither.' I glance at the clock. 'I need to pick up Lucas in half an hour, and I'll have to stop at the shops, otherwise there'll be nothing for dinner.'

'There'll be food at the party tonight,' she says flatly.

I slam my hand against my forehead. 'Hell. I forgot about that.'

'Carrie called when you were in Johnny's place to remind us.'

'She tried to call me too. Can't we feign food poisoning or something?'

'We can't let her down,' she says. 'Well, I can't. You've got an excuse.'

'It's fine. I'll brave it. Lucas won't forgive me if I don't take him. Alan's dressing up as Santa if the kids are good.' I roll my eyes. 'Lucas has been going on about it.'

'I could take him,' she suggests.

'Thanks, but I'll have to face them all on family occasions in the future. Our sister is marrying my ex's brother. You couldn't make it up, could you? What happens when they have kids? I don't want Lucas to miss out on his cousins. Because he sure isn't going to have a brother or sister.' I sigh heavily. 'I just can't get the image of Dean's caved-in head lying on that kitchen table out of my head.'

'Me neither.'

I read the message on the card again but it doesn't make things any clearer.

All I know is, Dean is dead and Johnny has mysteriously disappeared. And I need to work out if and how these two events are connected before whoever is behind them comes for me, or my boy.

FORTY-EIGHT

I stand in the shadows alone, waiting for Lucas to come out of school. Facing other parents remains a no-go.

My boy stands on tiptoes, searching above the other children buzzing around the playground. He spots me and his face lights up. My heart contracts. He waves. How I adore that boy. I'm so lucky to have him in my life. The sides of his coat flap and his blond curls bounce as he weaves at speed through the other children waiting for their parents. 'Did you get it, Mum?' He launches himself at me like a rocket. 'Did you?'

'I did.'

'Where is it?'

'In the car.'

He grabs my hand. 'You're the best, Mum.'

My efforts pay off. He runs straight to the lounge when we arrive home and has the disc in the console before he has even taken his coat off.

India follows me into the kitchen. She drops her bag on the floor, slumps in a chair at the table and drops her head in her hands. 'This is a nightmare. I can't stop thinking about him. All that blood.' She shudders. 'I can't believe it. Less than a week ago, I slept with a man who's now dead.' She hugs her arms around her body. 'And not just dead, but brutally murdered. I still think we should go to the police.'

'Just calm down. It's too late now.'

'When his body is found, do you think it'll make the national news?' she asks.

'I don't know. You said he was a loner.' We're whispering as if Lucas can hear us. 'His body might not be found until he doesn't turn up for work.'

'But don't you think he would've made arrangements to see someone while he's back?'

I shrug. 'I need a drink.' I go to fill the kettle but stop. Someone is banging on the front door. 'Who the hell is that?'

We glance questioningly at each other. I discard the kettle and step into the hallway.

I hear Carrie's voice before I even get to the door. She bangs again. 'Han, open up.'

I unbolt the door. 'What the hell? You scared the life out of me.'

She barges past me and spins around. 'What are you playing at?'

I close the door and bolt it. 'What do you mean?'

India stands at the top of the hallway. 'Carrie!'

'What's going on?' I ask, confused at my sisters' exchange.

Carrie turns to me when we get to the kitchen. 'Why did you go and see Dean?'

I glance at India.

'I'm sorry,' India says. 'I told her when you were in Johnny's apartment.'

Carrie prods my shoulder. 'You go and see a man who threatened to murder you right before my wedding. Why would you do that?'

'He threatened to murder you?' India says, glaring at me. 'When? You never told me that.'

I roll my eyes and puff out a large breath. 'When he accused me of being involved in Charlie's death. It was a bluff. My solicitor had words with his solicitor.'

The stress of the past five days takes its toll. Tensions are sky high, floating on clouds of uncertainty, albeit for different reasons. An argument erupts. It's unlike the three of us to argue. We've always had a close and loving relationship. 'You've always said he was dangerous. I can't understand why you'd go and see him.' Carrie is shaking. 'I'm getting married in three days. You could ruin everything.'

'I had to go and see him,' I cry.

'Let's all calm down,' India says.

Lucas silences us. 'Mum, can you come and sit with me?' He clutches the game console in his tiny hands at the kitchen door. 'I don't want to be on my own.' He's picked up on all the stress.

India jumps at the opportunity to get away. 'I'd love to come and sit with you. How about we play a game together?' They disappear out of the room. That's India all over. She'll always try to duck out of a confrontation.

'I can't believe you told her the truth about Charlie. It was our secret, Han,' Carrie cries. 'We agreed. We never tell anyone. You tell one person, and they tell someone else, and it spirals. Before you know it, you'll be in deep trouble. And so will I. Lying to the police carries a prison sentence.'

As if I need reminding.

'You know I never wanted anyone to know about the part I played in what happened that night,' she says.

'You didn't do anything.'

'Technically, I should've gone to the police as soon as you told me what had happened.'

'Sisters don't turn each other in, Carrie. Anyway, I had to tell India.' I momentarily close my eyes and squint. My head is throbbing again. I lean against the side of the sink.

'Why? Why did you have to tell her?'

'She was insisting that we go to the police when we found Dean's body.' I lace my fingers and place them on my head. 'I can't be linked to another man's demise. Especially not the brother of the first man I was linked to. The police will question me again. I can't afford for that to happen. I mean, it doesn't look good, does it? I could lose Lucas. I won't let that happen.'

She gets more and more worked up. 'You spilt our secret, Han.'

'I'm sorry,' I shout. 'But there's more for me to worry about than that now!'

She glares at me.

'It's all very strange, though. Don't you think? Johnny met with Dean last Friday. Johnny ghosts me, and now Dean is dead. I'm scared.'

'Of what?'

My bottom lip quivers. 'Scared that Johnny isn't actually in Wales.'

'Where do you think he is, then?'

'I have no idea.' I stifle tears. 'This is karma, isn't it?'

'What do you mean?'

I lower my voice as if the walls are taking in my secrets and are going to relay them to the world. 'Payback. Payback for what I did to Charlie.' My throat tightens. 'I left him for dead, when I could've saved him.'

'One moment of madness from our youth, and this is where we are.' Carrie's voice softens. She asks more questions about our visit to Dean's house. 'He must've been involved with some bad people to end up like that,' she says. 'You need to be careful, Han. What if someone saw you there today? Whoever did this to him could come after you.'

'I don't want to talk about it anymore.' I clutch my forehead. 'My head is killing me.'

'Promise me something.' She places her hands on her hips.

'Can we at least get my wedding over with before you do anything stupid again.'

'I'm sorry, OK. But you know India would never say anything to anyone.'

'I need to go. Are you coming tonight?'

I nod. 'I'm not in the mood, but Lucas wants to go.'

'The American family have arrived.'

I groan. Angela's sister, her husband and their son, his wife and three sons, arrived from New York last night. They were going to come to my and Johnny's wedding but had to cancel last minute because a vomiting virus had swept through the family.

'The triplets are pretty manic.'

'We'll be there.'

When she leaves I go upstairs to shower. The day has left me feeling dirty.

But however hard I scrub I can't wash away the fear that's riding through me.

The fear that Johnny has met with the same fate as Dean.

FORTY-NINE

'Are you OK?' India whispers as I drive to Angela and Alan's house, checking my rear view for the fifth time.

'Never been better.'

'No need for the sarcasm.'

'Sorry.' I drum my fingers on the steering wheel, not wanting to explain... either my imagination is playing games with me, or someone is following us.

'Are we there yet, Mum?' Lucas pipes up from the back.

'Almost, darling.'

I can't determine the make of the car, but it's still behind us.

'How long?' Lucas asks.

'Not long,' India says. 'Let's play I Spy.'

'Na! You're all right.' He absently kicks the back of my seat.

I'm sweating, despite the coldness circling the car. 'Don't kick, darling.' I turn on the stereo. 'Give him my phone,' I instruct my sister. I look in the mirror. The car is still there. 'Choose some music, Lucas. Make it something jolly.'

'Can't I just play a game?' Lucas asks.

'You've had enough screen time for today. Put some music on.'

He chooses a George Ezra tune and sings along.

I glance in the mirror. If I'm not mistaken, the car behind us is a Mercedes. The same car Johnny drives. I gasp.

'What?' India asks.

'Look at the car behind us,' I whisper. 'It's been following us since we pulled out of my road.'

She grabs the back of my seat and swings her body around. 'What car?'

I look in the mirror again. But all I can see is blackness. I turn my head, searching through the back windscreen. The car skids.

'Han, what're you playing at?' India grabs the dashboard. 'We don't need any more drama today.'

I swallow the ball of unease that is scratching my throat. 'I could've sworn... never mind. It's nothing.'

For months after Charlie's death, caught in a vicious cycle of guilt and relief, I often thought Dean was following me. Even though I knew it wasn't possible because he'd returned to the oil rig. The same anxiety is tormenting me again. It's crippling. I clutch my head. I can't seem to work out what is real or not since Saturday.

'Are you sure you're OK to drive?' India says. 'We could always get a cab back. Then you could have a drink. We both need it.'

I shake off her suggestion. Alcohol is the last thing I need in my fragile state.

When I pull into the driveway of Highland Hall, the marquee is lit up like Winter Wonderland. India takes Lucas in the house, while I sit for a moment, taking deep breaths. The journey here has added to the deepening sense of dread swirling within me. I could've sworn someone was following us. And I could swear it was Johnny.

* * *

I turn out of the drive and race across town to Johnny's apartment. It was him. I know it was. My pulse is racing as I drive straight to the car park. It's full. I get out of the car, leaving the engine running, and search for his car. It's there, in his allocated parking space. A layer of snow covers the roof. That car has been nowhere since I moved it the other day.

My heart sinks. This is all sending me crazy. I return to my car, disappointed, and drive back to Angela and Alan's house.

* * *

The rhythmic sound of jazz music filters into the hallway when I go inside. Alan must've put that on. He's an avid fan and often attends jazz evenings held at the local theatre.

The triplets are chasing Tom down the stairs, squealing like mice. Tom grabs Lucas and gathers the triplets. He introduces them to us. 'They've been as manic as this since they got back from the park at four o'clock.'

They aren't identical, but it's hard to tell the triplets apart. It's like three of the same kid running around. Lucas is unusually shy, but Tom encourages him along to the snug, a room that used to be the playroom when he and Johnny were kids, but is now a chill-out room for watching TV.

Carrie and India appear as I'm taking off my coat. Carrie's face is flushed. 'Where the hell have you been?'

'Sorry, I had to go back to get some tablets. I've got a headache.'

She eyes me curiously. 'There's some here you could've had.'

I brush off her suggestion with a shrug.

'I need to tell you something.'

My stomach turns another three-sixty. I don't like the troubled tone in her voice. 'What's happened?'

'We've heard from Johnny.'

The hairs on my arm rise.

Carrie squeezes my shoulder. 'He's not coming to the wedding.'

'Oh!' is all I can say. He told them but not me.

'He thinks it's for the best.'

'I guess it is.'

'The coward could've told her himself,' India says.

'I'm quite pleased, to be honest,' Carrie says. 'It would've been awkward.'

My eyes swell with tears. 'OK.' My voice cracks. 'You're probably right. Who spoke to him?'

'Alan.'

I run my hands through my hair. I don't think this day could get any worse.

She tugs at my arm. 'Come and meet Angela's sister and her husband, Bert. It'll take your mind off things. Their son and his wife have gone to London to see a show and left the triplets to run riot here.' She links one arm through mine and the other through India's and takes us to the kitchen. 'Angela and her sister, Diane, couldn't be more alike.'

I take a deep breath and walk into the large, warm kitchen where Angela and Diane are drinking wine at the breakfast bar. Bert, a broad guy with a round belly and a hearty laugh, is talking to Alan, drinking a bottle of Bud.

Carrie was right. Angela and her sister Diane look so much alike, they could be twins. They are even dressed similar in smart trousers and cashmere jumpers. Angela strokes Ruby's red, silky fur. 'Yes! You are a beauty, aren't you, darling?' Angela coos, smoothing the dog's ears. Ruby wags her tail, revelling in the attention.

Diane toys with a strand of pearls resting on her ample bosoms. She tells me how sorry she is about the unfortunate circumstances. 'I'm glad you came this evening. It's nice to meet some people before Carrie and Tom's big day.'

'As I told Angela,' I say, 'Tom will become my brother-in-law on Saturday. I'll be forever connected to this family, so Johnny and I will find a way to work through this.'

'You're a better person than I am, my dear,' she says. 'I don't think I could be so calm about the situation.'

She hasn't got a clue.

I try my best to stay engaged as the small gathering gets going. Angela has put on a generous spread of food, and Alan circles with champagne, filling glasses. When he goes to the fridge to get another bottle, I approach him.

'How did Johnny seem?' I ask.

He squints. 'Sorry?'

'When he spoke to you and told you he's not coming to the wedding. How did he seem?'

'I didn't speak to him. Tom did.'

'Oh. Sorry, I thought it was you. I must've misheard Carrie.'

'You need to get into your Santa costume now, Alan,' Angela calls out. 'I'll get the pizzas ready for afterwards.'

He salutes to his wife and leaves the room.

The conversation grows louder as my head pounds for escape. I'm relieved India is here. She steals the attention, telling Diane about her travels, allowing me to fade into the background.

'I had no idea how boisterous these boys would be without their mum and dad to keep them in order,' Angela whispers in my ear. 'Thank you for coming tonight, Hannah,' she continues. 'I didn't realise you were such a tough cookie.'

She doesn't realise how tough.

I stare around the large room with exposed wooden beams and copper pots hanging from a rack on the Aga. I've loved this room ever since Johnny first brought me in here. I swallow hard at the memory. It was the first time I came into the house. Angela and Alan were away on holiday, and Johnny invited me in after work one evening and gave me a guided tour of the vast house before making me a cup of hot chocolate. It was the day after our first date, and I fell in love with how he danced nervously around, meticulously preparing the drink as if he wanted to make everything perfect.

The boys' excitement revs up a gear, cheers exploding into euphoria.

'I guess the gift-giving fella has arrived,' Bert says, with an avid laugh.

We file out of the room to join the festivity in the snug. The boys are racing around as if they've eaten a family bag of Skittles each. It's chaos, but Alan, dressed convincingly for the part and adopting a compelling voice, produces a sack of presents and tells them to behave. Otherwise, he won't be back on Christmas Eve.

Lucas is beside himself with excitement. I genuinely smile for the first time today. It often amazes me how someone who was conceived in such an abusive relationship can bring so much joy. 'Look, Mum,' he shouts above the mayhem. He waves a book at me. 'I've got a new planets book.'

'We can read that when we get home,' I say.

'Now you boys need to come and have some pizza,' Angela says when Santa leaves, promising to return if the boys all behave themselves. They scuttle off, leaving me with Carrie and Tom tidying up.

'Why did you say Alan spoke to Johnny?' I ask Carrie.

'What?' she says.

'You told me Johnny called Alan to say he wouldn't be at the wedding.' I stare at Tom. 'But Alan said you spoke to him.'

'I did,' Tom says.

'You told me it was Alan,' Carrie says.

'No, I never.' They start arguing.

'You weren't listening properly,' Tom says.

'So what did Johnny say to you?' I ask Tom.

'He feels bad,' Tom replies. 'But he said he'll see you next week when the wedding is over and everything has calmed down.'

'You told me that he said that to Alan,' Carrie says.

'You're wrong.'

Carrie erupts as if she's having some kind of a breakdown. I've never experienced her go at Tom like this. She tears him to shreds. Her reaction stuns me. The wedding nerves have taken a firm hold. Unless there's something more that she's not telling me.

Tom raises his voice. It's awkward.

'I'll leave you to it,' I say, backing out of the room.

FIFTY

Morbid thoughts race through my head after learning that Johnny isn't coming to Tom and Carrie's wedding.

And they all lead me to the same conclusion.

Johnny isn't in Wales.

I'm now convinced something terrible has happened to him, or he's got himself involved in something he shouldn't have. Perhaps Tom knows more than he's letting on and is protecting him in some way.

After I've settled Lucas and read him a couple of chapters from his new planets book, I frantically scan the newspaper I found in Johnny's apartment. I've been wanting to do it since we arrived back with it earlier but didn't get a proper chance. Maybe it's nothing. But after rereading the article highlighted on the front page, I'm compelled to look through the rest of the paper.

I should have listened to my gut when he didn't show up at the church on Saturday. I turn another page. There must be a reason why he had a copy of this hidden under his bookshelf. Before I know it, I'm lost in stories of a dementia resource centre, dogs that have been seized as the police tackle hare coursing and a local restaurant that's up for an award.

But it's an article about a local woman who was left paralysed after an accident that piques my interest. It's the woman who sent Johnny the plant.

Rachel Radcliff once enjoyed life as a physical education teacher at Mountview secondary school. She was busy planning her upcoming marriage to her childhood sweetheart, Luke Radcliff, when they attended the wedding of Rachel's university roommate and the horrific accident took place, breaking Rachel's back and injuring her spinal cord.

'You never think this is going to happen to you,' Rachel said, when I interviewed her at her adapted home north of Peterborough. 'I lost everything in that accident.'

She remembers the moment the consultant told her that she'd never walk again. She was in denial at first. 'Oh, yes, I will,' she told him, because, she said, that's the kind of person she is. 'I'm a true believer in mind over matter.'

But as the weeks turned to months, Rachel had to face the reality. 'My destiny was to spend my life in a wheelchair. I was angry, which led to depression. I was a nightmare to be around. I even hated being with me, so I broke off my engagement and didn't speak to anyone apart from my parents for almost two months.'

It was only when her mum candidly told her, 'At least you're alive, Rachel,' that Rachel started to claim back her life. She reunited with her fiancé, got married, and set up The Sinclair Foundation, which helps people recovering from spinal cord injuries.

Another wedding guest, a childhood friend of the groom, later died from his injuries sustained during the accident, when the marquee came crashing down, trapping him under a table. Other guests at the wedding suffered numerous minor injuries, ranging from broken bones to cuts and bruises and multiple fractures. One guest was left blind in one eye.

'I still have nightmares about that day,' Rachel said. 'The franticness of it all. The loud crash. The screaming. The sheer panic as everyone tried to get out of the wreckage.'

Questions were raised about whether the marquee was properly staked and secure. The company that constructed the marquee, Mortimer Events Ltd, was investigated, but was found to have an impeccable safety record and had followed all manufacture specifications during the construction process. Their staff carried out a health and safety inspection after assembling the marquee, and left adequate instructions and evacuation plans were given to the wedding planner. High winds on the day, which reached twenty-four miles per hour, were blamed for the tragedy which left three children without a father, a man blind, and a woman seriously disabled.

Mortimer Events. I've heard that name before, but I can't think in what context. I fire up my laptop. I type *Mortimer Events Ltd* into the search engine. Several articles appear, detailing the wedding and disaster I've just been reading about. I scan the articles.

Then I find it.

The connection I knew I'd discover somewhere.

Mortimer Events Limited is no longer in operation. The owner and director, Angela Caxton, dissolved it shortly after the marquee incident. She replaced it with another company,

High Hall Events Limited. The arm of her business empire responsible for the erection of their marquees.

I type *Sinclair Foundation* into the search bar. Google directs me to a website about spinal cord injuries. A picture of a young woman, Rachel Sinclair, early thirties, with curly blonde hair and a bubbly expression heads the landing page.

I read her journey from PE teacher to the founder of The Sinclair Foundation. So Rachel Radcliff's maiden name was Sinclair.

Rachel Sinclair. Rachel Radcliff. I rack my brain, wondering if I missed Johnny mentioning her name before. Or if any of the Caxton family have.

But I'm certain I've never come across that name before, and I can't work out why Johnny kept his dealings with her a secret from me.

FIFTY-ONE

Full of unease, I try to frame it all in my mind. Angela dissolved a company that played a part in a man's death and left several people seriously injured and some disabled. One of those people, Rachel Radcliff, née Sinclair, set up a foundation that Johnny recently made a very generous donation to.

India appears, her hair wrapped in a towel.

'I've found it,' I say. 'There's an article about the woman who sent the plant to Johnny.'

She sits and shuffles her chair around the side of the table until it's touching mine.

I jab my finger on the newspaper article. 'Take a look at this.'

India studies the article.

My leg jiggles while waiting for her to finish reading.

'Poor woman.' Her lips twist to the side. 'Why do I get the feeling you're going to tell me this Mortimer Events is connected to Caxton Events?'

'Because your gut instinct never fails you.'

'It does,' she scoffs. 'My gut instinct told me Dean Ferguson was a decent guy.'

'Mortimer Events Limited no longer exists. It was owned by Angela and was the company she set up that erects the marquees on behalf of Caxton Events. She replaced it with High Hall Events, presumably because she didn't want the association with the accident. Johnny told me about what happened, but he played it down somewhat. It was a rough time for the company. He was on holiday when it happened, but it still affected him badly.'

'What did he tell you actually happened?' she asks.

'There was a freak storm that caused the marquee to collapse.'

He clammed up when I asked him more about it, and I stopped asking. I for one know how someone feels when a subject is off-limits.

I continue. 'I've heard it mentioned in the office on the odd occasion, but now I think about it, it's always pretty hush-hush.' But I've read all the online articles about it. I pick up the newspaper and wave it at her. 'But I can't work out if that's the reason why Johnny kept this.' I puff out a large breath.

'Good grief, Han. You witnessed a bloke with his head caved in today, and now you've got the bandwidth to look into all this.'

'I just can't help thinking there's a connection. Call it intuition.'

'Connection. How?'

'Johnny going AWOL, and then Dean worming his way into your life. I can't help thinking that was a road map to me. Then this newspaper article. The donation. It's all like pieces from a jigsaw puzzle that don't quite match.'

She rests a hand on mine. 'Perhaps because, Han, they are different puzzles.'

She's wrong. I know she is. 'But what if something has happened to Johnny, and he needs my help?'

I don't know what's worse: the looks of pity people have

been giving me since the weekend, or the one she is giving me now. She thinks I've lost my way.

She points to the newspaper. 'Why is the article on the front page circled?'

'Look carefully.' I point to the front page of the newspaper. 'The whole article isn't circled, only a part of it. I don't know. Perhaps he didn't want to draw attention to what was inside.'

I stare at the floor.

All I've ever wanted is a peaceful life.

But all I seem to do is attract trouble.

But this is all on another level.

Dread gnaws at my insides.

I have to find out what's going on.

India shakes her head. 'So, you think this is in some way connected to Johnny and Dean?'

'I don't know, but it's made me suspicious.' I pause. 'I'm scared.'

'Because of what's happened to Dean?'

I nod. 'And for Johnny.'

And for Lucas.

Because something tells me this is all going to come back to me.

FIFTY-TWO

Every night is the same. I lie awake until the early hours, thinking of Johnny.

I've wanted so badly for Saturday to arrive, so I can see him and talk to him. Now I don't know when I'll see him again.

If I ever will.

I bat the sinister thought away.

My head is fuzzy when I get into work on Thursday morning. Everything is an effort. Raised voices are coming from Angela's office. As I pass, I see Tom standing by her desk. She spots me. They stop talking as if they're discussing me. She calls my name, summoning me into her office.

I step inside. If I'm not mistaken, there's an atmosphere.

'We were just going over the Red Glow Engineering project, as the director called yesterday and is coming in today,' she says. 'I sent them the quote, and they're keen to move forward with their exhibition on the twelfth of January. After being let down by the other company, though, he has several questions and wants reassurances from us. We need you to join us at one thirty, please?'

'No problem.'

'Can we have a quick debrief now?' she says. 'The three of us.'

I slide my bag from my shoulder. 'Sure.'

'I'll get some coffee.' She leaves the room.

I take the chair beside Tom. 'How's Carrie this morning?'

'That was some outburst last night, wasn't it?' He rolls his eyes. 'The stress is getting to her. She'll be fine after the wedding.'

'Can I ask you something?' I say.

He glances up from the file. 'What about?'

'The marquee accident. The one involving Mortimer Events. What happened?'

He raises his eyebrows. 'Wherever did this come from?'

'Johnny never really wanted to discuss it, but I came across this newspaper article about it, and I wondered what happened.'

He repositions himself in his chair and puts his forefinger to his lips. 'Shh. Don't let Mum hear you talk about it. A man died, and some people were left with lifechanging injuries. She gets really upset. She felt she was to blame.'

'Why?' I ask.

'I guess she felt somewhat responsible. She owned the company that supplied the marquee.'

'But I thought a freak weather storm caused the accident.'

'It did.' He nods adamantly. He taps his pen on the desk, faster and faster. 'Mum and Dad just took it really badly. Dad, especially. He had another heart attack over it, for Christ's sake. It was partly why we hired you. To ease the load to help them get back on their feet. Dad wanted to close the whole business down after it happened. Give it all up. It caused a rift between him and Mum. Did Johnny not tell you all of this?'

'No.' I shake my head. 'Not all of it.'

'They decided on a rebrand in the end.' He studies my face. It's uncomfortable. 'What newspaper article?'

'One I found at Johnny's apartment when I was picking up my stuff.' It's a lie, but I don't want to admit I've been there again. 'So that's why Mortimer Events was dissolved?'

'Pardon?'

I spin around.

Angela stands in the doorway holding three cups of coffee. 'What did you just say?'

'It's fine, Mum,' Tom says. 'Leave it.'

'I heard Mortimer Events mentioned.' Angela's face is flushed. I can't tell if it's from the heat in the room, or if it's because of the conversation she has joined. 'Why are you talking about that?'

'I'm sorry,' I say. 'I came across a story about one of the victims and was just curious about what happened.'

'We don't talk about it,' Angela says. 'It was a very dark time for this family. We've put the whole episode behind us.' She holds my eye contact. Her voice is even and controlled. 'I'd rather you didn't discuss it again.'

FIFTY-THREE

Angela is agitated. The mention of Mortimer Events has unnerved her. She plonks the coffee on the desk and promptly begins the meeting.

Tom is miles away, as if he's already on the sunbed in Barbados for his and my sister's honeymoon. For an awkward quarter of an hour Angela harps on about the way she wants to run the lunchtime meeting with the new client.

After the meeting, I try to steel myself to catch up from being away from my desk yesterday. But no matter how hard I try, I can't focus. A jovial atmosphere buzzes across the office, but I can't summon the motivation, or mood, to join in. Everyone has been invited to the wedding, and Angela decided, as a gesture of goodwill, to grant everyone an extra day's annual leave tomorrow. Everyone is revelling in the thrilling anticipation of an upcoming long weekend.

Everyone, except me.

I can't concentrate on anything work-related. I keep googling the local news where Dean lived, fearing that his body has been found, but nothing is reported... so far. I turn to the marquee accident, rereading the articles I found last night.

Every few minutes, I glance around. I'm being ridiculous, but I sense Johnny is watching me. I study his desk with a sense of sorrow. This time last week, he was sitting there.

When Jenna heads up to the kitchen just before noon, I grab my opportunity.

I strike up a conversation, which isn't difficult given how talkative Jenna is. She pats her plus-sized belly, rambling on about the dress she had planned to wear on Saturday that is now a little on the tight side. 'I'm just useless at sticking to diets.' Giggling, she takes a plastic container out of the fridge. She lifts the lid and shows me the contents of a tuna fish salad. 'Is it any wonder I can't stick to them? How unappetising does that look?' She takes a packet of dried soup from her pocket and empties the contents into a cup.

'Can I ask you something, Jenna? I know it's a sensitive subject.'

She looks at me quizzically.

'It's about the marquee accident that happened before I joined the company.'

'Ah, the incident that shall never be mentioned. What do you want to know?'

'I recently came across a newspaper article about it, and I wondered what happened. Why it's so hush-hush.'

She pours boiling water into the cup, stinking the kitchen out with the rich, meaty smell of chicken soup.

'All above my pay grade, I'm afraid. They were dark times. Terrible. Tragic. Johnny was away at the time, but Angela, Alan and Tom all went into overdrive trying to secure the reputation of the business and its future. They were locked away in Angela's office for hours on end. There was fallout. Some of the staff couldn't hack it and left.'

'But the company was cleared of any wrongdoing.'

'Absolutely. Everything was crossed and double dotted. But the damage had been done. They had to close the company and have a whole rebrand, which didn't come cheap, I can tell you. Between you and me.' She taps her finger against her lips. 'Angela nearly had a nervous breakdown over it. Partly because Alan had a heart attack, which she believed was caused by the whole incident. It was his second heart attack, so it really freaked her out.'

We continue chatting, but she reveals nothing more than I already know. If she's telling me the truth, that is. But there's no reason for her to lie.

Leaving Jenna to her Cup-a-Soup, I return downstairs and sit staring at Johnny's desk. I'm missing something here.

He needs my help. But at what cost to me and my darling son?

I call India. She was already up when I left this morning. She had planned a day in London, shopping and lunching with a friend but cancelled, unable to face it after yesterday. As noon approaches, despite having phoned her five times and left messages, she still hasn't called back. It's not like her. I tell myself to stop fretting. I'm like an overprotective mother. She's an adult who can look after herself. Perhaps she decided to go to London after all. I try to call again, but there's no answer.

* * *

I grab my coat and leave the office, racing home as fast as the slush-covered roads allow. As I pull up to the T-junction leading to my house, I notice a Mercedes in my rear-view mirror. The same as the other day.

Johnny! My heart contracts. It's Johnny.

I slam on the brakes. The car behind honks its horn. The loudness makes me squirm. The driver presses his finger to his temple as he passes me. My mind is playing tricks on me. It's not Johnny. The man is at least twice his age. And it's not even a Mercedes.

I find India practising a yoga pose on the living room floor. She appears deep in concentration. I wave frantically. She startles and removes one of the wireless in-ear headphones. 'What the hell, Han? You scared the hell out of me.'

'I need you to come with me.'

She removes the other headphone and untangles herself from the yoga pose into a standing position. 'Where are we going?'

If I answer her, she might not come. 'I'll tell you in the car.'

I ignore the distant, 'For heaven's sake,' following me along the hallway. She calls after me, asking again where we're off to, but I'm already out of the front door.

The passenger door opens. India jumps in. 'Are you going to tell me where we're going?'

'Johnny's apartment. But I want you to come with me. Quickly. I don't have much time.'

'Why?'

'Because I'm too scared to go on my own.'

FIFTY-FOUR

'What's brought this on?' my sister asks.

'Johnny was my soul mate, India.'

An icy shiver runs through me.

When did I start referring to him in the past tense?

'We kept nothing, absolutely nothing, from each other.'

But, of course, this isn't true. I never told him about what happened to Charlie. He thinks Lucas's dad was the result of a relationship that went wrong. When we first met, I was too ashamed to admit to the domestic abuse. And, right or wrong, once I'd told the lie, I felt compelled to carry it on.

'From the minute I saw Dean with you at the church, and Johnny didn't show, I've had a niggling feeling that something terrible has happened to him. Now he's not coming to his brother's wedding. You'd think he'd show for that.'

'Not really. Think about it. It'll be awkward. She'd never admit to it, but I reckon Carrie doesn't want him there. I don't think she wants the drama on her wedding day. I'm not being horrible, but I wouldn't put it past Carrie to have told Tom to get in touch with him and tell him to stay away.'

'I don't buy it. What about the fact that he arranged to meet

Dean the day before we were meant to get married? No. I don't buy that he's in Wales. There are too many unanswered questions, too many coincidences.'

'But he told Tom he was.'

'Perhaps Tom is protecting him. I need to get to the bottom of it all.'

'Oh, Han! I get the feeling you need to leave all this for now. Dean's dead! Is that not enough? Let the dust settle. Get through the wedding. Then perhaps things will become clearer.'

'I can't.'

'You're scaring *me* now.' India bites her lip. 'You don't think Johnny murdered Dean, do you?'

I raise my voice, incredulous. 'Johnny would never have done that.'

'You don't know, Han. We could be playing with fire here and end up getting dreadfully burnt.'

I raise a hand from the steering wheel, shutting her down. 'Then there's all this stuff with Rachel Radcliff – Sinclair – and the marquee.'

'Then we should go to the police.'

'After what we found yesterday? No way. No way.'

She slumps in the seat as if resigning herself that I'm not giving in. 'You've already searched his apartment.'

'I was only looking for the game for Lucas. I came across that newspaper by accident.'

'Why don't you just speak to Carrie? She is our sister, after all. Perhaps she knows more than she's letting on.'

'This wedding means the world to her. I can't be seen to spoil her day. I'd just look like the bitter bride who didn't get her groom. She'll never forgive me.'

'Fairs. Angela, then. Or Alan. You get on well with him. Or what about Tom?'

'If I'm being honest, now I've found out about all this

marquee incident and Rachel Radcliff, I don't know if I trust any of them: Angela, Alan, Tom – the lot of them.'

'What do you mean?'

I shrug. 'I know Tom and Carrie's wedding is the priority now, but they don't seem particularly concerned about Johnny's disappearance.'

'Perhaps they don't like talking about it in front of you?'

I shake my head. 'No, it's more than that. And, it could be me, but when I'm in the office, I feel as if they are talking about me behind my back. I'm starting to think the whole family is a bloody nightmare. I have to ask what Carrie is marrying into. What did *I* almost marry into? And what kind of family are we joining?'

'Good grief, Han. That's quite a statement.'

She's looking at me as if I've gone crazy.

Perhaps I have.

FIFTY-FIVE

I pull up in the road adjacent to Johnny's apartment with a sense of déjà vu. My pulse is racing. I can't believe I'm here again.

We enter the front lobby, hoping Betsy, or any of the other neighbours, won't catch us. I'm not up for another heap of sympathy. We climb the stairs to Johnny's apartment. I ring the bell in the vain hope he'll open the door, but I don't wait for an answer.

India grabs hold of the sleeve of my coat as we enter. 'Wow! This is lush. No wonder he's so particular about it. It's lovely.'

I call out Johnny's name.

We wait. There's no reply.

'Let's start looking.'

India shivers. 'What're you actually looking for, Han?'

'That's the thing. I'm not sure. But if someone was in here poking around then it must've been pretty important. I'm going to start in his office with his paperwork.'

'What do you want me to do?'

'Search around the kitchen and in the living room. It's not that big an area. It shouldn't take long.'

'But I don't know what I'm looking for.'

I shrug. 'Anything that looks suspicious.'

I return to Johnny's study. I can't believe I was here less than twenty-four hours ago. It feels like days. The three rose petals remain by the foot of the desk. I shake my head. It's another reminder of why I'm here. It doesn't make sense.

Sadness consumes me to see the book *A Father's Guide To Loss* I found dog-eared the first time I was here. 'Oh, Johnny,' I whisper.

An odd sensation overcomes me. I'm transported back to the night I lost our baby and he held me in his arms until I eventually stopped crying. It's as if I can still feel him holding me. Rubbing my brow and telling me it would all be OK. We would get through this together. We would have another baby one day. We've been so close during our short time together, I can't imagine life without him now.

I swallow the lump in my throat and hunt methodically through the documents in the filing tray. Details of our house purchase top the pile, with a picture of our dream home in the corner. I stare at it in disbelief. It's as if the devil has put it there to twist the knife of torment lodged in my heart another ninety degrees. I thumb through the next layer of correspondence: a solicitor's letter, bills, a parking ticket. I do a double-take. Johnny never mentioned that. Maybe he never thought to. The remainder of the documents in the pile are run-of-the-mill admin. I comb through the drop files in the bottom drawer of the desk. Nothing. I search the bookcase... again nothing.

India appears at the door. 'I can't see anything of interest.'

'Neither can I.'

'What about his bedroom?' she says.

'That's next.' I nod towards the door.

We leave the study and head up the half-turn staircase. My heart is beating in my ears. A reminder that being here is wrong, but I carry on.

The bedroom still smells of Johnny's eucalyptus shower gel.

'Wow! It's got a roof terrace. It's a proper bachelor pad.' India peers through the doors leading to the outdoor space, while I rummage through Johnny's drawers. Seeing his clothes gets to me, confirming that the anger I've felt towards him has totally morphed into outright fear. I stare at his wedding suit hanging in a bag from the wardrobe door, and his shoes beneath that have now collected a layer of dust.

'Have you checked the back of the wardrobes?' India asks. 'Any false panels?'

'Whatever for?'

'You never know. I met a guy in Bali whose mum worked for MI5. She was a spy but told him and his dad that she worked in an IT role. They only discovered the truth when she was shot in the line of duty.'

'Johnny was hardly a spy, India.' I shake my head. It's not like her to dramatise. 'He had a full-time role with Angela and Alan's company. I think I'd have known if he was working elsewhere.'

She twists her lips to the side. 'Just saying.' She steps into the dressing area, slides open one of the mirrored wardrobe doors and parts Johnny's clothes, feeling the area behind. 'Just checking for any loose panels.'

'For Christ's sake, India.' I walk to the bed, drop to my knees and search beneath. I find a pile of Johnny's car magazines he loves to read. I pull them out.

India interrupts me. 'Good grief, look at this,' she calls.

I turn to her pulling a box out of the wardrobe. She removes a Christmas present, beautifully wrapped in expensive paper and ribbon, and reads the gift tag. '"To my beautiful wife. All my love, Johnny."' She pulls out another one. 'This one has the same message. Looks like you were due to be spoilt this Christmas.'

A sickening thought enters my head. 'If they're meant for me.'

India pulls a face. 'Who else would they be for?'

'What if they're meant for someone else? What if he's got another wife, and that's why he couldn't go through with the wedding?'

It's the first time I've seen India sincerely laugh since last week. 'Oh, come on. Get a grip. That's the most absurd thing I've ever heard. Totally bonkers. He obviously knew he was going to be busy with the wedding and the house move, so he got his Christmas shopping done early.' She pauses. 'You're serious, aren't you?'

I can't speak. My mind is in overdrive. She's right. It's an absurd thought. I'm being overdramatic.

'You're crazy, absolutely bonkers. Here, catch.' She chucks one of the presents at me. I swoop down, managing to catch it by my feet. 'Open it,' she demands.

'I can't. It feels wrong.'

'If you don't, then I will. I'm not going to leave here with you having that insane notion in your head.' She marches to my side and locks the other two presents she's holding between her knees. She grabs the present from me, unloops the ribbon, and tears off the paper. 'See!' She waves a bottle of Chanel N°5 in my face. 'Your favourite perfume.'

She takes the other two presents from between her knees, slots one under her arm and opens the other. It's an Amazon box. She opens it to find a smaller box and then another like a set of Russian dolls. She opens the last box to find another, that looks like a jewellery box. 'Open it.'

Hesitantly, I lift the lid. My heart melts at the sight of a pair of sapphire and diamond earrings that match my engagement ring. My voice wavers. 'I was looking at these in a shop in the Cotswolds when Johnny took me and Lucas for a weekend away in the summer.' I bite my lip. 'He must've bought them for me.'

'And you thought they were for another woman.' She returns to the box and pulls out another three presents. '"To Lucas. Happy Christmas. Love Johnny."' She shakes her head, laughing. 'I think you can wipe the attempted bigamy from your mind.' She returns to me and gathers the presents. 'Guess we'd better rewrap these for when Johnny comes back.'

'I'm scared, India.' I drop down on the edge of the bed. I'm shaking, and the constant nausea has taken a firm hold. 'Really scared he might not come back. That something dreadful has happened to him.'

My sister joins me, perching on the edge of the bed. She ties the ribbon back around the wrapped bottle of perfume. 'Come on, Han. Get a grip. You're letting your imagination run away with you. Let's get going. There's nothing here.'

I shake her arm off me and glance at my watch. 'I'll have been out for more than an hour by the time I get back to the office.' I grab the magazines and go to replace them under the bed when I notice something in the middle of the pile that isn't a magazine. 'Wait. What's this?'

I pull it out, a large sealed envelope with *Rachel Radcliff* written on it.

FIFTY-SIX

'That's Johnny's handwriting.'

India nudges my elbow. 'Open it.'

'Do you think I should? I've, in effect, broken into his home and am now snooping through his stuff that he evidently didn't want anyone to find, otherwise he wouldn't have hidden it under the bed.'

'We didn't break in. You used your key.' She shrugs defiantly. 'Remind yourself why you came here in the first place.'

'You know, I've been thinking. What if Dean believes he found some proof that I left Charlie for dead that night, and he gave that to Johnny?'

'You're overthinking things.'

'I'm so confused.'

'If he'd had anything, he'd have gone to the police before going to Johnny. Stop being paranoid. Open the envelope.'

'I don't know. It feels wrong. What if he suddenly comes back?'

'Just open it.'

I finger the seal. 'Once I do, he's going to know.'

'So what. You say you were concerned for his safety. Listen,

LEFT AT THE ALTAR

you were dumped at the altar. I think you've got the latitude to do whatever digging you please.'

I hesitate.

She huffs and removes her phone from her pocket. 'Let's see how you open an envelope without someone knowing.' Her fingers glide over the keyboard with speed. 'Here we go. Steam from a kettle. But you need to be careful not to wrinkle the paper. Put it in a freezer. That might not work with all adhesives. Do you have a hairdryer here?'

I shake my head.

'It says to use a hairdryer. The heat softens the glue and you can easily peel away the flap. Let me take it back to yours, and I'll do it while you're at work this afternoon.'

I sink the palms of my hands into my eye sockets. 'I don't know.'

'We're taking it. Come on. We can return it later.' She hauls me off the bed. 'Let's get out of here. It's giving me the creeps now.'

I glance at my watch. 'Damn! Look at the time. We need to hurry.' I stuff the envelope in my bag.

We hurry down the stairs. I lock the front door, wondering if I'm doing the right thing taking Johnny's personal property. Then I think of the petals on the bed in that hotel room, the tickets to Disneyland, and the perfume and earrings I've just found.

All reminders of why I came here.

And why I need to find out what's in this envelope.

If he's in some kind of trouble, it could mean life or death for him.

'I've got a few things I need to do first,' India says when we get in the car. 'I've got a Zoom call with a hotel in Bali for a potential promotion.' She often gets invited to spend a night at luxury hotels in exchange for promotion on her Instagram and TikTok accounts. With over a million followers, she has built herself a profitable business. 'It's a popular five-star one, as well. If I can get my foot in their door, it could open lots of others for me.'

I start the car, set the heating dial to maximum, and pull into the road. It's snowing again. The unsteady roads slow my speed. 'I'm going to be late.'

'Take it easy,' India says, a pleading undercurrent to her tone. 'We want to arrive back in one piece.'

My phone rings. It's Angela.

'Aren't you going to answer it?' India says.

'No! I don't need her to stress me out more than I already am. I shouldn't have left the office when there's an important client coming in.'

When I drop her off, I say, 'Call me as soon as you've opened it.'

'Why wouldn't I?' She climbs out of the car and taps the roof. 'Drive safely. You're scaring me.'

I arrive back at the office at five past one.

Angela pounces at me. 'Where've you been, Hannah? We've got an important client meeting. Did you forget?'

'I'm sorry. The roads are atrocious.'

She throws me a stern look. 'Good job our client called to say they're running late as well, then, isn't it? Get yourself up to the meeting room as soon as, please.'

I hurry to my desk, dump my bag, pick up a notepad and pen and rush upstairs. Angela is already waiting in the meeting room.

'I know you've a lot going on, Hannah. But you gave me your word that you wouldn't allow the circumstances to affect your work.' She's being incredibly cold.

Redness creeps up my neck. 'I haven't.'

She goes to speak but Jenna and Tom enter with two stout

men, the new clients, who prove demanding as the meeting progresses. I'm full of unease and fidgety, conscious of the number of times I look at my watch. My mind is on that envelope, wondering if India has opened it yet. I'm so scared it contains something about me. Something Dean gave to Johnny last Friday.

When the meeting ends, Angela asks me to remain seated while she sees the clients out.

After she and the others leave, I call India, but the call goes to her voicemail. She must still be on her Zoom call. I drop her a text:

Have you opened it yet?

When Angela returns, she firmly closes the door and perches on the side of the large meeting room table. 'I'll come straight to the point, Hannah. I'd like you to take some time off.'

I'm not sure I heard her right. 'Sorry?'

'You're not yourself. You hardly contributed to the meeting. A few of your emails have been sloppy.' Her tone softens. 'I understand why. You have a lot to deal with at the moment.'

The knot in my stomach tightens. I hope she's not trying to work me out of the company. Mortgage payments, soaring heating bills, my car insurance renewal all rush through my mind. I can't afford to lose this job. I panic. 'Obviously I've been a little unsettled, but I'm on my game, Angela. I don't need time off.'

'I insist. Wrap up any outstanding issues this afternoon.'

'But what about this new client? You're so busy, what with Johnny being away. And after today, Tom won't be here until the new year.'

'We'll cope. Johnny had already booked time off for you next week to take you away.'

'But, I—'

Her posture stiffens. She's such a hard-nosed business woman. 'I said, Hannah. Wrap up any unfinished business this afternoon. Then go and enjoy time with your sister for her big day. And you can take next week off.'

Nausea charges through me. I clutch the edge of the desk. She can't do this to me. I consider defending my corner. I'm perfectly fine to carry on working. But Angela is one of those people with whom you have to know when to back down for your own good.

'You'll still be paid, and you don't need to take it as annual leave. Just rest.' She stands. 'Or go away if you can. You've been through a tough time. A change of scenery will do you good to come to terms with what's happened.'

With that, she abruptly leaves the room, not allowing me to get another word in.

It's as if she wants me out of the way.

FIFTY-SEVEN

I sit in silence, considering my next move. I wonder what Johnny would tell me to do. I close my eyes tightly, shaking my head. I can't think about Johnny coming to my rescue anymore. That boat sailed last weekend.

I return downstairs. My head is in a whirl. I can't help thinking this is the beginning of Angela trying to get me out the organisation. Three missed calls from India pop up on my phone.

'It opened a dream,' she says when I get hold of her. 'I'll easily be able to reseal it. You'll never be able to tell it's been opened.'

'And?'

'It's all to do with that marquee accident.'

'What about it?'

'It all looks very formal. Lots of legal jargon concerning the investigation. I can't say anything particular sticks out to me.'

Disappointment brings a heavy sigh. 'I'm coming home soon. I'll take a look.'

I end the call and glance around the office. Alan is standing at Tom's desk. They are in deep conversation and staring at me as if they're discussing me. When they see me looking, they turn away.

I stand and march towards them. 'Is everything OK?' I ask.

'Sure. Why?' Alan says.

'You appeared to be talking about me.'

Alan's face tightens. He frowns. 'Oh, Hannah. Of course we weren't. I was just saying to Tom how good the marquee looks.'

My gaze follows his finger pointing to the marquee beyond the window by my desk.

'It's the first time I've seen it all lit up in the dark.'

I step backwards. 'I'm sorry.'

'Are you OK, Hannah,' Alan says, 'You look dreadfully pale.'

'I'm fine,' I mutter and return to my desk.

Perhaps Angela is right.

I do need a break.

This has all got too much.

But the thought of spending a week alone at home is more depressing than being here. It's not as if India will be there. She has other plans.

Following Angela's orders, I tie up all outstanding issues, type an *out of office* message for my emails and switch off my computer. An eerie foreboding overcomes me. My actions are purposeful, as if deep down I know I'm never coming back here.

I hurry to my car, eager to get home, but Carrie calls me from the marquee. 'Come and look. We've got the lighting working at last.'

I clench my jaw. My head has started pounding. I need to take some tablets.

Carrie meets me halfway across the vast lawn. My boot hits a large stone. I stumble. 'The ground's rock hard,' I say.

'I had the guys lay some salt earlier. I'll get them to spread some more. The last thing we need is someone slipping and breaking their neck on Saturday. I'm getting really nervous.' She giggles like a heady schoolgirl.

I think back to this time last week. I was just as excited.

She drags me into the marquee. It looks spectacular. I don't want to be here. I want to grab Lucas and take him away somewhere. Anywhere as long as it's far away from here.

'You've been working hard,' I say.

Light shimmers from four gigantic crystal chandeliers hung from the covered scaffolding bars, casting a beautiful warm glow across the tables. The stems of fake lilies swathe the tall arched windows cut into the walls. And it's surprisingly warm from the large heaters positioned outside that blow warm air into the huge internal space.

'It's looking great, isn't it?' Carrie beams, looking around the place. 'Just how I imagined it.'

'Angela is insisting I take next week off,' I say.

'What a great idea.'

'But, I—'

She chats incessantly, all wedding-related. I can't stand it. The more she talks, the more my head pounds. My vision blurs. 'I need to go,' I say. 'I need to get Lucas.'

'Don't be late tonight.'

'Tonight?' I say.

'Tonight at mine. Everything's ready.' Her neck twitches. She's talking fast. A sure sign her nerves have taken hold. 'All our favourite snacks. Bottles of champers chilling in the fridge.'

I can't bear it. 'I'll say now. I'm not staying too long. Lucas is tired. And so am I.' That's an understatement. I can't even remember being this tired after Lucas was born, when he didn't sleep for the first three months. 'We want him to be on top form for Saturday.'

I find her another fake smile. I shouldn't be faking it. My sister has been painstakingly planning tonight for months, down to the time we're going to call for a pizza takeaway. An evening for her, India and I to spend together. It was the only night the three of us could spend alone together, with Lucas, of course.

But I'm not at all excited.

All I want to do is crawl into a ball and hibernate under my duvet until this is all over... until I've had a chance to face Johnny again and put this nightmare behind me.

But reality is telling me that isn't going to happen anytime soon.

FIFTY-EIGHT

India has separated the contents of the envelope into three neat piles, each about a centimetre thick. There must be over fifty pages in total. 'Johnny's certainly been doing his homework. This mostly relates to the accident. There are a few other documents that I can't work out which pile they belong to.' She takes a sip from the large glass of wine she has poured.

I could kill for a drink right now. My stress levels are at an all-time high, but I need to drive us to Carrie's, so I opt for a can of Diet Coke.

India picks up a bundle and waves it. 'Here we have various excerpts from the case. The accident. The level of injuries sustained. Details of the guy who died. It all makes pretty murky reading. The poor couple this happened to...' She grimaces. 'On their wedding day! You'd be scarred for life, wouldn't you?'

She places the bundle back on the table, tidying the edges, before picking up another ream of papers. 'These are reports from Caxton Events: office paperwork, health and safety reports, legal stuff I don't understand. You'll know more about this than me.' She aligns the edges of the pile and places them at ninety degrees on top of the first bundle. 'Then we have abstract pages that don't seem to fit into any part of the investigation, so I can only assume they've randomly made their way in here.'

'What's your gut feel here? What do you think Johnny was up to? Is the donation he made to Rachel Radcliff's foundation mentioned anywhere?'

'I was going to come onto that. There's been correspondence between the two of them. And get this – the donation was for twenty-five thousand pounds.'

My eyes widen, and my jaw drops. 'What! Where did he get that kind of money from? All our funds were tied up in our house purchase.'

'And wait for it.' She whisks a sheet of paper from the pile. 'It looks like the plans for some kind of centre for spine-injured people.' She places the sheet of paper in front of me and takes another piece from the pile displaying a computer-generated image of a building with a large signage across the front: *The Sinclair Foundation*. 'And there's email correspondence between Johnny and Rachel. It looks like they were working on a plan to get this centre up and running.'

'So you think the donation was more of an investment?'

'I'm not sure.'

Lucas appears. 'I'm hungry, Mum. Can I have something to eat?'

'Darling, I'm sorry.' The fist of mothers' guilt punches me in the gut. I've neglected him these past few days. 'We're going to Aunty Carrie's soon. We'll be eating when we get there.'

'But I'm hungry now.'

I snatch a banana from the fruit bowl on the side of the table, but it's seen better days.

'Yuk! It's all brown. I don't want fruit. I had an orange at afterschool club.'

I find him a packet of crisps in the back of the cupboard.

He grabs it from me. 'Thanks, Mum. You're the best.' He races back to the living room. I cringe at the sound of a PlayStation game springing into action. I squeeze my eyes shut tightly for a moment. The sounds remind me of when Johnny and he used to play games together. They were such good times. I was so happy.

Twenty-five thousand pounds – I'm incredulous.

I sigh and turn to my sister. 'What about Dean, is there mention of him anywhere by any chance?' I shudder. Every time that man enters my thoughts, or I say his name, I feel physically sick.

'Nothing. Zilch.' India shrugs. 'And I keep checking the news. There's been nothing on any channel about his body being found.' She slides the stack of papers towards me. 'Here you go. Knock yourself out. I need to get on. That call with the hotel went well.'

'I'm sorry. I should've asked.'

'We can catch up later.'

I sip my Diet Coke and browse through the papers. India was correct. The case files don't make pleasant reading. I don't understand much of the legal jargon used but photos from the scene of the accident are alarming. Some are official photos, taken by what appears to be some kind of investigation team. But it's the pictures people took on their phones at the time and later posted online that bring tears to my eyes, as does the thought of Johnny giving Rachel all that money without my knowledge.

I continue reading. The company was, it appears, cleared of any wrongdoing. It seems, however, that Johnny has meticulously gone through every piece of paper, marking them up in places, although his notes mean little to me.

I'm on safer ground with the office documents which appear in order. Tom carried out the risk assessment and completed all the health and safety documentation. Other papers not associated to the accident have made their way into the file. I study them intently. They are dated around the time of the accident, as is the copy of a rogue email with copies of Tom's and Alan's diaries of the week of the incident.

I turn to the payment made to The Sinclair Foundation. There's an acknowledgement of receipt and a handwritten note Johnny hurriedly penned from a meeting he had with Rachel last week, when he should've been at work. He wrote it in a hurry as the writing, although undoubtably his, is untidy.

I don't know what hurts more – that he met this woman without telling me, or he gave her twenty-five thousand pounds from money that could've gone towards our new home.

I return to the letter confirming the receipt of funds. Rachel Radcliff's email and phone number are at the top of the page. I consider emailing her. Perhaps she can fill in the blanks.

I grab my phone.

I have to speak to this woman. Now.

Because I have nowhere else to go.

My hands tremble as I call her number.

She answers after three rings. 'Hello.'

I falter. I'm not sure how to introduce myself. 'Is that Rachel Radcliff?' I ask to buy some time.

'Who is this?' Her voice is gentle, as smooth as honey.

I tell her that I came across a newspaper article about her foundation and would like to know more about it. We chat. It's an easy conversation, as if we're two old friends catching up after not speaking for a while. I'd like to get involved in her work, I tell her.

I arrange to go to her house tomorrow morning. It's out of character for me to be so forward. Carrie's going to kill me. She has booked for us to go to a spa. Appointments she arranged last year. I was looking forward to going with my sisters, but am now dreading it because the spa is in the grounds of Maple Manor, where Johnny and I should've spent our wedding night.

'It'll have to be early, before ten o'clock as I have an appointment,' Rachel says. 'Or later in the day. I should be back by three o'clock.'

'I can be there for a little after nine. Is that too early?'

'Nine it is.'

I end the call and get ready to go to Carrie's.

I can't believe I've arranged to meet this stranger.

But Johnny gave her twenty-five thousand pounds and never told me about it.

Then he disappeared.

I have to know why.

FIFTY-NINE

Twenty-five thousand pounds.

I still can't believe it. Why Johnny didn't tell me about this revolves around my thoughts as I toss and turn for most of yet another night.

My thoughts turn to Dean, and his head lying in a pool of blood on that kitchen table. I retrace the journey to his house and torment myself with thoughts about someone seeing me and India looking through his kitchen window.

I break out in hot sweats, but within seconds of discarding the duvet, my skin prickles from the chill in the air. I pick up my phone again and check the news, looking for a mention of Dean's body having been found, but there's nothing.

My head pounds. My eyes burn from the lack of sleep. I reach into the bedside cabinet and take a couple more paracetamol.

India is sitting in the lotus pose on the floor in the living room when I get downstairs in the morning. Lucas is playing on the PlayStation. He's been fixated with that damn console since I brought it back from Johnny's. I wish for the hundredth time I'd left it there.

My heart aches for my son. Usually, we spend a lot more time together. We play board and card games, cook, or go for walks, and in the summer, potter in the garden together. I need to give him more attention when Carrie and Tom's wedding is over. 'Shall we go out for the day on Sunday, darling?' I ruffle his blond hair, my fingers catching in a clump of curls.

His eyes remain fixed on the screen.

'Lucas!'

He still doesn't look at me.

I raise my voice. 'Lucas! Answer me.'

'What?'

'Let's go to the park at the weekend.'

'If it's snowing, can we build a snowman?'

'Sure. Off that thing now. We need to go.'

He ignores me.

'I said now, Lucas. I don't want to get cross.' My firm gaze bores into him. He gets it. I don't use that look often. I don't need to. He's such a good kid. But when I do, he knows it's time to comply. He discards the controller, switches off the TV and wanders off.

India stands and elegantly stretches her hands above her head.

'I'll be there as quick as I can,' I say.

'Carrie's going to go nuts. Especially after yesterday.'

I had to bail early from Carrie's last night because of the building pressure in my head that I was scared was going to explode into a migraine.

'Just stick to the plan. Tell her I had to pop into town after dropping Lucas at school. I'll head straight to the spa when I'm done.' Rachel's house is about a twenty-minute drive away, a little more perhaps in this weather. 'I won't spend long there. I should be back for ten. Ten thirty at the latest.'

'That's too late. Our appointments start at ten.'

'I'll be there. I've booked you a cab for nine thirty, so you can go straight there.'

'I'm concerned about you going somewhere that's connected to all of this. Can't you at least wait until after the wedding? Then I could come with you.'

'I'm fine.' The tone of my voice tells her to leave me be. Rachel is hardly a threat.

She follows me into the hallway. 'You're not thinking straight. Carrie will know something's up when I turn up in a taxi. You know what she's like. This isn't a good idea. Why don't you go after the wedding?' She repeatedly grabs my shoulder. 'Then I could come with you before I fly back to Australia.'

'I'm honestly scared something has happened to him. I can't waste another day.'

'At what cost? You're only going to piss off Carrie, and you could be putting yourself in danger.'

'He's the love of my life, India. I have to help him.'

SIXTY

After dropping Lucas at school, I drive to Rachel's house. Another hard frost hampers the journey. Gritter lorries have taken to the roads, spreading their load, but shiny signs of black ice still appear here and there. Flakes of snow flurry in the cold air, reminding me of the recent fateful journey to Dean's house. Was that only two days ago? My mind wanders, returning to his battered head lying on his kitchen table, and intrusive thoughts ask if Johnny has met a similar destiny.

I arrive at Rachel's modern semi-detached house at a quarter past nine. It's snowing heavily. The windscreen wipers swipe away flurry after constant flurry. I could get stuck here, snowed in, and miss my sister's wedding. I brush the rash thought aside. I'm overthinking things again.

I park beside her wheelchair-accessible vehicle and take the wide concrete path cut into the driveway that leads to the front door. The bitter depth of winter cuts through the thick fabric of my hooded coat. I shiver.

The house appears quiet as if no one is in. I press the doorbell and wait, stamping the snow from my boots on the doormat. Finally, there's movement from inside the house. The front door slowly opens, and the woman I recognise from The Sinclair Foundation website appears.

Rachel has the same curly blonde hair and a bubbly expression as in her photo, and her warm smile reaches her aqua-blue eyes. She looks snug and cosy in a thick turtleneck jumper. 'I'm sorry to have kept you. I couldn't get my mum off the phone.' She rolls those beautiful eyes and shakes her head. 'She's a bit of a fusspot.' Manoeuvring a one-hundred-and-eighty-degree turn in her wheelchair, she sweeps out her hand to invite me in. 'Close the door behind you, would you, please?'

I push the door to. The banging sound echoes along the wide hallway. Suddenly, I feel vulnerable. India was right. I shouldn't have come here. I'm being irrational. Rachel is hardly a threat. But then I realise it's what she could reveal further about Johnny that's making me feel so exposed.

Her wheels move as smoothly as legs along the vinyl tiles to the kitchen. 'Can I get you a drink? Coffee? Tea? I'm having a coffee.'

'I'll go for the same. Strong, black, please.'

It's going to be a very long day.

Her kitchen is spacious, adapted with lowered countertops and adjustable shelving.

She's a talker, her voice as mesmerising as her appearance. She makes two cups of coffee and delivers them to the kitchen table on a tray she balances on her lap, explaining how she ended up in a wheelchair and how it inspired her to set up The Sinclair Foundation.

'I wasn't wholly honest with you on the phone yesterday,' I blurt out.

Her bubbly smile disappears. Her arms move to the wheels of her chair.

'It's OK.' I lift my hands. 'I'm only here to find out some information on the marquee accident.'

Her posture stiffens. 'Are you a reporter?'

'No! Nothing like that. You sent a plant to Johnny this week.'

Her face holds a deep frown for a few seconds before relaxing. 'Ah! And you're his new wife. Of course! I thought I recognised your face from somewhere. Johnny showed me a picture of you when he was last here.'

My heart is heavy as the confusion grows. 'When was that?'

'Last week.' Her brows knit together, and her eyes rise to the left. 'Monday.' She pauses. 'No it wasn't. It was Tuesday. Tuesday evening.'

Johnny was here last week, and he never told me. And not only did he not tell me. He lied to me. He told me he had a client meeting last Tuesday and would be back late. I can't work out why he would've lied to me. Or perhaps he simply dropped in here on his way home.

'I was surprised when he told me he was getting married on Saturday.'

'The wedding didn't go ahead.' I fill her in. 'He told his family he'd gone to Wales, but I don't know if that's true.'

'Why would they lie?'

'I'm not saying they did.' I can't conceal the desperation in my voice. 'I'm thinking that he might have lied. For what reason, I don't know.' I can't believe I've opened up so much to this stranger, but there's something about her. Perhaps it's because she's been put through the mill – experienced severe trauma the same as me – that allows me to trust her.

She sips her coffee. 'So he didn't turn up at the church and didn't even call you?'

'He sent me a text.'

She raises one eyebrow. 'I find that hard to believe. From what he told me, he couldn't wait to marry you. He was positively gushing about you.'

My hand clutches my chest.

'What do his family say?'

I suddenly wonder what she thinks of me. This random woman who has turned up at her doorstep under false pretences. 'Do you know who Johnny's family are?'

She squints. 'What do you mean?'

'Johnny Caxton. Angela Caxton, who owned Mortimer Events, is his mother.'

Surprisingly, she nods. 'Yes. Of course I knew that. That's where the donation came from.'

I frown. 'I thought it came from Johnny personally?'

She shakes her head. 'No. No. It came from Caxton Events. They've been keen to help with the foundation. Johnny is helping me get the centre up and running. He arranged for the plans to be drawn up.'

'When did he first approach you about this?'

'A few months ago. He said he was visiting a client one day and saw an article about me in a newspaper in their reception. He reached out. I was a bit reticent at first. I wasn't sure how I'd feel about anyone connected to that family helping me out. I hated them so badly for so long while the investigation into what happened was ongoing, especially Angela Caxton, that by the time it was all over, I didn't have any hate left inside of me. They did nothing wrong. Move on with your life and play the cards you've been dealt, my mum told me. It's the only way to come out the winner.'

I can relate to this.

'The anger was killing me. I had to find forgiveness. It was an accident. No one was to blame. It was an act of God, as they say. When Johnny showed up, he was so genuine and so adamant he wanted to help, I couldn't refuse. I'm so keen to get my foundation up and running, I need all the help I can get.'

I can't understand why Johnny didn't tell me all this.

'So have you shared your concerns with his family?' she asks again.

'It's difficult. My sister is marrying Johnny's brother.' I hold up a hand. 'I know. I know. It's all very complicated.'

'Yes. Johnny did tell me. He and his brother were each other's best man.'

'That's right. But Johnny's not going to their wedding now. My sister didn't want him to be Tom's best man anymore, and he decided it's best he stay away.'

'Did they make up before that happened?'

'Make up? What do you mean?'

'Johnny mentioned he and his brother had a bad argument. I thought it was about the wedding.'

He never mentioned anything about an argument with Tom to me. Or perhaps he did, but I was so caught up in the wedding, it didn't register. I wonder if that's why Tom has chosen another of his friends to be his best man.

I thought Johnny and I told each other everything.

It seems we've both been hiding things from each other.

SIXTY-ONE

I stay longer than I should with Rachel. I'm so captivated by this woman, and what she has to tell me, that I forget to check the time.

Snow is still falling when I pull out of the driveway. Carrie will be delighted. If it continues, she'll get her white fairytale wedding.

The conversation with Rachel hurtles through my mind as I journey to the spa. The fear that Johnny hasn't simply ghosted me intensifies. But no matter how I try, the pieces of this puzzle still don't fit together.

I drive up the long gravel driveway to the spa at the side of Maple Manor. India had suggested to Carrie that we find another venue for our treatments. All the staff will know about the wedding that didn't happen. But finding a place to accommodate all three of us at such short notice wasn't possible.

Dark memories surface from when I returned here in my wedding car with Alan last Saturday. It's cutting. I've lost so much.

I fantasise that it's not too late. We can come back from this. I know we can. If I can find Johnny, I can explain. I'll open up about Charlie. I'll tell him that I left for dead the man who physically and mentally abused me, when there was a slight possibility I could've saved him. He'd understand. I know he would. I can see that now. We can move on. Rebuild our lives. I know we can.

I hurry into the building. It has the bygone charm of the main hotel, beamed ceilings and oak wooden flooring, but has been modernised with clean line furniture and soft furnishings. It's ten forty-five. Carrie and India are having their massages. How I could do with a massage right now. My muscles are tighter than the strings of a harp. But it's too late to join them, so the young therapist dressed in a dusty pink tunic and matching trousers takes me to the treatment room housing three pedicure stations that line the far wall. 'Take a seat, and I'll bring you a drink.' She pulls a remote control from a pocket at the side of the chair and hands it to me. 'If you press the top button, the chair reclines. Relax and your sisters should be with you in a few minutes.'

Relax. She hasn't got a clue.

I take two paracetamol and close my eyes, trying to switch off, but there's not a moment's reprieve. It's stifling. Dean's smashed-in face refuses to leave me alone, as if it's punishing me for doing the wrong thing and leaving him like I left his brother seven years ago.

The door opens. My sisters appear in white fluffy dressing gowns and matching slippers. Carrie stands in front of my chair, her hands on her hips. 'There you are! What the hell happened to you?'

'I'm sorry. I had to sort something out and got held up.'

Her face reddens. 'What was so important that it couldn't wait?'

'I had a few bits to get in town. I'm here now.'

She raises her voice. 'It's not good enough. You missed the massage, which cost me a fortune.'

'I'll pay.'

'It's not about the money.' She flails her arms. 'How many days have the three of us spent together in the past seven years?' Her emotions spiral, just like they did on Wednesday night with Tom. What's got into her? 'This was meant to be our morning.'

India rests a hand on her shoulder. 'Leave it. It doesn't matter.'

'It does matter.' She shakes off India's hand. Tears fall. She's being totally over the top. 'It's not fair, Han. This is my day. You will be at the rehearsal this afternoon, won't you?'

'Of course I will.'

'If you ruin—'

A knock at the door saves me from further rebuff. Six therapists walk into the room. 'Ready for your treatments, ladies?'

Carrie wipes her face with the back of her hand. There's an embarrassing silence.

'We can't wait,' says India. She guides Carrie to sit down and chats away. Her conversation brushes away the awkwardness.

The therapists giggle like schoolgirls at the mention of any wedding-related small talk Carrie makes. I should be enjoying this, but the whole experience is marred by my perfect world that has collapsed around me. I try to rest while one of the therapists fiddles with my hands and another with my feet, but I'm too on edge.

After the treatment, we stop – according to Carrie's punctiliously planned timetable – for a quick lunch in an intimate café set in a conservatory adjoining the back of the building. Our table shares the breathtaking views across the large lake and surrounding gardens that I marvelled at from the terrace of my wedding suite last weekend.

Stuck with that view for the next half hour isn't an option, so I rush to occupy the chair on the far side of the table, so my back faces the outside. Carrie has already pre-ordered a platter of our favourite sandwiches, followed by a selection of miniature cakes that I'd usually find rather appetising. I love cake.

'Three glasses of prosecco?' She looks from India to me.

'Why not?' I can't face alcohol, but I daren't disagree with her. I'm not hungry either, but I force down a sandwich, feigning enjoyment. I laugh when they do, fake excitement for the long-awaited wedding tomorrow, pretending I can't wait.

Lucas enters my thoughts. I place the fork on the plate. The need to hold my boy close to me is overpowering. I want to go and fetch him from school right now.

'What's up, Han?' Carrie asks. 'Have you got a headache? Make sure you bring your pills with you tomorrow, won't you? We can't have you ill. It'll ruin the day.' She babbles on, talking about the wedding. It's suffocating. It's only when she excuses herself that I get the chance to speak to India.

'She's full-on today, isn't she?' India says.

'I guess I was the same last week.'

'So?' she asks. 'What happened?'

I brief her on my visit to Rachel's. 'The money didn't come from Johnny. Caxton Events gave the foundation twenty-five thousand pounds.'

She raises her eyebrows. 'Why?'

I shrug. 'Angela's very generous. Perhaps she harbours some guilt about what happened.'

I don't notice Carrie approaching the table. 'Guilt? Who's guilty of what?'

'Me. I feel guilty for missing the massage.'

'It's fine. What's done is done.'

I wish I could tell her the truth about where I really went this morning. But I can't. She's high enough maintenance as it is today.

She smiles. 'I forgive you.'

'I want to ask you something. That marquee accident a few years ago. What actually happened?'

Carrie crosses her arms. 'Why are you bringing that up?'

'I came across a newspaper article about it, about a woman who was left paralysed. I was just interested to know what happened.'

'It was a terrible time. No one talks about it. It was so stressful. Angela blames Alan's second heart attack on the whole situation.'

'She's given the foundation a twenty-five-thousand-pound donation,' I say.

Carrie's eyebrows jump. 'Has she? How do you know?'

'Johnny told me.' Another lie, but she doesn't need to know about my trip to Rachel's.

'You probably know more than me, then.'

'And did Tom say anything to you about him and Johnny having a big argument last week?'

She frowns. 'No! He never mentioned anything to me. What was it about?'

So Tom and Johnny both wanted to keep this from us.

SIXTY-TWO

'I know this can't be easy for you, Han,' Carrie says when she meets me and India at the church.

'I'll be fine.' Memories from when Johnny and I arrived here for our own wedding rehearsal are torturing me.

'Are you really sure about doing the reading?' Carrie asks.

'I've already said. I'll be fine.'

'You sure? You're not going to mess it up, are you?'

'I've been practising.' Yet another lie. They're tumbling out of me like a stream of sewage water. For over a week I haven't looked at the reading I'm meant to stand up in front of the congregation and deliver tomorrow.

The last time was the Thursday evening before the wedding, when I practised it in front of Johnny at his apartment. He was sitting on his sofa, legs stretched out on the coffee table, with a glass of wine from the bottle we were sharing. He'd taken a chair from the dining table and made me get up on it as if I was standing at the lectern in the church. 'Don't be nervous, darling.' He gave me a big smile. 'You can always look at your own husband at the front of the crowd.'

My own husband!

Carrie squeezes my arm. 'Are you listening to me?'

'Sorry?'

'India said she'll do your reading if you want.'

'I will, Han. I can practise it tonight,' India says.

'I said it's fine.' The words come out sharper than intended. 'I'm sorry.'

'I know you don't want to hear this, Han, but I could kill Johnny.'

If he's not already dead!

I wipe the morbid thought from my mind.

Carrie's voice cracks. 'Not only did he ruin everything for you, but it's put a damper on things for us. Tom's so cut up about it.'

'Don't let it spoil your day,' I say.

We're the last to arrive in the church. The rest of the wedding party are talking to the priest. It's a beautiful church, welcoming and spiritual. It's why Johnny and I chose it for our wedding, too.

Carrie and Tom embrace, and she produces a typed list of everything she wants covered during this session.

I approach them. 'What do you want me to do?' I ask.

Tom shifts from one foot to another, chewing his lip. He is avoiding eye contact with me. Something's bothering him. 'Are you OK, Tom?' I ask.

He snaps at me. 'Why wouldn't I be?'

'I just—'

The priest joins us. He acknowledges me with a silent nod. He's a rotund guy with a cheerful face. Not that he can cheer me up at the moment. He outlines the plan for the rehearsal. I zone out, counting rectangles in the parquet flooring, while I listen to the same talk from when I was last here. An intense shiver shoots down my spine. It's as if Johnny is around somewhere, watching the proceedings.

'Let's all practise how we'll enter the church,' the priest says.

I robotically follow the sequence of events, wearing a smile, but it's thin and flaky. The priest directs my sister and Tom through the ring exchange. I fiddle with my engagement ring. I've been thinking about taking it off, but I can't bring myself to. It's as if a tiny part of me still believes Johnny is going to come back to me. I bite my lip and stare at the belt holding up my jeans. I close my eyes and think of my baby. Voices whirl around me. The church spins. I grab hold of the side of a pew.

I startle at Alan's voice and the gentle touch of his hand on my shoulder. 'This can't be easy for you. You're doing great.'

* * *

After we've practised speeches and the exit sequence, we head to the small pub less than a minute's drive away, where we all went after the rehearsal for my and Johnny's wedding. The wedding party gather around the far end where Angela has arranged a spread of finger food.

Luckily, I have an excuse not to stay long. 'I need to get going,' I say, earlier than I need to, but I can no longer put on an act. 'I need to pick Lucas up from school.'

Carrie clutches India's forearm. 'You can stay. I'll drop you off later.'

On the way out of the rattly back door, someone grabs my arm. I turn to see Tom. 'Can I have a quick word, Han?' He stands close to me, too close, invading my personal space.

I pull my arm away, but he clutches onto it. 'You're hurting me,' I say.

He eases his grip, but he doesn't let go. His body is still and tense. 'Why have you suddenly got such a keen interest in the marquee accident?'

I'm taken aback. Not just by his words but by the sinister look in his eyes.

He glares at me. 'Carrie told me on the way here that you were asking about it again. She tells me everything, Han. Everything.' The darkness in his eyes intensifies. It's unsettling. I've always got on well with Tom. But he's frightening me. 'I told you everything you need to know the other night. It was before your time, and, anyway, it's a family matter.'

A family matter.

His words are a slap around the face. I snatch my arm from his grip. 'You think I'm no longer part of this family, Tom. But don't forget you're marrying my sister, so I'll always be a part of it.'

I turn and storm out of the door, not giving him the chance to respond.

SIXTY-THREE

'He's hiding something. I'm telling you.'

India removes her coat and chucks it on the sofa. 'I thought he appeared jittery at the pub, but he's getting married tomorrow, Han. It must've been a pretty dire episode for the family to go through.'

'He hurt me!' I lift the sleeve of my pyjama top and show India the markings on my arm. 'When I've put Lucas to bed, I'm going to look through all that paperwork again.'

'Oh, Han. Leave it until after the wedding. You'll only wind yourself up even more. Look at you! You're exhausted. Have a bath. I'll put Lucas to bed. Then we can watch a film and get an early night.'

'There's something in those papers, and I'm scared it has something to do with where Johnny is now.'

'Even if it does, what good can come of it tonight? I'll go through it again with you at the weekend. Let's just let Carrie enjoy her wedding tomorrow. We'll see them off on their honeymoon, and then I'll help you.'

'Don't you think we should warn Carrie?'

'Warn her of what?' Her eyes widen. 'Han! Listen to yourself. At this stage, you've no cast-iron proof of anything. If you say something to her, you'll only drive a wedge between the two of you.'

Lucas bursts into the room. 'Mum. Can I play a game?'

I get up. 'Not tonight.'

'Why not? Please.'

'No more tech tonight, darling. I'm going to make hot chocolate for us, then I'm going to read you a story. Your aunty is getting married tomorrow, and we all need an early night.'

'That's right, buddy,' India chimes in.

'Can Aunty India read to me tonight?'

'Special treat. We both can,' I say. 'Let's have hot chocolate first.'

'I'm going to get my pyjamas on,' India says.

I pick up Lucas. He's getting too heavy, but I'm savouring the special moments while I still can hold him in my arms. I take him to the kitchen, where I fill a saucepan with milk and put it on the cooker to boil. The pile of papers on the table catches my eye. India is right. I am exhausted. But I'm still going to go through it all again tonight.

I stand Lucas on a chair and help him spoon hot chocolate powder into three mugs. I pour in an inch of milk and find him a spoon to stir the mixture. He chats away.

My stomach flips.

I was hoping it wouldn't happen.

Apart from his brown eyes that he unmistakably inherited from Charlie, and his blond curls, there's been little resemblance to his father to date. But as his facial features have matured, he's beginning to look like him. The gentle curve of his chin has changed to form more of a point, and his cheekbones have become more prominent. I hug him tightly, silently praying he doesn't grow to look any more like his dead father. I don't need the reminder of what I did in my face for the rest of my life.

'You're hurting me, Mum!'

'I'm sorry, darling.' I release my hold and pour the heated milk into the mugs. As I'm filling the third one, India appears at the door holding her phone against her chest. The alarm plastered across her face like a layer of unbecoming foundation tells me something has happened.

She playfully elbows Lucas. 'Where's my hot chocolate?'

Lucas jumps off the chair, purposely landing with a thud. He laughs. The chair legs scrape along the tiled floor. The sound goes right through me. I stare at India. She shakes her phone at me and mouths, 'Dean.'

My heart jolts. 'Why don't I take these into the living room, and you go and choose the books you want us to read to you.' I steer Lucas towards the door, not taking my gaze from my sister.

'I want my drink first,' Lucas protests.

'It's too hot. By the time you've chosen the books, it'll have cooled down. Go on. Off you go.'

India steps aside to let him pass. He runs off.

'What's happened?' I ask my sister.

'Dean's body has been found.'

SIXTY-FOUR

I don't need a mirror to know my cheeks have drained of all colour. I feel as pale as she looks. 'When?'

'Last night, apparently.'

'Do they know who did it?'

'It's not on the national news, only the local channel.' India summarises the brief article out loud. 'The police have launched a murder investigation after the discovery of the body of local man Dean Ferguson, yesterday afternoon.' She puffs out a hard, fast breath. 'This is dreadful, Han.' She vigorously rubs her forehead. 'His body was found by a friend after Mr Ferguson failed to turn up to meet him and subsequently didn't answer any of his calls. People who saw anything suspicious should contact the police. Oh, hell, Han. What if someone saw us?'

'Calm down. There was no one about.'

'What were we thinking to leave him?' She groans. 'The police will go through his phone history and be able to tell he had contact with me. They'll be after me. That will drag you into the whole affair when they find out you are my sister, and his connection to Charlie.' She drops down onto one of the kitchen chairs. 'This is hell.'

'I've already thought all this through. You had nothing to do with his murder. And neither did I. You have nothing to worry about.'

'That's not the problem. I'm more worried about someone having seen us at his house and having to lie to the police about it. I knew we should've called them when we were there.' She chucks her phone on the table, laces her hands and slams them on her forehead. 'This is absolute torture.'

'No one saw us. The house is in the middle of nowhere.'

'Let's just come clean now,' she says. 'That's the best thing.'

'I can't. We can't. What the hell do we say? We found a dead's man body and ignored it. Come on. You're not thinking straight.'

'I'm going back to Australia. I'm going to change my flight and fly out Monday when the wedding is over.'

'Now that *will* look suspicious! Let's just calm down. When the police find out you had a relationship with him, they'll want to speak to you. And that will lead them to me. Then they'll discover my connection to him. We can't lie and say we never went there in case of the small chance someone saw us, or CCTV caught us in the area. So we say we did go there to have it all out with him and find out what he was playing at, but there was no answer. We don't have to say we found him dead.'

Lucas bursts into the room and shoves two books at me. '*The Kid Who Came From Space* and *Shark in the Park*,' he squeals in excitement.

'Two of my favourites.' I try to infuse energy into my voice, but it emerges as a high-pitched whine. 'Let's go and snuggle up on the sofa and read.' I place the three mugs on the tray. My hands are shaking so much, I spill the drinks.

'Silly Mummy,' Lucas yells.

India grabs a cloth and wipes up the mess, shaking her head at me.

In the lounge, Lucas sits between us on the sofa. India's eyes meet mine over the top of his head. A meeting of shared agony. I take deep breaths, trying to control the anxiety in my voice as I read the story of the boy with a new telescope. When I finish, I kiss the top of Lucas's head and hand out the mugs of hot chocolate. 'Now drink up,' I say. 'One more story, and it's bed. You've got a big day tomorrow.'

'Why's your voice all funny, Mum?' He stares up at me. His beautiful brown eyes, and his innocence, make me want to cry.

'Is it? I didn't notice.'

While India reads *The Kid Who Came From Space*, Johnny's kind and loving face haunts me. I ball my fists and hold them to my mouth, biting my knuckles as I think about him meeting Dean last week, and the conversation between the two of them that led to Dean's death and Johnny's disappearance.

There has to be a connection.

And I fear it all has to do with the Caxton family.

SIXTY-FIVE

'You look stunning,' I say, trying to contain the whirlwind of different emotions in my voice. My body is here, but my head is in several other places.

Roughly this time last week, Carrie was helping me into my wedding dress in the hotel suite at Maple Manor, and the same tingling excitement mingled with nervousness had been rushing through me as it is my sister at this moment.

I continuously stifle yawns. It was well past two thirty before I turned the lights out this morning. I'd gone through the papers in that envelope twice more but could find nothing to spark a reason as to why Johnny collected all those documents.

'That's a pretty dress, Aunty Carrie.' Lucas looks cute in his grey suit and waistcoat, and a vibrant green bow tie that matches India's and my bridesmaids' dresses. I feel like a stick of asparagus. 'You look like a princess.' He wraps his skinny arms around my legs. 'So do you, Mum.'

Carrie gives a coy smile as she spins one-eighty in her A-line wedding gown with a beaded bodice and long beaded sleeves. 'Let's get some photos.'

I'm not sure who is more troubled: India or me, but we're

both doing a remarkable job at covering up our fear and exhaustion, helped by how fast the morning has whizzed by. Hairdressers and beauticians have waved their magic brushes and helped to conceal the anxiety we're all feeling for different reasons.

Before I know it, we're walking down the aisle. It's awkward. Tom and I haven't spoken since the altercation after the pub, and he refuses to meet my eye. I grit my teeth. I can't ruin my sister's day, but I'll be having it out with him tomorrow.

It's hard to suppress my emotions when the happy couple exchange their vows.

What kind of family am I now officially part of?

They've chosen traditional vows, whereas Johnny and I had written our own vows, concrete promises of riding the highs and lows of life together forever.

I touch my belly.

This is the year of loss.

* * *

When we arrive back at the marquee, Lucas approaches me with the triplets and their grandmother, Diane, who he's been hanging out with. Along with Angela and her daughter, she kindly agreed to look after him for the day with the triplets.

'Mum, we're bored. We want to build a snowman.'

The four of them jump up and down like a court of kangaroos. 'Can we,' one of the triplets says. 'Can we?'

I shake my head steadfastly. 'Not in those lovely clothes. You'll ruin them.'

Diane laughs. 'Exactly what I told them.'

'Please, Mum. Please,' Lucas begs.

'I said, no, darling. You can't have your photo taken in muddy clothes.'

All four of them kick up a fuss, a chorus of pleases I satiate with promises I'll help them build their snowman tomorrow morning, when we return here for the send-off breakfast. The last official wedding celebration to be endured.

My appetite is shot to pieces. I pick at the melon wrapped in prosciutto starter and hardly touch the mini-Christmas dinner served afterwards, or the oddly coloured green cheesecake that matches our bridesmaids' dresses. India doesn't eat much either. We made a pact before we left the house that we wouldn't speak about Dean today, but we can't help constantly exchanging looks of confusion seeped in dreaded fear. And I can't help checking my phone to see if there's any further news related to his body being found.

Alan steps in for our dad and delivers the father-of-the-bride's speech, a variation no doubt of the one he'd planned for me last week. I can't look, only listen. Tom stands next. His speech is packed with adoration for his beautiful bride, the love of his life. But when he thanks the bridesmaids, his vision remains fixed on India.

I contemplate what Johnny wrote in his speech but quickly banish the speculation from my mind. I'll never find out.

Roddy, the best man, addresses the guests and begins his speech, explaining how he and Tom met at school. 'He got into a fight with Johnny.'

Gasps sound across the marquee, tinged with a ring of awkwardness at the mention of Johnny's name, but that could be my imagination. 'I was head boy and had to pull them apart. I told them it was crazy for brothers to fight.'

Alan leans into me. 'I'm sorry, Hannah. I asked everyone not to mention Johnny today.'

Roddy drops his cue cards. At first, I think it's part of the ploy to entertain the two hundred guests. The cards spill to the floor. I lean backwards in my chair, staring at him at the other end of the top table, bending to scoop them up. 'Silly me!' he says. The young children in the crowd giggle. 'Now they're all out of order.'

His words strike a chord in me. But I can't work out why. 'I'm such a donkey.' He laughs. 'Just give me a sec.' He shuffles the cards into the correct order and continues his speech. 'People have travelled far and wide. We have Carrie's sister India, who has travelled all the way from Australia. Angela's sister and her family, who come all the way from the States. Pike and his missus, who've flown down from Scotland. And Alan's brother and his wife, who drove across the country for six hours from Dumfries yesterday.' He picks up his half-empty glass. 'Ladies and gentlemen, let's raise a toast—'

I stop listening.

Dumfries.

My mind goes into overdrive as I make the connection.

I need to get home.

The rest of the day drags. All I want to do is go home and qualify my thoughts. Tune myself in to Johnny's workings within that envelope.

I go through the motions – clapping when the bride and groom cut the ivory and gold seven-tier wedding cake and pretending to enjoy watching their first dance. I've never wanted to be elsewhere so badly.

The DJ changes the music to dancefloor fillers, Abba followed by, ironically, 'I Will Survive'. Didn't he read the script? It's a wedding for goodness' sake.

Lucas chases his new friends around the dancefloor.

Of course I will survive. I have a child.

Thankfully, Carrie and Tom depart early, and I can escape, too. I'm grateful Lucas doesn't protest too much. He's had a busy week and is as shattered as me. Angela's eagle eyes see me slipping away.

'Leaving so early?'

I keep the conversation short. 'I've got a migraine coming on.'

'I understand. Today couldn't have been easy for you.' Her kindness catches me off guard. Only forty-eight hours ago, she kicked me out of the office. But I know all too well that the mask of compassion can easily fool.

* * *

When I get home, my head is killing me. I pop a couple of pills. I need to stay focused. After removing my bridesmaid dress, I slip into my pyjamas and settle Lucas before hurrying downstairs to the envelope I hid in the dresser in the kitchen.

I carefully remove the contents and find the sections I need.

I was right.

It was there in plain sight all along.

Tom never carried out the health and safety check on that marquee.

He was responsible for Rachel's spinal injuries and that man's death.

SIXTY-SIX

'I don't know what you're getting at,' India says when she finally gets home and I show her my findings. It's well past one o'clock. She took one for the team and stayed until the bitter end.

'Can't you see?' I point at the piece of paper. 'Tom supposedly completed a health and safety inspection report of the marquee that he signed and dated. But it's all a sham. Johnny was onto him.'

She pours a glass of water. 'Onto him? I don't follow.'

'Tom couldn't have carried out the health and safety check because he was in Dumfries the day before the accident, and he stayed in a hotel there that night. It's a six-hour drive away, and he had another meeting on the journey back the following day that he definitely attended. There's an email to prove it. That's why there's a copy of the Dumfries hotel receipt here. Johnny had been collecting all this evidence.'

India blinks. Her tired brain appears to be trying to process it all.

'And what's more. Remember when Roddy dropped his cue cards during the speech? When he picked them up, he said they were out of order. Something about that resonated with me.' I lick my finger and thumb through the papers until I find the relevant ones to show her. 'The health and safety report numbers for that period are out of sequence, further proving that the one for the marquee incident was forged.'

'So, what are you saying?'

'Tom wrote that report at a later date. He never carried out that health and safety check. He covered his tracks by faking the report.'

'These are pretty hefty allegations, Han.'

'But it makes sense.'

'But I thought it was proved that unexpected high winds caused the accident.'

'Yes, but I think there must've been something wrong with the construction that a safety report would've picked up. I reckon Johnny saw the newspaper article, which rekindled thoughts of the accident. Something didn't sit comfortably with him, so he started digging. Look at the donation. He wanted the company to do their bit in doing something good.'

India remains confused. 'But surely he would've told you all about it?'

I sigh. 'I don't know. Perhaps he wanted to spare me the grief, or perhaps the family were dead set against the donation. So he blackmailed them, and didn't want me to be any part of it. That's why Tom's been so defensive about me asking about the accident.' I take a deep breath and slowly release it. 'I'm scared his family have done something to him. And now I'm scared Tom's onto me because I've been asking about it. And it's why Angela wanted me away from the office.'

Her mouth opens. 'How can you say that? They're our family now.'

'Think about it. After the accident, they've been desperate to maintain the success of the company. Who knows what end they would go to.'

'But doing something to Johnny? No, Han.'

'I've told you Tom's been acting strange towards me.' I drop my head backwards and stare at the ceiling. 'I don't know what to think anymore.' I can't separate my thoughts. They are all tangled into a mess of grief and sorrow. 'I'm scared for Carrie, as well. What kind of family is she now mixed up in? Are we now mixed up in?'

'Do you think you should go to the police now?'

She's fixated with involving the police. I need to make her see sense. It's a route I simply can't go down.

'I've said before, the last people we need meddling around at the moment is the police.' I pause, before asking, 'Do you think Carrie knows?'

'I doubt it.'

'You never know. She would've done anything to ensure that wedding went ahead.'

'What are we going to do?'

'Have it out with Tom. And find out where Johnny really is.'

SIXTY-SEVEN

I awake to another pounding headache. Thump. Thump. Thump. I try to lift my head off the pillow, but a sharp pain cuts me to the quick. This is not the time for a migraine. I have to be on my best game today. I need to take some tablets, fast. Otherwise, I won't stand a chance of powering through the day.

Lucas flies into the room as if he's been catapulted. He slams his hands on the bed. 'Wake up, Mum. We're going to build that snowman.' He dances from foot to foot.

The sound of his voice cuts through me. It's excruciating, like someone is shaking a set of maracas in my ears. My eyeballs hurt to stay open. But I won't be beaten. 'Go and get me a glass of water, can you, darling, please?' A whisper is all I can manage. 'And please be quiet. My head's hurting, and Aunty India is still asleep.'

'No, she's not, she's downstairs.' He bounces out of the room.

Reaching out an arm, I pat the bedside table, fumbling to locate my phone. I text India to come and help me. Some tablets and an hour with my eyes closed then I'll have to assess the situation. Either I'll be bedridden all day, or I should be able to struggle out of bed.

'Get me some tablets,' I whisper when she arrives with a glass of water. 'They're in the drawer. I can't move my head.'

'You look dreadful.' She pops two paracetamol from the packet.

'I need four. I can't afford to be ill.'

'You can't take four.'

'I do when it's this bad.' Taking four makes me groggy and kills my appetite, but it's the only way to murder this beast.

Murder.

The word intensifies the pain.

'You need to go to the doctor's, Han. Get some prescription medication. You can't carry on like this.'

'It's the stress. I'll be OK after I've spoken to Johnny.'

If I ever get to speak to him again. The little sleep I managed to get last night was filled with grotesque dreams of Johnny's body lying on a cold slab in a morgue.

An hour later, I stagger out of bed. It's freezing. I've managed to ward off a full-blown migraine, but I'm lightheaded and feel queasy. I want to go back to bed, but there's no time. I've been thinking of nothing else all night. I need to get to Highland Hall and find out what the hell is going on.

I look in the bathroom mirror as I clean my teeth. Heavy bags shadow the area beneath my eyes, and I'm deathly pale. I apply some mascara and blusher and throw on warm clothes.

Downstairs, Lucas is holding a carrot, raring to go. 'Hurry up, Mum. They'll be waiting for me to build the snowman.' He waves the carrot at me. 'I've got the nose.'

I drive us to Highland Hall. The nausea I've felt since I got out of bed refuses to subside. The deep sense of foreboding inching through me isn't helping. I go through the Caxton family in my head: Angela, Alan and Tom. And now my sister, officially a member of the Caxton clan, wondering who I can trust anymore. I'm so wrapped up in a heavy blanket of suspicion that I'm second-guessing everyone.

India opens a packet of chewing gum and offers a piece to me.

The queasiness intensifies. I gag. I clutch my tummy.

No way. I can't be.

My hand moves to my breast.

I gasp.

I remember this feeling from when I was pregnant with Lucas, and earlier this year when I fell pregnant with our angel baby: the tender breasts, the extreme nausea, and the aversion to the smell of anything minty.

I panic.

I'm not ready for another baby.

SIXTY-EIGHT

I touch my other breast.

I am.

I'm definitely pregnant.

I've put it down to wedding nerves and the aftermath of Johnny leaving me, but it's why I've been feeling so sick. Fresh terror grows within me. I don't want to have a baby on my own again.

My mind is whirling when we arrive at Highland Hall. Alan directs us to the boot room. 'The boys are eager to build this snowman,' he says with an affectionate roll of his eyes. 'Carrie and Tom are on their way.'

The boot room is a large, windowless wood-panelled room at the side of the main house. It contains an array of discarded family coats, shoes and boots from years gone by. They are used by visitors who like to go walking around the grounds. I've always found it rather creepy in here. The gloomy light doesn't help.

Angela greets us, fussing around the highly animated triplets, who are dressed in matching red snowsuits with fur hoods. Lucas adds to the cacophony of excitement, which is doing nothing for my fragile head and queasiness.

I brush my hand over my belly.

This could be it.

The glue that sticks me and Johnny back together again.

Angela hands me a bag. 'I forgot to tell you. I found these cheap online and bought them for the triplets and thought Lucas might like one. He hasn't got a snowsuit, has he?'

Her generosity takes me aback. I eye her warily, recalling what I've discovered about this family. 'That's so kind of you.'

I zone out. The thought of having another baby alone is frightening.

Angela waves a hand in my face. 'Are you listening, Hannah? Does Lucas have any boots?'

I shake my head. The triplets are all wearing snow boots. 'Only trainers, but I've brought a spare pair he can change into.'

'There're some of the boys' old snow boots somewhere.' She crouches and searches one of the boxes beneath a built-in clothes rack that runs the length of the wall. 'Alan's been tidying up in here.'

Lucas is so euphoric that he's going to be dressed the same as the triplets, he can barely contain his excitement. The noise level rises. Angela tells them all to quieten, but it's a fruitless request. They fool around, pulling faces at each other like clowns. 'He put some stuff in the cellar. Go and take a look, would you, please? They'll be in the large trunk at the far end if they're there.'

I grimace as I open the door. A sour smell hits me. It adds another layer to the nausea that's making me retch. I grope for the light switch. A ladder with nine or ten rungs acts as makeshift steps as the staircase collapsed a few years ago. I slowly climb down, precariously clinging onto each rung, relieved when my feet hit the concrete floor. The dank smell is overwhelming. Or is that something stronger? It smells of a dead rat down here.

I worm my way around boxes, old tins of paint and disused pieces of gardening equipment, holding my nose, until I find the large trunk.

'Have you found them?' Angela calls down. Her voice echoes around the gloomy-lit space.

The smell is getting unbearable. I need to get out of here before I'm sick. I rummage through the stack of old coats and footwear until I come across some children's snow boots. I check the size. Twelve. That'll do.

I return upstairs. 'I think there's a dead rat or something down there. It smells dreadful.'

'Not again!' She shakes her head irritably. 'We had one a few months ago. It's these old houses. I'll get Alan to take a look. If you want to go outside, wrap up warm. It's freezing out there.' She pulls a basket from the shelves below the hanging coats. 'There're plenty of hats and gloves in here.' She sifts through the contents, picking up items and dropping them. 'Help yourself.'

I consider joining the boys. The fresh air might help clear my head. There's too much going on in there. I need to clear the noise and work out what's important now.

Because things have changed.

SIXTY-NINE

Carrie and Tom have arrived when we return to the kitchen. I fade into the background energy of the newlyweds, gagging at the smell of cooked bacon. I go to fetch a glass of water, grabbing the side of the butler sink when another tide of nausea depletes me.

People merge into small groups, picking at the buffet breakfast. 'If anyone's cold I've lit a fire in the living room,' Alan calls out. A cork flies across the room as he cracks open a bottle of champagne to toast the happy couple.

I've finished my glass of water when Tom appears beside me. The panic and hormones and the situation I'm now in get the better of me. I need to find Johnny more than anything.

'I know what you've done,' I whisper, although with all the noise no one can hear me.

'What?'

'You've got blood on your hands.' I can't believe I'm being so brave.

'What *are* you talking about?'

'You forged the health and safety check documentation for that marquee accident.'

His face pales. He glances around the room. Everyone is engrossed in conversation. He takes hold of my arm, forcing me around so our backs are turned to the room.

'The marquee collapsed because something was wrong with the setup, wasn't it?' I say. 'You were just lucky there was a storm that day, and you had the weather to blame for the accident.'

'What are you on about? There was a full investigation. The company was exonerated.'

'But if your negligence was proven, you'd be facing a manslaughter charge. Coupled with the forged documents, you'd be put away for a very long time. And Caxton Events would be no more.'

'You're talking absolute rubbish. Caxton Events had nothing to do with the situation.'

'But the owners did!'

I contain the volume of my voice, but I can't hide the emotion. 'Johnny was onto you. I know he was. You were in Dumfries the day you were meant to carry out the health and safety check on that marquee. And you stayed there that night. Johnny had it all worked out. He wouldn't want you going to prison, but he would want the wrong put right. Rachel told me you two had argued. So what really happened to Johnny, Tom? Because I sure know he's not in Wales.'

'You're deluded,' he snaps. 'Your sister was right. You're crazy.'

'What?'

'My brother didn't want to marry you. Full stop. Deal with it.'

A hand stabs my shoulder. We both startle. 'What are you two talking about?' Carrie frowns. Her eyes flit between the two of us.

'We were just talking about Roddy's speech yesterday.' Tom repeats one of the best man's jokes. 'Hannah was just going to check on the boys, weren't you?' He takes Carrie's hand. 'Come on, wife. Let's mingle.'

Crazy. Carrie called me crazy?

I go to grab my sister's shoulder but stop. This isn't the time or the place.

I can't stay here any longer. I'm going to get my boy and go.

From the selection of footwear lined up in the boot room, I find a pair of Angela's wellie boots. They are a little on the large side, but they'll do. I pull a woolly hat and a pair of thick black gloves from the basket she showed me earlier, and head outside.

The freezing air catches in my throat. My feet are numb from the cold, and I can't stop shaking. I need time to think about my next move.

Tom is as guilty as hell. Anyone else would go to the police. But I don't know what to do for the best.

The sky is as grey as my mood. Snowflakes fall on my face. The triplets are rolling an ever-increasing ball of snow to make the body of the snowman. 'Where's Lucas?' I panic, scanning the grounds. The snow absorbs my voice. They don't hear me. I run to them. 'Where's Lucas, boys?'

One of the triplets breaks free from his brothers. 'He's gone to get some twigs for the snowman's arms.'

'Where?'

He points to the small, wooded area beyond the gardens. 'Over there in the trees.'

Irrational or not, fear rushes through me. A wave of panic telling me that I shouldn't be letting my boy out of my sight.

I hurry towards the dense tree area, the fallen snow hindering my steps.

Lucas appears at the entrance, his red snowsuit like a drop of blood against the white of the snow. I call out his name, telling him to hurry up. He runs towards me holding out an arm. 'I've found some treasure, Mum!'

He hands me a small brown velvet box.

It's at this moment I know for sure I'll never see Johnny again.

SEVENTY

I don't know how I prevent myself from collapsing.

Lucas's face is bright red from the cold. His teeth are chattering. 'Open it.'

I can't let him see what's inside this box. I pretend to lift the lid off. 'It's stuck.' I grab his shoulders. 'What did I tell you about staying where I could see you?'

'You're hurting me, Mum.'

I release my grip. 'Where did you get this from?'

His face crumples at the urgency in my voice. He points to the wooded area. 'In there.'

'Where in there?' I'm shouting.

The sight of his trembling bottom lip stabs at my heart. 'By the logs,' he mutters.

I kiss his flushed cheek. 'Hurry back to the others and finish that snowman, darling. We need to get going.'

'It's too hard. Come and help us, Mum.'

'I'll be there in a bit.'

He tootles off, picking up speed.

I wait for him to join the boys before I wade through the snow. My legs are weak and wobbly with fear. I keep checking behind me to ensure Lucas hasn't decided to follow me. But he has rejoined the triplets.

The sky has darkened. It's eerie around here and reminds me of when India and I went to Dean's house. I identify the logs Lucas was talking about and rush to them, checking every couple of steps to ensure I'm alone. I perch on the knee-height pile and bend over to catch my breath. More than ever, I need to remain calm. A noise makes me sit bolt upright. The hairs on the back of my neck stand to attention. I glance around me, but there's no one in sight.

It's only then that I can stomach opening the box.

I breathe deeply, shuddering as I release each breath. With shaking fingers, I lift the lid.

My bottom lip trembles at the sight of Johnny's and my wedding rings. I glance around frantically. He's here. I know it. It's as if I can feel his presence, his voice in the wind whipping around me.

Where are you, Johnny?
What have they done to you?
'What are you doing?'

I turn, confronted by Tom's large frame hurtling towards me. He looks like a hunter seeking his prey. 'You can't be here!' he gasps.

I stand. 'Why not?' My eyes sting with tears. 'Why can't I be here, Tom?' I'm beyond upset. My world is caving in on me, and I'm convinced the person responsible is standing before me.

He's breathless. 'It... it's dangerous. We... we've laid snares for the rabbits.' He stammers. 'They... they've been digging up the garden. Damn nuisance.' His gaze flits deeper into the trees. 'Just get out of here.'

'You've deceived me, Tom Caxton. But not anymore.' I stretch out my arm, holding the open box in my shaking hand. 'Where's Johnny, Tom? What have you done with your brother?'

'Christ, Hannah. Where did you find that?' He reaches to take the box, ignoring my rebuke.

I swipe my hand out of the way, vigorously shaking my head. 'Cut the innocence. I know what you are, Tom. You're a murderer.'

He takes a single step backwards, blinking. 'Hannah, you're upset. This whole business has taken its toll on you. It would anyone. Come back inside. Let's join the others. It's freezing out here.'

I spin around, scanning the area for any disturbance in the snow-covered ground. There, about twenty metres to the right of where we're standing, is a small mound – could it be? 'Johnny?' My voice is a whisper lost in grief.

I turn back to Tom, my eyes wide, incredulous, questioning. 'Murderer,' I yell.

He glares at me, the word momentarily shaking him.

Tears sting my face. The realisation I've felt for a while – that something truly terrible has happened to Johnny – hits me harder than I can bear. 'Murderer!' I scream again.

Tom thrusts back his shoulders. He juts out his chin, sneering down on me, his voice cold and heartless. 'Well, it takes one to know one, Hannah!'

SEVENTY-ONE

My voice shakes with rage and grief. 'What's that meant to mean?'

Tom's countenance has changed. His eyes bulge with evilness. 'You murdered Charlie Ferguson. I know you did.'

My stomach turns. How does he even know that name? 'What're you talking about? Who's Charlie Ferguson?'

His head jolts backwards. A raucous laugh fills the cold air. 'You know, they say that blood is thicker than water. But it isn't when it comes to marriage. Carrie told me all about what happened to Charlie.'

I stand stock-still, silent, trying to digest his words.

'It's troubled her, you know. Deeply troubled her for all these years. That her own sister left her fiancé for dead, and then lied to the police. She broke down earlier in the week and confessed all... after a little encouragement from me.'

'No!' I say. It's all I can manage.

Carrie! How could you?

'But, you see, I already knew about Charlie.'

I stare at him in disbelief. 'I don't know who you mean.' I'm not the least bit convincing. Snow falls. I brush flakes from my face.

He smirks. 'Oh, I think you do.' He paces up and down in front of me. 'I coaxed the truth from Carrie.' He glances around as if checking no one can hear our conversation. 'Her truth, anyway. But her truth isn't the real truth, is it, Hannah?'

I grab at the pile of logs for support. 'I don't know what the hell you're on about.'

'Don't take me for a fool. Johnny had a visit from Dean Ferguson last Friday.'

The mention of Dean's name strikes another bolt of fear through me. Dread weighs me down. It's making me feel dizzy.

'He was due to meet Johnny on Friday. He planned to tell him that the woman he was marrying was a murderer.'

'You're lying. Johnny wasn't here on Friday afternoon. He got stuck in traffic.'

'Yes! But he rearranged to meet Dean after he dropped Lucas off with Mum and Dad.' He clears his throat. 'You pushed Charlie off that balcony that night, didn't you, Hannah?'

My voice is full of raw panic. 'That's not true.'

'Oh, I think it is. Carrie thought so, too. That's why you ran away at first.'

'Carrie said that?'

He smirks. He's toying with me.

'What did Dean say to Johnny?'

'He didn't say anything.' A look of venom forms on his face. 'They didn't get to meet.'

'What? Why?' He's confusing me. 'Where is Johnny, Tom?'

'My own brother was going to betray me.' His hands ball into fists. His eyes bulge. He looks as if he has lost his senses.

'Betray you? How?'

'It seems you've already come across the evidence he was collecting.'

I gasp as the realisation dawns. 'It was you who came to Johnny's apartment last Sunday morning, wasn't it?' I rub my forehead, trying to work out the course of events. 'You never went to the hotel that morning, did you? You went to Dean's house.'

He claps. The round of applause echoes around the woods like thunder. 'Of course I went to the hotel. I'm not stupid. Like you had to that night you killed Charlie, I had to cover my tracks. I told Carrie I was going to the gym before the hotel. I just didn't tell her I never made it to the gym and where I went instead.'

I think back to last Sunday morning, when I was with him and Carrie at their house. He was agitated. But I put it down to everything that had gone on. He was meant to be enjoying his upcoming wedding. Instead he'd been left to clear up Johnny's mess. 'But you wouldn't have had enough time.'

'It's surprising how far you can get on a Sunday morning when there's no traffic on the road.'

I'm panicking. 'What have you done to your brother, Tom?'

He scoffs.

I slowly shake my head. I need to keep my wits about me.

I've been so wrapped up in Johnny, I never noticed before.

How dangerous this man standing before me is.

SEVENTY-TWO

I can't believe I got this guy so wrong. He's been like a brother to me. 'So how was Johnny going to betray you?'

'Your perfect Johnny was threatening to expose the cover-up if I didn't agree to his stupid bloody donation. He was going to tell Mum and Dad about me faking the health and safety report. Alan wouldn't have let it lie. It would've been the end of the company. The company my mum and me have worked our arses off to build.'

My mind is spinning in circles. 'So Angela's in on this?'

He points a finger at me. His voice is as bitter cold as the air. 'You keep my parents out of it. They know nothing.'

'But they agreed to the donation. That's why you were so mad with Johnny. They sided with him over you.' I pause, preparing myself. 'So what has happened to Johnny, Tom?'

'It was an accident.'

'What was?'

'We had a fight.'

'And?'

'He hit me.'

'And?'

'He bloody hurt me. So I shoved him back.' He shrugs. 'He fell awkwardly,' he adds matter-of-factly as if he's reciting a line from a storybook.

I can't believe this man has fooled us all this past week. He's been stressed, yes. But I put that down to pre-wedding nerves and Johnny supposedly dumping me at the altar!

'Where?' I gasp. My chest is so tight I'm struggling to breathe. 'Where did this happen?' I have to know where my Johnny took his last breath.

'In the office. By his desk. There was nothing I could do.' His face remains as cold as stone. I no longer know this man.

I press my gloved hands on my forehead and drag them down my face. 'Where is he now? What've you done with him?'

He glances at the pile of logs.

A chilling sensation freezes my bones. I let out a low scream. 'He's under these, isn't he?' I touch one of the logs. 'You're evil. You murdered him! You're a murderer.'

His face contorts. 'As I said. It takes one to know one.'

I catch my breath. 'And Dean? What happened to him in all this?' My hand shoots to my mouth. I gasp as the realisation dawns. 'He was there. He saw, didn't he? He came to meet Johnny at the offices and witnessed you murder him.'

'The fool tried to blackmail me.' He gives another manic laugh.

The pieces of this troublesome puzzle I've been trying to solve are finally falling into place. I haven't been going mad. I've been right all along. 'He tried to blackmail you, so you murdered him as well.' I think back to Dean turning up at my door that night. 'Hannah! Hannah! I need to talk to you.'

'He fell in love with your sister, you know. He sought her out to find you, not realising he'd fall for her. He came to tell you about what happened to Johnny, but your reaction scared him off. Thankfully. You did me a favour there, so, thank you.'

I want to wipe that smirk off his face. 'How did he find me?'

'Through Carrie's Facebook page.' He eyes me curiously. 'How do you know he's dead?'

I refuse to betray India. 'I read about it in the news.'

He shakes his head and laughs. 'You're such a liar, Hannah Young. Hell knows how you've managed to escape prison all these years.'

'Stop turning this on me. You murdered Dean because he witnessed what you did to Johnny and was going to expose you! He came to tell me that night. I know he did.'

'You really are a good little detective. Perhaps you should join the police now you're out of a job. Coz you're not coming back.'

'I don't give a damn about Caxton Events anymore.'

He gives a throaty cackle.

'You've been following me, too. Why?'

He jilts his head forwards. 'That's your paranoia. I always said to Carrie there was something not quite right about you.' He points a finger to his temple and turns it in circles. 'There's a screw loose in that crazy head of yours.'

'You're the devil.'

He snarls in my face. 'Then you're the devil's sister-in-law.'

I stare at him, incredulous. 'You made up things about Johnny to keep me from suspecting you. He was never a womaniser, or unreliable. And he never felt trapped. How do you think you're going to get away with it? What happens when the police find out Johnny really is missing, Tom? When he doesn't come back from Wales. Because Alan will report it at some point. They'll know he never went to Wales from his phone records.'

'Johnny's phone is now at Dean's house.'

I pause, processing what he's just told me. 'You've set Johnny up for Dean's murder?' I'm stunned at the gravity of his betrayal. 'But Johnny's phone will be full of evidence about what you did.'

'You don't give him, or me, enough credit. We only conversed face-to-face about the marquee incident.'

'You'll never get away with it,' I cry. 'You faked all those text messages from him as well! How could you?' I drop the ring box. I bend to pick it up.

He shoves me. 'Give that to me.' He scoops the box off the ground.

I try to grab it. 'No. It's mine.'

'We can't afford to leave any evidence.' He straightens up. 'So let me tell you how this is going to play out, Hannah Young.'

I can't bear to look at him. I drop my head. I have to get away from here.

'If I go down,' he says, 'then so do you.'

I slowly lift my head. 'What?'

'If you go to the police with any of this, then I tell them that you murdered Charlie.'

'That's hearsay, Tom. And you damn well know it. You don't have an ounce of proof. Neither did Dean.'

'You're still denying it!' He scoffs. 'It's irrelevant now, anyway. And even though Carrie doesn't know for sure that you murdered Charlie, she knows you left him when you could've saved him. You left a man for dead. And I will tell the police as much.'

I stare at him, speechless.

'That's right! If I go down, so do you, Hannah. And so do your sisters.'

SEVENTY-THREE

'Sisters? What's India got to do with this? You'd really throw your new wife to the dogs?'

He nods and laughs. Turning on his heel, he tosses the velvet box in the air like a ball and catches it before placing it in his pocket and heading for the house.

I spin around, engulfed by an eerie sensation. I touch one of the logs. My Johnny is here. I want to get down on my hands and knees and remove every log until I find him.

But for now I have to think of my boy.

I have to protect Lucas.

He needs me here.

Not behind bars.

And so does my baby.

The snow intensifies, flakes as large as pennies, and the sky darkens to a deep threatening grey. I rush to Lucas and the triplets, trying to repress the sickness pushing through me. 'We need to go in. The weather's getting too bad.'

'No!' the four red-faced boys call out in unison.

'We have to finish, Mum,' Lucas says. 'We still have to make our snowman's head.'

'Be quick, then.'

I turn on my heel. I can't leave it here.

I stomp back to the boot room.

Tom is brushing snow off his shoes as I enter. He peers over his shoulder. 'I reckon there's going to be another big dump of snow. Don't you? Perhaps Carrie and I should make a move to the airport a little earlier. What do you say?'

It's as if the conversation we've just had never happened.

'My feet are wet through,' he says. 'So are my blimmin' socks.'

I'm astounded at the conversational tone to his voice. I clench my fists.

He walks towards the cellar. 'Mum said she thinks there's a dead rat down here.' He stops at the entrance and glances into the cellar.

He thinks I'm going to let this rest.

A darkness overcomes me. A shadow as leaden as the sky. The same threatening sensation that overcame me the day I discovered I was pregnant with Lucas.

My boy. My baby.

I have to protect my children.

And myself. I promised myself I'd never have another man controlling my life again.

Tom sticks his head into the cellar and sniffs. 'Crikey. I see what you mean. It stinks down there.' His hand scrambles to find the light switch.

Sometimes the opportunity presents itself.

And a reassuring whisper flutters in your ear, telling you that you have nowhere else to go.

A serene calmness overcomes me, like a reassuring blanket of comfort that wraps itself around me and tells me everything will be OK.

I advance at a pace, launching myself at my brother-in-law.

And with my gloved hand, thrust him hurtling into the darkness of the cellar.

SEVENTY-FOUR

His skull cracks on the bricked floor below. The sound is as sickening and shocking as it is satisfying. There's no way he could've survived the fall.

But I need to make sure.

I should know by experience.

There's no use in a job half done.

Taking deep breaths, I peer into the darkness of the cellar. Think. Think. 'You have to think on your feet here, Han,' I mutter to myself. I can't go down there. I look around me. Think!

I switch on the light and lean over the threshold. Luck is on my side. A telling comfort that I've done the right thing. The lower rungs of the ladder are lying atop Tom's legs. It must have given way when he fell.

I wait a few minutes, just to make sure.

I can't make the same mistake a second time.

From what I see, his head lies in a pool of blood the same as Charlie's that fateful night. I heave. So much blood. I crouch on my haunches and stare intently at his upper back, ignoring the blood, looking for the rise and fall of his chest. But there's no movement. I watch intently for another couple of minutes.

I'm safe.

He's gone. He must be.

I move aside a pile of the triplets' clothes and sit on the wooden bench, willing myself not to be sick. Coldness seeps deeper into my bones. I drop my heavy head into my hands. My voice whispers in the winter quietness, 'You did it for your boy, Hannah. Your boy.' I touch my belly. 'And your baby.'

Getting up, I walk to the back door, and stare out the glass panel.

Life goes on.

The snowman stands, his stone eyes glaring at me as if he has witnessed what I've just done. The four boys are coming in, their little legs wading through the snow. I rush to the cellar door and recheck below.

I turn off the light but leave the door slightly ajar.

I'm pretty sure I'm safe. Again.

SEVENTY-FIVE

SEVEN YEARS AGO

I waited seven days after my period didn't show. A torturous week I spent hoping and praying as my breasts swelled and the queasiness intensified.

But I knew.

I'd read online about the tender breasts and extreme tiredness in the first trimester. And then there was the sickness that tortured me from dawn until I succumbed to sleep each night.

On the way home from work the previous night, I'd popped into the pharmacy and bought the kit. Those tests are more accurate if taken first thing in the day, I'd read online. Charlie had been particularly attentive that morning. He always was after one of his outbursts that left cuts and bruises beneath my clothes, and scars in my head that had no chance of ever healing. 'I'll make it up to you, babe,' he whispered, stroking my hair. 'Dinner tonight.'

My heart thumped in my ears like the sound of a loud drum. I didn't dare remind him I wanted to go to a friend's birthday – a night that had been arranged before we'd even got together. He wasn't in the right mood.

'I'm meeting the lads after work, but I'll be home by seven.

I'll go shopping today. Steak and chips, your favourite.' He ran his forefinger from the bruise on my neck up to my mouth and traced it around my lips. 'What do you think?'

'Sure.'

'I love you, babe.' He kissed my neck. The tingles those kisses caused in the early days no longer appeared. They got lost along the way in the beatings and constant verbal abuse that left me numb to his touch. 'It won't happen again. I promise you.'

I nodded and, heaven knows how, or why, I managed to smile.

When his truck roared out of the driveway, I ran to the toilet and collected the sample. Three minutes later, it was confirmed.

Another life was growing inside of me.

* * *

All day, I considered my options while helping the older people in the care home where I worked. I had to find a way to escape the cage he'd locked me in. And not only for me anymore. His words echoed in my mind as I dumped a serving of mashed potato beside a piece of cod in parsley sauce. *You can never leave me, you know, babe. You and me, we're good together. I'm never going to let you go. Never.*

But that was before I'd found out I was pregnant.

I'd been trying to pluck up the courage to leave for a while. But now there was no turning back. I had another life to consider.

But I had nowhere to go. My dad was dead and my mum in a home because of her early-onset dementia. India was travelling, and Carrie was about to join her for a few weeks in Asia. A trip I'd planned on joining, but Charlie put paid to that. My friends had all disappeared over the months I'd been with him. He'd made sure of that. I had some savings. Twenty-pound notes stuffed in a sock he didn't know about. A few weeks more, and I'd have enough to disappear to the seaside. Dunwich, where our parents took us on holiday when we were kids. He'd never find me there.

* * *

When I arrived home that evening, I stifled tears to see his truck parked at the side of the desolate driveway. He'd told me he was meeting his mates. I'd planned to sneak out before he got home, to meet Carrie and give her the birthday cake for our friend and be back before he returned. Now, he'd kick up a fuss about me wanting to go out again, and who knew how much that would flare his anger.

I trudged into the bedroom. It was freezing.

'That you, babe?' What was once a sound of pure delight now made my skin crawl.

I dropped my bag and walked to the double doors that opened onto the flat-roof balcony where Charlie was sitting on the railings. An outside light flicked on as I moved towards him. Smudges of white powder covered part of the plastic table beside a half-smoked joint balancing on the rim of an old chipped bowl.

Bile shot up my throat. His behaviour was always worse on the nights he took drugs. I knew I was in for a beating.

He turned to look at me. 'Where've you been?' he roared.

'Work.'

'Don't lie to me.' I could see it in his eyes – the unruffled calm before the storm of abuse.

I knew what was coming. The verbal abuse had begun; it was only a matter of minutes before it turned physical. He'd be off those railings before I'd even taken my coat off, and I'd be up against the wall with his hands around my neck.

LEFT AT THE ALTAR

He took the final puff of the cigarette he was smoking, flicked the butt into the air and turned his back on me.

'I thought you were going out,' I said.

He could detect the surging fear in my voice. I was sure of it. 'I came home early. Thought I'd have a few beers here with you.'

I felt my belly as darkness overcame me.

Sometimes the opportunity presents itself.

A moment of madness for which you have no control, helped by the reassuring whisper in my ear that my actions were for my baby.

I marched towards him.

And I pushed him.

I'll never forget the gasping sound. The sharp suction of air as he tried to clutch hold of the railings for his life, his eyes full of terror. But his body was already too far gone. His hands flapped as he grasped the thin night air, and he plunged to the hard ground.

The sickening thud from the patio below brought me to my senses.

I gripped my stomach with an intensity so strong, I gagged.

Now my child was safe.

And he'd never lay a finger on me again.

SEVENTY-SIX

I stoke the fire in the log burner. The fire I threw the pair of Angela's gloves on that I borrowed earlier. I can't have my DNA or traces of any fibre found on the deceased's body. What a saving grace that Alan lit it this morning.

I sit in the armchair by the crackling fire.

'I know this is difficult for you,' the female officer says. 'But could you tell us when you last spoke to your brother-in-law?'

Her voice is soft, unlike her male colleague, who sounds as if he's a heavy smoker. His skin, tinged yellow and crinkly, is a giveaway, too. They sit beside each other on the leather sofa, sipping tea that Angela's sister has just served.

While waiting for them to question Carrie, Angela and Alan, I methodically prepared what I was going to say when my turn came to face the firing line of their questions. I've lost Johnny. But those emotions need to wait. My priority is my son and my unborn child. I need to concentrate on staying around for them. I'm just grateful he left this earth still thinking of me as his princess.

'This morning.' I tell them about going outside to check on Lucas and bumping into Tom in the thicket. I need to cover all bases, layered with as much of the truth as I can pull off. 'He told me I had to get away.'

'Get away?'

'Out of the thicket. He said something about traps being laid for the rabbits. They'd been a nuisance.' I consider telling them about the box containing the wedding rings, but carefully does it, Han. They must've already found the box in Tom's coat pocket. Let them ask me about it, not the other way around.

As if he can read my thoughts, the male officer speaks. 'We found a jewellery box containing what we believe are you and your... your...' He stumbles, unsure how to refer to my dead fiancé. Not that they know he's dead yet. I need to be patient. I'll give them a little help along the way. But when the time comes, they need to believe they found out about Johnny's murder themselves.

The female officer butts in. 'Johnny.'

The male officer nods. 'Johnny's and your wedding rings.'

I gasp. 'Is that what was inside that box? My son found it in the thicket when he was looking for some twigs for his snowman. I couldn't open it, so I gave it to Tom.'

He frowns. 'So you'd never seen it before today?'

'No. Johnny and I chose our rings together, but he collected them from the jeweller the morning before the wedding, after they'd been engraved.' Thankfully, this is the truth. We were meant to go together, but I'd been too busy, so he'd gone alone.

I was really upset at the time, but sometimes you don't realise that fate has a part to play in how life pans out. I never was meant to go with him to pick up those rings.

I tilt my head sideways. 'What was it doing in the woods?'

'We're not sure, but it's something we'll be looking into.' The female officer repositions herself on the sofa. 'Tell us about your relationship with your brother-in-law.'

I sit in one of the pair of leather wingback chairs, biting my lip and shaking my head. 'We were close.'

'How close?' she asks.

'We worked together. And socialised a lot because... well.' I shrug. 'I was marrying his brother, and he was marrying my sister. I loved him like a brother.' I feign a snuffle. 'This is awful. I still can't believe it.'

'Can we ask you about what happened with Johnny?' the female officer asks.

I wipe my nose with a tissue from the box on the table. 'He went to Wales, but it doesn't add up. All I got from him was a text.'

Here we go. This is for you, Tom.

And for Johnny. Justice for my Johnny.

And for my Lucas. I've protected him once before, and I'll protect him again. I can't leave him without a mother. I won't.

'But I went to his apartment and found...' I tell the officers about the book and the Disneyland tickets, and everything else that doesn't equate to what Johnny did to me. Then I back off. I've dropped a few breadcrumbs, now let them navigate their way to finding out what really happened to Johnny Caxton and Dean Ferguson.

There'll be more questions along the way. Of course there will be. But I'll have them covered. Like I had them covered the night Charlie died. All I need is a little time and space to think all this through. Everything happens for a reason, my mum used to say. I'm now thankful Angela has given me the week off work. My mind races for what I need to do in the coming days. Returning that envelope to Johnny's apartment has to remain a priority.

'Did you ever consider going to the police about Johnny?' the female officer asks.

'What would've been the point? He was in contact with his brother. I trusted what Tom told me. Why? Do you think something's happened to him?'

'Rest assured,' the male officer says. 'We'll leave no stone unturned as we conduct our enquiries.'

'Thank you.' My bottom lip quivers, and that I'm not faking.

They conclude the interview. They'd like me to go to the station to make a formal statement.

'Of course. Is it OK if I do it tomorrow? I'd like to take my son home now. He's been through a lot.'

'We understand. Tomorrow's fine,' the male officer says. 'We're sorry for your loss, Hannah. What a terrible accident for the family, especially for your sister.'

'Tragic,' I say. 'We all loved Tom.'

I leave them and go to fetch Lucas with a deep sense of justice.

Do I feel any remorse for what I've done?

Yes, of course. I never intended for any of this to happen. But Tom led me down a dark hole I had to find a way out of.

I rest my hands on my belly.

As any mother would understand.

We'd do anything for our children.

Absolutely anything.

A LETTER FROM AJ CAMPBELL

Dear reader,

I want to say a huge thank you for choosing to read *Left at the Altar*.

I loved writing Hannah's story. If you enjoyed it and want to keep up to date with my latest releases, just sign up at the link below. Your email address will never be shared, and you can unsubscribe anytime.

www.bookouture.com/AJ-Campbell

In doing so, you will also receive a copy of my gripping short story 'Sweet Revenge'.

As for all authors, reviews are the key to raising awareness of my work. If you have enjoyed this book, I would be very grateful if you could leave a short review on Amazon, Goodreads and any other social media platform you are active on. I'd love to hear what you think, and it makes such a difference in helping new readers discover one of my books for the first time.

The inspiration for this story came from seeing a bridal car driving on the outskirts of our local town one day. I thought to myself – I wonder how it must feel to get to the church and for your husband-to-be not to turn up! I went home and started plotting, and Hannah's story came to life. It was as simple as that. Observing an event and making up a story based on a potential outcome. And then the twists just kept coming!

All my novels undergo a rigorous editing process, but sometimes mistakes happen. If you have spotted an error, please contact me so I can promptly correct it.

I love hearing from my readers – you can get in touch via my Facebook and Instagram pages.

Best wishes,

Amanda X

facebook.com/AJCampbellauthor
instagram.com/ajcampbellauthor

ACKNOWLEDGEMENTS

I'm thrilled to be part of the Bookouture team for the publication of *Left at the Altar*, my eleventh published psychological suspense thriller.

It takes a team to write a book, and I must first thank my very talented editor, Natalie Edwards. This has been the fourth book we've worked on together. I've learnt so much from you, Natalie, and it's been a pleasure to work with you again on another twisty tale. And thank you to Team Bookouture for everything you've done to help get the finished product into the hands of readers.

To my brilliant beta readers – Mr C, Dawn H, Christine H, Sally R, and John B – thank you for helping me to develop the story and spotting the plot holes! I always value your opinions and suggestions. I'm blessed to have you so close by my side. And Jen Vance, thank you for your help with the research of Hannah's character.

Thank you to my ARC team and all the book bloggers who read and review my books. Where would I be without you? Your support, as usual, has been incredible, and I thank you from the bottom of my heart for everything you do for me.

To my readers: I couldn't continue writing for a living without you. Every day, I'm grateful that you found me! I hope you love Hannah's story as much as I've loved writing it.

And finally, thank you, Mr C, for everything you do for me!
Amanda X

PUBLISHING TEAM

Turning a manuscript into a book requires the efforts of many people. The publishing team at Bookouture would like to acknowledge everyone who contributed to this publication.

Commercial
Lauren Morrissette
Hannah Richmond
Imogen Allport

Cover design
Head Design Ltd.

Data and analysis
Mark Alder
Mohamed Bussuri

Editorial
Natalie Edwards
Charlotte Hegley

Copyeditor
Janette Currie

Proofreader
Becca Allen

Marketing
Alex Crow
Melanie Price
Occy Carr
Cíara Rosney
Martyna Młynarska

Operations and distribution
Marina Valles
Stephanie Straub
Joe Morris

Production
Hannah Snetsinger
Mandy Kullar
Ria Clare
Nadia Michael

Publicity
Kim Nash
Noelle Holten
Jess Readett
Sarah Hardy

Rights and contracts
Peta Nightingale
Richard King
Saidah Graham

RAISING READERS
Books Build Bright Futures

Dear Reader,

We'd love your attention for one more page to tell you about the crisis in children's reading, and what we can all do.

Studies have shown that reading for fun is the **single biggest predictor of a child's future life chances** – more than family circumstance, parents' educational background or income. It improves academic results, mental health, wealth, communication skills, ambition and happiness.

The number of children reading for fun is in rapid decline. Young people have a lot of competition for their time, and a worryingly high number do not have a single book at home.

Hachette works extensively with schools, libraries and literacy charities, but here are some ways we can all raise more readers:

- Reading to children for just 10 minutes a day makes a difference
- Don't give up if children aren't regular readers – there will be books for them!

- Visit bookshops and libraries to get recommendations
- Encourage them to listen to audiobooks
- Support school libraries
- Give books as gifts

There's a lot more information about how to encourage children to read on our websites: **www.RaisingReaders.co.uk** and **www.JoinRaisingReaders.com**.

Thank you for reading.

Made in the USA
Middletown, DE
02 September 2025